W9-DAR-474

ESCAPE TO LOVE

Alice Wootson

ARABESQUE

★BET BOOKS™

BET Publications, LLC
http://www.bet.com
http://www.arabesquebooks.com

ARABESQUE BOOKS are published by

BET Publications, LLC
c/o BET BOOKS
One BET Plaza
1900 W Place NE
Washington, DC 20018-1211

Copyright © 2003 by Alice Wootson

All rights reserved. No part of this book may be reproduced, stored in a retrieval system, or transmitted in any form or by any means without the prior written consent of the Publisher.

If you purchased this book without a cover, you should be aware that this book is stolen property. It was reported as "unsold and destroyed" to the Publisher and neither the Author nor the Publisher has received any payment for this "stripped book."

All Kensington Titles, Imprints, and Distributed Lines are available at special quantity discounts for bulk purchases for sales promotions, premiums, fund-raising, and educational or institutional use. Special book excerpts or customized printings can also be created to fit specific needs. For details, write or phone the office of the Kensington special sales manager: Kensington Publishing Corp., 850 Third Avenue, New York, NY 10022, attn: Special Sales Department, Phone: 1-800-221-2647.

BET Books is a trademark of Black Entertainment Television, Inc. ARABESQUE, the ARABESQUE logo and the BET BOOKS logo are trademarks and registered trademarks.

First Printing: June 2003
10 9 8 7 6 5 4 3 2 1

Printed in the United States of America

2003

CHICAGO PUBLIC LIBRARY

R01929 44071

ESCAPE TO LOVE

Angela tried not to notice the sweat glistening on Trent's bare back. She never was good at purposely not noticing something.

His muscles rippled as he positioned another piece of wood on the block and raised the axe. His shoulder muscles stood out as if waiting for her to use them for an anatomy lesson. Or in some other way. As if she could shove aside what the sight was doing to her insides; heating them hotter than the wood would be in the iron stove: as if teaching an anatomy lesson was what was in the front of her mind.

She clinched her hands behind her to keep from doing something stupid like going over to him and stroking her hands along the muscles glistening in the sunlight as if they were waiting for her; beckoning to her.

Chicago Public Library
Bucktown-Wicker Park Branch
1701 N. Milwaukee
Chicago, IL 60647

**BOOK YOUR PLACE ON OUR WEBSITE
AND MAKE THE ARABESQUE
ROMANCE CONNECTION!**

We've created a customized website just for our very special Arabesque readers, where you can get the inside scoop on everything that's going on with Arabesque romance novels.

When you come online, you'll have the exciting opportunity to:

- View covers of upcoming books

- Learn about our future publishing schedule (listed by publication month and author)

- Find out when your favorite authors will be visiting a city near you

- Search for and order backlist books

- Check out author bios and background information

- Send e-mail to your favorite authors

- Join us in weekly chats with authors, readers and other guests

- Get writing guidelines

- AND MUCH MORE!

Visit our website at
http://www.arabesquebooks.com

CHICAGO PUBLIC LIBRARY
WEST TOWN BRANCH
1271 N. MILWAUKEE AVE
CHICAGO, IL 60622

R01929 44071

To all of you readers who have taken time to write to me and encourage me, to my local paper and the colorful locals in the news who provided the basic premise of this story, and especially to Ike who is still happy to be driving Miss Alice and to accompany me as I follow my dream.

One

The world outside the twenty-seventh floor window had been blanketed with darkness for hours. The April night pressing against the wall of glass facing Angela Baring offered a spectacular view of the downtown Philadelphia skyline in the moonlight, but she didn't notice it. The hum of the computer in front of her joined with the hum of the building's heating and cooling system and whatever else kept the building alive. If it were not for these sounds, silence would fill the room and crowd against her, even though she didn't notice any of those sounds, either.

She frowned as she stared at the computer screen. Something was wrong with her calculations; her figures were definitely off. She needed this information as part of her final project for class, but she didn't want to spend any more time on it tonight. The more she worked on it, the worse it got. She shook her head. It was bad to be a business major and not be able to find what must be a simple glitch in the math. This was basic math she was working with—something a high school student would be able to do.

She deleted a line, stared at the text that was left, and put the line back. She stared again, and then gave the print command. *I'll check the hard copy at home tonight and again tomorrow if necessary.* As the pages flowed from the printer she looked at her watch.

"Why does it always take longer to put it onto paper than it takes to think of it?" Even if she weren't alone in the room, she doubted if she would have gotten an answer.

When she had decided on her final project, it had seemed

so simple. Set up an imaginary company, but use the figures from Hunter's Beer Distributors for her paper. She hadn't checked with Mr. Hunter, her boss, but then she wasn't using his company, only some of the figures; so she hadn't seen a problem. She had assumed that Mr. Hunter had used a competent accountant. She sighed. Big mistake on her part.

Angela gathered the papers into a folder, took her purse from the bottom desk drawer, and turned off the light. This Friday had ended the way her Fridays usually did: a hot date with a computer printout and fooling with numbers instead of a tall, dark, and handsome male.

She thought about Dwight. *How much longer will he be understanding about the hours I put in with the job and with my schoolwork instead of with him? How much longer before he decides that I'm not worth his time and moves on to somebody else?*

She had worked hard to get him to notice her. He was her first real boyfriend. She smiled. They had been getting closer until she decided to go back to school. She swallowed hard. They could be close again if he'd just be patient for a little while longer. She sighed. Maybe she could work on her paper before and after she saw him tomorrow night. She missed being with him. Softness showed on her face. He was *The One;* he just didn't know it yet, but he would. Soon, she hoped. He only saw her as his latest girlfriend. As soon as she got home, she'd call him. He could come over tonight. Why should they wait until tomorrow?

She gathered the papers spread over the top of the desk and, hugging them to her, closed her eyes. Dwight was the special one for her—her soul mate. She sighed again. Was she ready to take that final step to intimacy that he had been urging her to do for months? She pushed down the nervousness and doubt that tried to fill her mind. Did she want the same thing that he did? Maybe she was nervous thinking about it because it was a new experience that she was considering. She sighed. She needed a commitment from him before she went any further. She hoped she could make him understand that.

Yes. She nodded. *I could work on my paper after Dwight leaves.* She smiled, hoping it wouldn't be for a long time. They had a lot of catching up to do. She chewed at her lip. *Or* she thought, *I could stay up all night Sunday to finish it.* It was her final paper, but everything was finished except for what she had been working on this evening. She frowned. *Where did I go wrong in my calculations?*

Tonight, when they were together, she'd remind Dwight that the semester was almost over and that her graduation was close. Then they would be able to spend more time together and move their relationship forward. He'd understand. *Isn't he as ready for a commitment as I am?* She sighed. She hoped so. Why would he spend so much time with her if he wasn't?

She got as far as the elevators when she sighed again and returned to the office. All her class work was on that floppy. Even though nobody else would be in the office before she got in on Monday and she didn't have a computer at home, she'd still feel better with the disk in her hand.

The way this semester is going, she thought, as she walked down the hall, *I could have rented a room instead of an apartment.*

Lately, she only went home to sleep and grab her meals. Simple, quick-to-fix meals. Her stomach growled as if to remind her that even that would be welcome right now. Maybe she could fix an omelette for Dwight when he came over and they could eat together.

Angela walked down the hall. The light was on in Mr. Hunter's office, which wasn't unusual. He often had late meetings, although Angela didn't understand why running a beer distributorship was so complicated. She shrugged. He was the boss and it wasn't any of her business. Her job was to run the office.

She grabbed the disk, slipped it into her bag, and went to wait for an elevator. She smiled when the light came on over first one elevator and then another right after.

"Nick must be making his rounds." Her smile widened. "At least I'll be gone before he can tease me about the building owner charging me rent for living here."

She thought about the elderly security guard as the elevator doors slid open and she stepped inside.

Nick had been working here when she started four years ago. He was the grandfather she never had and he often kept her mind from the fact that she had no family.

The doors opened on the first floor, but Angela didn't get out. Instead, she groaned and leaned against the wall. If it was true that people get more forgetful as they get older, in about ten years—at the ripe old age of thirty-six—she wouldn't be able to remember her own name.

She thought for about ten seconds, then pushed the button to take her back up. That other folder wouldn't do her any good on her desk. She needed it so she could finish her paper this weekend.

Angry voices, hurled from Mr. Hunter's office, reached her while she was still halfway down the hall. Sounds separated into words as she got closer to the private door that allowed him to leave without going through the reception area where her desk stood. She walked closer.

"How did you think you could get away with something like this? Did you think Mr. Franks wouldn't find out? You think he's stupid or something?"

"No. No. I-I just ran into a bind. I'll pay it back, I swear. Every penny of it. I'm good for it. I just need a little time."

"Mr. Franks, he said he can't trust you no more."

"Look. Let me talk to him. Okay? It won't take long. Just let me talk to him."

"Mr. Franks said not to bother him with this no more. He said he's through with it." The speaker waited for Mr. Hunter to take his turn talking, but he didn't make a sound. "Sorry," the man continued. "Nothing personal. You know how it is. I got a job to do."

Angela hesitated. This wasn't the first time that heated words had spewed from Mr. Hunter's office. One time, during a particularly loud argument, she went in to see if he was all right. He yelled at her and told her to go back to her work. Her feet felt as if they were moving through thick mud.

She could see Mr. Hunter through the partly opened door.

He took a step backward. She watched as the other man came into view. She had never seen him before. A chill rippled through her, but she shook it off. It must be okay for him to be here. Nick wouldn't have let him in unless Mr. Hunter had said it was all right, would he?

All she wanted was to get her work from her desk and leave. That's what she should do: get the folder and leave. Still she stood, as if riveted in place, watching a play, and she had to see what would happen next.

Just get the folder and leave. Get it and get out of here.

She didn't. Another shiver rippled through her. Monday she'd look for another job. Something wasn't right here. She had kind of felt it for a while, but the work wasn't hard and there wasn't much of it and the pay was good, so she had ignored her instincts. Now she could no longer convince herself that everything was okay.

She watched as the man reached into his pocket. He took a step toward Mr. Hunter. When his hand came out holding a gun, Angela couldn't move. Mr. Hunter's words kept coming, but Angela didn't know what he said. All her concentration was focused on the other man's hand. She stayed in place as he fastened something onto the gun barrel.

The sound of three soft thuds bursting through the narrow opening of the door freed her from her spot. She drew in a hard, loud breath and backed away from the door, slowly at first, then she turned and ran, knowing her sneakers would let her run fast, but also knowing that sneakers didn't really let a person sneak.

Mr. Hunter's door crashed open against the wall but Angela didn't turn around.

"Hey. Wait a minute." The man's words flew at her and pushed her to go faster. A thud chipped the plaster from a spot on the wall as she turned the corner and ran into the hallway leading to the elevators.

"Come back here. Let's talk about this." His voice followed her. She heard the anger hiding under his words.

Angela dashed the short distance into the open elevator. She fastened herself to the side, wishing she were smaller.

She pressed the Close Door button and continued to push it even as the doors obeyed her. A bullet smacked through the door and a small hole appeared in it and the back wall just as the elevator started down.

The man's shouts reached her as the elevator took her away from him. The last thing she heard was a string of curse words.

"Hurry, hurry," she urged the elevator as if her words would make it go faster.

The elevator stopped on the first floor and she squeezed through the doors before they fully opened. *Nick would help her*. She dashed toward his desk. *He had a gun*. The chair stared at her.

"Nick. Where are you?" Angela walked forward a few more inches as if, when she got closer, he would magically appear. She stopped when she saw a trickle of red oozing across the floor, coming from behind the desk. The hum of the other elevator slipped into the air.

Angela glanced at the front door, which suddenly seemed miles away. The outside looked tantalizing close, but she didn't have time to go behind the desk, buzz the door open, and get out before the elevator finished its trip. Even if she did, where would she go? It was too far to the corner and this section of center city Philadelphia was deserted at night. The creaks and hum of the elevator grew louder.

She ran away from the desk, around the corner, and down the hallway. She was near the next corner when the sound of the elevator door opening pushed her to run faster.

She pulled at the first door. Locked. She ran to another. The same. The back exit was too far away and the hallway was too straight. And every door was locked. She shivered as she prayed.

"No sense running." Hard words stabbed into the air. "Ain't nobody here but us, but you saw that, didn't you?" He was still around the corner, but his voice was getting closer, looking for her.

"Look. I know Tim Hunter didn't pay you nothing much. How 'bout we make a deal? I know we can work something out."

I can imagine what kind of a deal he has in mind, she thought.

She hesitated, but not to consider his offer. Then she ran a few more steps down the hall and pulled the fire alarm.

Bells blared, but they didn't drown out the man's curses or his running footsteps coming toward her. He was still around the corner, but not for long. A few more seconds and . . .

She turned the doorknob of the janitor's closet and almost fell over when it opened. She gave thanks as she darted inside. Bless Jesse for not locking it. She eased it shut behind her and ran her hand along, first below, then above the knob. No bolt. She knew there was no logical reason for putting a bolt on the inside of a closet door, but she wished somebody had been illogical just this once.

She stood still, barely breathing, afraid to move, afraid of bumping into something in the dark. The footsteps slowed outside the door. Angela slowly wrapped her hand around the knob and pulled it toward her, trying to do an imitation of a bolt. She closed her eyes and prayed that she was doing a good job.

Sirens wailed closer and closer. One more string of curses hurled from the man, then footsteps ran away from outside the closet door and faded toward the back of the building. Angela stood where she was—afraid to breathe deeply, afraid he'd come back, afraid.

The sound of shattering glass filled the air outside her space. The mix of many voices and weighty footsteps reached her. She took a deep, wobbly breath, gave another silent prayer, and dared to leave her sanctuary.

Two

"Hey, Jim. What's up?"

Trent Stewart spoke to the fire chief standing with three other firefighters near the doorway. He worked his way around two others who were folding hoses that snaked along the floor.

"We responded to an alarm. Didn't find a fire, but did find a dead man behind the desk. My people didn't touch anything, of course, after we concluded that he's dead. We also have a witness. I think she came out of the utility closet around the corner."

"Am I the first?"

"You beat the uniforms here. Where were you? Waiting down the block?"

"Almost. I was on my way home from the Community Hero Recognition Dinner when I got the call."

"That explains the tux. I thought maybe they changed the dress code on you." He laughed.

"Don't talk so loud. Some politician might think that's a good idea." Trent smiled back. "I'd better get to work. Where's the witness?"

"Over there." Jim stepped to the side and pointed.

Trent looked at the young woman hunched in the chair against the wall. *Just a kid. What was she doing here this late? What's she doing here at all?* He watched as she struggled to take slow deep breaths and let them out just as slowly. He wouldn't yank away her hope by telling her that deep breaths didn't work. "Did she say anything?"

"She made me show her my ID." Jim smiled. "As if I'd

wear this outfit if I didn't have to. Then she started apologizing for pulling the alarm. I don't know how much of a witness she is. I can't even get her name from her."

"I take it there was no fire?"

"Not even a burning match."

"Do you think she did it?"

"My gut tells me no, but . . ." He shrugged. "Who can tell nowadays?" He smiled. "Probably you. That's why you get to dress clean and I eat smoke for a living."

"Tell that to somebody who doesn't know that you turned down the chance to be fire commissioner. Let me try to get her story."

"Fine. We're out of here."

As Trent approached the woman, he reassessed his first opinion. She was older than the seventeen or eighteen that he had first guessed, but not by much. He frowned.

"Wait." She bounded from the chair, rushed past him, and toward the firefighters. "Wait. Where are you going? You can't leave me here. He might come back."

"Who?" Trent spoke, and the woman glanced at him as if she had just noticed him. Then she continued past him as if he weren't there. Trent followed her over to Jim.

"Mr. Stewart will take it from here," Jim said.

She glanced at Trent again and back to Jim. "Who is he?"

Trent stared at her. It had been a long time since he had been brushed off so thoroughly. He smiled slightly. He had to admire her. Even in her present mental state she was bouncing back.

"He's a police detective."

"He doesn't look like a policeman."

"I'm Detective Stewart." He reached into his pocket and she backed away. Her eyes widened. She looked ready to bolt out the door.

"Wait." He held up both hands. "I'm reaching for my ID. Okay?"

She looked back at Jim who nodded. Then she looked at Trent and frowned. Then she sighed. "Okay." She stood stiffly. Her gaze followed him as he reached into his pocket and pulled out his identification. She reminded him of a runner waiting for the starting pistol.

She took the tag that he held out and examined it. She looked from it to Trent and back several times as if he had changed a lot since his picture had been taken. Finally she gave it back to him.

"Okay now, Miss?" Jim stood just inside the door. Angela hesitated. "He really is a police detective. I've known him since high school. It's okay. Really."

"Okay." Her voice wavered as if it wasn't as sure as her word said. Her glance slid to the desk and stayed there as if she could see through it to the body on the other side— as if she wanted to. Trent eased himself into her line of vision.

"What's your name and what are you doing here this time of night?"

"I-I work here. I-I was working on an assignment. Not an assignment for work. A class assignment. I take classes. Night classes. I'm in college. I'm a business major. I work here, too, during the day. Upstairs. My classes are in the evening. Not tonight, though. Not on Fridays. On Fridays I work on my class assignments. Last semester I took classes on the weekends, too. That was what I was doing tonight." She shook her head. "I don't have a computer at home. I could work in the computer lab at school, but this is more convenient. Mr. Hunter knows I use the computers. He doesn't care." She frowned. "I mean, he *did* know and he *didn't* care. I-I mean . . ."

"Were you here alone tonight?"

"Yes. I mean no. I mean except for Mr. Hunter I was, but—but . . ." She gulped in air as if she was afraid a shortage was coming. Then she closed her eyes and let the breath out slowly, but took in another right away.

"Yes or no?"

"He shot Mr. Hunter."

"Who?"

"I-I don't know."

"How do you know he was shot?"

"He must have killed . . ." She frowned. "Is-is Nick dead, too?"

"The guard?"

She nodded.

"Afraid so."

"He was so nice to me." A tear slid down her face. "Nick was nice to everybody. He didn't have to kill him."

"Who did it?"

"I told you. I don't know his name. I never saw him before."

Trent turned as two uniformed officers came into the building. He recognized one. "Excuse me." He spoke to Angela, but he wasn't sure his words got through.

"Hey, Murphy. The firefighters were first on the scene and they made sure nothing was disturbed. Do what you have to do. I'll question the witness." He frowned. "At least I think she's a witness. So far I haven't gotten anything much out of her." He glanced at her and shook his head. She seemed lost again. Her arms were wrapped around her middle as if that was all that was keeping her from falling apart. He sighed and went over to her. This was going to be a long night.

"Let's go up to the office."

"No." She backed away from him. "I'm not going back up there. Maybe he decided to go back to Mr. Hunter's office. Maybe he never left the building." She frowned. "You know he had a gun?"

"Mr. Hunter?"

"No." She glared at him. "The man who shot him. He shot at me, too. Twice."

"That's Mr. Hunter?" Trent pointed toward the desk.

"No." She frowned. "I told you, that's Nick, the security guard. Nick Alberts. Mr. Hunter is my boss." She was having trouble breathing again. "He *was* my boss." Her stare found the security desk.

Trent blocked her vision. "What floor?"

"What floor what?"

A very long night. "What floor is Mr. Hunter's office on?"

"Twenty-seventh."

Trent called to Murphy. "I think we got another DB on

twenty-seven. Better check it out." Trent turned back to Angela.

"What's your name?"

"Angela. Angela Baring. I know it's against the law to pull a false alarm, but I didn't know what else to do. He was after me because I saw him. He was going to kill me. He did shoot at me. Two times." She shuddered. "Once in the hall upstairs. Then he shot into the elevator, but he missed me. You can check for yourself." Her eyes widened. "I couldn't get away. If Jesse hadn't left the closet unlocked, I'd be dead, too." She glanced toward the hall. Out there. *On Monday, they'd have found my body after they found Nick and before they found Mr. Hunter.* "How much is the fine? If it's a lot, will they let me pay a little at a time? Will I have to go to jail?"

"Well, Angela Baring, I don't think you have to worry about the false alarm. Why don't you start at the beginning?"

She took a deep breath and closed her eyes. Then she began.

"I was using the computer to work on my final paper for my accounting class. It's due on Monday. My paper, I mean. I graduate in May. I was . . ."

Trent took out a small notebook and began writing.

". . . and that's when I pulled the alarm and hid in Jesse's closet."

"Jesse's the janitor."

"Yes." She nodded.

Trent shook his head. It was frightening. He was beginning to follow her train of thought even though it wandered all over the track.

Murphy came back down and beckoned to him.

"You were right," he said, when Trent reached him. "There's a body on the twenty-seventh floor in the office of Hunter's Beer Distributors. Male, approximately forty-five to fifty years old. Shot once in the head at fairly close range. Another shot chipped the plaster at a corner and landed in the wall. A third is lodged in the back wall of one of the elevators."

"Okay," Trent said. "Let me get someone else over here to handle that end of it. I'm going to be tied up with her for a while." He glanced at Angela, who had retreated to a safe place in her mind, and added, "A long while." He took out his cell phone and made the call. Then he went back to Angela.

"We need to go to the station."

"I'm not leaving here. While I was in the closet, I heard him running toward the parking lot. He might still be out there. What if he's waiting for me? I saw him shoot Mr. Hunter and he knows it. He already killed two people."

"You'll be safe with me. I promise." Angela didn't move. "You can't stay here. You have to realize that. You'd be alone after we left. If you go home, how do you know he wouldn't find you there?" Panic filled her face and she looked around. Trent felt guilty for putting it there, but he had told the truth. She hesitated a few more seconds before she stood. "Good." He nodded at her.

She looked so frail that he had to struggle to keep from putting his arm around her. Still she might be the killer. He shook his head. No. No one was that good an actress. Not even the best in show business.

He had to get her to the door. She might be right. The shooter might be outside waiting for her.

He took a deep breath and moved toward her. Then, after another deep breath, he did pull her close, now, trying not to notice how soft her shoulders were even through her sweater. That was partly because the sweater was too big for her. *Who's was it? Roommate's? Boyfriend's? Men wore this style as often as women. Who was she, really?*

He moved a little in front of her as they neared the door. It wasn't hard to hide her. He was over six feet tall and she barely came to his shoulder. He wasn't heavy, but he had no trouble blocking her completely. He frowned. She was too thin. He usually liked his women with more meat on their bones. His frown deepened to a scowl. *Where had that come from? She was a witness. Technically she was a suspect, too.* He let out a harsh breath. He never, ever, got involved emotionally or physically with a case. Emotions were a distraction. He'd take her statement, turn her over to the chief, and then it was good-bye Angela Baring.

"Do you have a car?"

"I ride the bus."

"This time of night?"

"Do you think I take the bus because I want to?"

He stopped her at the door and stepped outside. After he was satisfied that no one was around who could harm her, he reached inside for her and coaxed her out. The night was more like June than April, but she shivered and hunched her shoulders as if seeking protection from the cold. Or trying to hide inside herself.

"You're doing fine, Angela. Don't fall apart on me now."

She didn't say anything, but her shivering backed off. Trent eased her into the backseat, then got behind the wheel. He looked around once more as he pulled away from the curb. There was the possibility that someone was watching them.

"Eighteen-thirty-one Larson Place. Do you know where that is?"

Trent glanced over at her, but immediately pulled his gaze back to the rearview mirror. He smiled. No one was behind them. *Did she do it?* The question popped up in his mind, but left right away. *She didn't. She couldn't have. If she did, why the alarm? Why wait around if she was the shooter?*

"Do you?"

What's that?"

"Huh?"

"What's at eighteen-thirty-one Larson Place?"

"That's where I live."

"I'm not taking you home."

"I have to go home." If she went home, maybe she could pretend that this never happened.

"We have to go to the station. I need for you to answer some questions."

"I already told you everything I know. Why can't I answer any other questions you have at my apartment?"

"The forms I need are at the station."

"You're going to give me a ticket for the false alarm, aren't you? That's why you're taking me to the police station."

"Angela, we have two dead bodies to account for. Forget the fire alarm, okay? Just forget it."

"Okay."

Her answer had no strength. Sitting hunched over, with her arms around her middle and her shoulders pulled up to her ears, she seemed to be trying to make herself shrink until she disappeared.

"We have to find out who did this. Okay? That's the only way we can solve this. We can arrest him and then you'll be safe."

She didn't answer. He glanced over at her again. She seemed to be staring out the window, but he was sure she wasn't seeing anything. "I'll try not to take too long, okay?"

She nodded slightly, but pulled her arms tighter around herself. He fought the urge to . . . He let out a hard breath. The sooner he got things sorted out, the sooner she'd be out of his life and the sooner he could move on to the next case and forget her.

Silence rode with them the rest of the way to the station. Now and then he checked in the rearview mirror, but no one followed them. Still, when he got to headquarters, he gave a long look in the mirror. Then he let his gaze slowly check all around as he pulled into the station parking lot.

Three

"Here we are." Trent turned off the motor.

"Where?"

"The station."

"Is it safe to get out?" Angela darted looks out the windows on both sides. Then she looked out the back window.

"I'll make sure." Trent got out without trying to convince her of the safety of a police station. He had learned a long time ago that some people had a feeling about this kind of thing sometimes. Maybe this was one of those times for her.

About a dozen patrol cars were parked and more were zipping in and out of the lot as he stood leaning against the open car door. Still, he scanned the surroundings slowly, including the buildings jammed together across the street. Lastly he let his gaze pan the rooftops.

He had been accused of being paranoid in the past, but being careful never hurt. Not being careful could get you killed. He had no idea what they were caught up in, but he knew it was more than something simple. Robbers would never go to the trouble of hitting a business like this. Even if Mr. Hunter was known to keep money on hand, the security guard at the door would make thieves go elsewhere. There were too many mom-and-pop stores around with no security at all. Even banks were more accessible than a business on the twenty-seventh floor of a center city office building. He frowned. *Common robbers didn't use silencers, either. Whatever it was she was in the middle of, it was big.*

He sighed and checked the street once more. Finally satisfied that she'd be safe, he opened her door.

Before she got out, her gaze darted around as if she couldn't decide where to look or as if she didn't trust him. He couldn't blame her. She didn't know him.

She got out and her gaze repeated the search. Then she dashed for the building, leaving him standing at the curb. He rushed to catch up.

When she stopped just inside the door, he had to put out his hand to keep from bumping into her. Then he had to make himself remember that she was part of his new case. *Then* he removed his hand from her back. He hesitated and looked around. Protocol dictated that he should keep her here in the main room, or at least start out here, but as frightened as she was, he wasn't sure how much he'd get from her if she kept checking her surroundings.

"Down here." He tried to lead her down a hallway, but she stood as if she had finally found a place of safety.

"Wait." She backed against the wall.

"For what?"

"These men." Her stare touched each person in the room.

"These are police officers."

"They have guns. How do I know the killer isn't a policeman?"

Rather than argue, he waited while she checked the face of every man in the large room. He doubted the shooter had been a police officer, but there were almost as many civilians in the room. Who knew? Maybe the shooter had been picked up for something else, like running a red light or a stop sign.

Trent looked around the room. Things were busier than usual even for a Friday night. If there had been a "limited capacity" sign posted on the wall, they would certainly have exceeded it. Finally, after checking everybody in the room a second time, she turned to him.

"Okay. I'm ready."

Chocolate brown eyes too large for her face stared at him. His glance slid to her mouth. Just the right size. If only. . . .

"Where do we go?"

Where would his thoughts have taken him if she hadn't interrupted? He took a deep breath. "This way." He led her down the hall and into the third room on the right. *She's a case, Trent. A new case. An open case.* He shook his head, trying to get rid of thoughts that didn't belong in his investigating mind, but not succeeding.

"Witness," he said to a man as they passed him.

"Who's he?" Angela took a step closer to Trent. Her side brushed against his. His common sense struggled for control.

"My boss." Her eyes widened at his words and he wished he'd said it differently. "He's the chief."

He got a legal-size pad from the top of the file cabinet just outside the room. Then he opened the door and let her in.

"Have a seat. Want a cup of coffee?"

"It would keep me awake." Her breath had ragged edges when she exhaled. She shook her head and sighed. "I-I won't be able to sleep, anyway. I keep seeing what happened . . . seeing him shooting Mr. Hunter." She took another breath. "I see it even with my eyes open." She blinked several times and struggled to breathe normally. "I know I'd see him if I tried to sleep." She swallowed hard. "What if he knows where I live? What if he comes after me?"

"It was probably just a robbery." From what she told him, he doubted seriously if it was as simple as that, but he could give her hope even if it was only temporary. He sat opposite her. "Okay. Let's take it from the beginning again."

An hour later he read back his notes to her and she nodded each time he stopped. He frowned. He knew it wasn't going to be just a robbery gone bad. He leaned back and stared at her. Being right didn't make him happy this time. His frown deepened.

"What? What is it?"

"Wait here a minute." At least she was alert enough to read his expression. "I have to go check on something." He looked from his notes to her and back to the notebook. Then he left the room.

* * *

She watched him go. Once he left, her shivering started again. The look on his face had been worse than that of the dentist when he had told her that she needed a root canal. She closed her eyes and leaned back in her chair. *Why did I have to forget that stupid folder? Or why didn't I let it wait until Monday? If I had gone out with Dwight tonight the way he wanted instead of staying at work. If I hadn't decided to take classes this semester. . .* She shook her head. "Ifs" weren't going to help her. She didn't know what was going on, but that man hadn't looked a robber. She hadn't come in contact with any that she knew of, but she doubted if many thieves wore three-piece suits and ties. She frowned.

Did *anyone* still wear three-piece suits? She swallowed hard. The killer did. She let out a hard breath. A silencer. That was what he fastened onto his gun as she watched. She shook her head again. Thieves didn't use silencers, did they? Why would they? What mess had she gotten tangled in?

She stared at the closed door. Maybe this was one of those cases where the criminal is caught the next day. Then she could get back to her life. She frowned. She'd have to find another job. She couldn't go back there even if the business stayed open. She frowned and shifted in the chair. Who would take over the distributorship? She swallowed hard. She wondered if Mr. Hunter's body was still up there? What about Nick? Was he still on the floor leaking blood or . . . ? She struggled to get her breathing under control again.

Nick had a family, but who would they call for Mr. Hunter? Who'd take care of his funeral? She didn't even know if Mr. Hunter had a family. He didn't have any pictures on his desk. She never took a call from a wife or kids. He never mentioned anyone. She didn't know anything about his personal life. She didn't know anything about him at all. The only talking they ever did was related to business, and they didn't talk much about that. She frowned again. Now that she thought about it, there hadn't been much for her to do there. *Was it really a front? Why hadn't I questioned it before? Why hadn't I noticed that we weren't busy enough for the company to stay so large.*

Mr. Hunter knew the Mr. Franks that the killer talked about. She could tell from the bit of conversation she heard between the killer and Mr. Hunter before the killer . . . *Don't think about that.* She forced herself to search her memory. *I never took a call from him; never heard his name before tonight. I never heard of Mr. Franks before tonight.* She took in a quick breath as her eyes widened. *Yes, I have.*

She leaned forward in the chair. Last Monday morning she had answered the phone. The caller refused to tell her his name, but, since he was so insistent, she had buzzed Mr. Hunter anyway. He had sounded nervous when she told him about the call even though she couldn't tell him who it was. Before Angela had hung up, she had heard Mr. Hunter call the man by name. Mr. Franks. Right after that Mr. Hunter had left his office. The temperature had been perfect, but he had been sweating as if his office were a sauna. When she asked where she could reach him, he told her he'd see her the next morning. *I have to tell Mr. Stewart.*

She sprang from her chair. Her face let go of some of the tightness. Maybe this would help get her out of this nightmare. She wanted to get away from what had happened as fast as she could. She still had a paper to write. She still had her future all planned. She still had her life. She swallowed hard. They'd catch the killer, put him in jail, give him a speedy trial like criminals always want, and it would be over. She'd never go near the office building again. She would find a job to take her through the end of the semester and it would last until she got a real job based on her degree. Maybe in time, she could forget all about this horrible mess and dead Mr. Hunter, and the floor painted with poor Nick's blood.

Angela rushed to the door. It opened as she reached for it. She stepped back as Trent walked in.

"I remember something else. Maybe it will help." She clasped her hands in front of her. "I'm sorry I didn't remember before, but I remember now. Maybe it will help you catch the killer." She noticed the thick book he held and frowned. She asked, "What is that book?"

* * *

"Let's sit back down." Trent followed her to the table and set the book down. He would listen to what had her excited, but from what he had just found out, no matter what she had to tell him, he knew that this case would be open for a long time.

Angela told him about the phone call last Monday. Hope filled her face as she talked. His jaw tightened. He was about to erase it. In the little time since he left her, he had found out more than what she had told him. And he had just started digging. No sense waiting to tell her.

"Mr. Hunter didn't own the business."

"What do you mean? The company's name is 'Hunter's Beer Distributors.' He's . . ." She stopped. "He *was* the largest beer distributor in the tristate area. He hired me. He signed my paychecks. Of course he owned the business."

"Franks was his boss. And *he* has people over him."

"I told you. I never met Mr. Franks. How could I have been working for him and not ever seen him?" She frowned. "You do believe me, don't you? I'm telling you the truth."

"I believe you. That's the way they work."

"Who? That's the way who works?"

"Please sit down, Miss Baring."

It wasn't often that he had good news for people with whom he came in contact. He wished this was one of those rare times. He tried not to notice how vulnerable—how innocent—she looked as she slowly sat back at the table. And she was innocent. After what he had just found out, there was no way she could be involved and the department not know it. Besides, she was a receptionist—an unsuspecting part of the front.

"What do you mean by 'they'?"

He stared at her a bit longer. Her skin looked like smooth milk chocolate. He always did have a weakness for chocolate. He forced his attention away from her. He wrapped his hands around the large book to keep from finding out if her skin felt as soft and smooth as it looked. She wasn't a suspect, but she was part of the case. An important part. Besides, there was that rule about not getting involved with anyone connected to a case.

Eight years ago, when he joined the force and read the rule, he thought it was a good idea. In his mind, he still did, but the rest of him . . . When he'd noticed how soft her lips looked, something had stirred inside him. It was the rest of him that needed to be convinced. Right now that rule was just a barrier. *Get away from there, Trent.*

He opened the book about a third of the way and turned it around to face her. "See if anybody looks familiar."

"Is this what they call 'mug shots'?"

"Sometimes."

"Is the killer in there?" She stared at the book, but she didn't touch it.

"You tell me."

He wanted this over with. He wanted to take her statement and hand her over to someone else. He wanted her out of his mind. He wanted to move on to the next case. Mostly, he wanted a way to make himself believe all of that, believe that *she* wasn't what he *really* wanted.

"Start on that page and study the photos carefully. Let me know if anyone looks familiar. Take your time." *But hurry up so I can try to get you out of my thoughts.* He let out a hard breath.

Maybe he had been at this job too long. Maybe after he left the Marines he should have used his educational funds to take business courses instead of working toward a degree in criminal justice. He was good in math. He could have used a business degree to get a job that required nothing from his training in the Special Forces Unit. He could have been working in an office. She could, too. Maybe in the same office, or at least in the same building. Then she wouldn't be as off-limits to him as she was now.

He watched her focus on each picture and stay there as if the test would come later and this wasn't it now. Then she moved her attention to the next. He didn't want to think of what would come after she identified the shooter.

He looked as she turned the page. Three or four pages more and she'd be there if he was right. He hoped he was wrong, but he doubted it. He was seldom wrong about things like this. That fact didn't please him now.

She examined two more pages, flipped to the third, and gasped. He let out a harsh breath. No, being right did not make him happy.

"That's him." Angela leaned back in her chair, away from the book. Her finger shook as she pointed to a picture. She kept her hand away from the page as if afraid that, if she touched it, the man would grab her and pull her in like something from a horror movie.

Trent went over to her. "You're sure?"

"Yes." She nodded rapidly and struggled to find air.

"Maybe you should look at the rest of the pictures to make sure."

"I don't have to look at any more pictures. That's him. That's the man who killed Mr. Hunter." She forced her gaze from the picture of the man who changed her life. She stared at Trent. "You knew, didn't you? That's why you skipped so many pages."

"I suspected it was him." He shrugged. "I had to make sure." He lifted the phone from the wall. "Yeah. Pick him up. I hope we're not too late." He hung up and went back to the table, but he didn't sit down.

"Who is he?"

"He works for some people. You don't need to know his name."

"What people?" She frowned. "Why are you being so vague? What aren't you telling me?"

"Some people are laundering drug money."

"Laundering drug money? The mob? The killer is part of the mob?" She jumped up. The chair tumbled over, but she wasn't aware of it. She backed up until she was against the wall. "The mob? I work for the mob?"

"You worked for Mr. Hunter. Besides, that's an old term. The so-called mob of the old days has a lot of competition for the drug trade nowadays."

"Drugs?" She frowned and shook her head. "Uh, uh. I can't believe it. Mr. Hunter was always together. I mean, he didn't smile much, but neither do I. If he used drugs, wouldn't he have acted strange? I would have noticed something funny.

I'm not an expert or anything, and I don't have much free time, but I watch a little television. I've seen how users act. Don't they nod or act spaced out or something? Mr. Hunter didn't act that way. He acted . . ." She paused. "He acted normal. All the time."

"You're talking about junkies. Just because somebody sells drugs doesn't mean he uses them. In fact, most dealers don't use. They can't afford to lose control. It's a business."

"Mr. Hunter sold beer. *That* was his business. I know because I saw the office records." Then she said, "Once he left a file folder out and I . . ." She stared at Trent. "I had to look at what was inside to see where to file it. I saw the inventory. I saw how much beer was in the warehouses. I knew how much was at each location." Her sentences ran together as if she was afraid of losing the connection.

"Anything can be worked out on paper."

"That file that I saw . . ." She frowned and her words came as if they had run out of power and were waiting for her memory to supply some more. "Mr. Hunter was upset that I saw it. He told me never to touch anything on his desk. Told me to forget what I saw." She shrugged. "I didn't understand, but he was the boss." She shrugged again. "But why did they kill him? He was making a lot of money for them."

"We're not sure. I suspect he was making more money for himself than he should have. Besides, it was all on paper. Most of the money came from them."

"He was stealing from them? From the mob?"

"Like I said, we're not sure. We'll know more after we pick up the shooter."

"What happens now? How long do I have to stay here? Can I go home?" Her eyes widened. "Are you going to arrest me for working for the mob? I didn't know anything about it. I swear."

"We know. I'm not going to arrest you."

"Then I want to go home. Do I have to sign a paper or something before I can leave? What happens now? I don't have to stay here until you catch the killer, do I? How long will that take?"

"Wait here. I have to go check on something."

Trent let out a heavy breath when he got outside the room. Getting arrested would be the least of her worries if she knew all of the facts. A plan formed in his mind that went against his usually sensible thoughts. It dug in and forced his common sense to disappear.

As he walked to the chief's office, he wished it were farther away. Maybe then he would have time to put together a convincing argument against what he was going to suggest. He shook his head.

There was no reason the chief should do what he planned to ask him to do. In fact, he should deny it right away and Trent should accept that. The chief was a stickler for protocol and what Trent wanted was so far away from routine procedure that he knew the chief wouldn't be expecting his request. He, himself, was surprised at what he intended to ask. He took a deep breath and opened the office door. He would ask anyway.

"We got a hit from her." He explained what happened. Then he took a deep breath and stated the improbable.

"I want this case."

"What do you mean? You have it."

"I mean after this part is over. I want her assigned to me until it's over."

"We don't know how long it will take."

"I know that."

"I can't leave you on one case. You're finished with it."

"I don't have to be."

"I can't do what you're asking."

"Sure you can."

"It could take months. Years. I can't authorize that."

"I need to protect her."

"We have a procedure in place for that."

"We both know what can happen to that procedure."

"We've corrected that problem."

"Chief, I want this assignment."

"Can't do it."

"Okay." Trent set his badge on the desk. Then, staring at the chief, he laid his gun beside it.

The chief looked at Trent's career staring at him from the desk. Then he stared at Trent. "What's this woman to you? What aren't you telling me?"

"Nothing. There's nothing else to tell. I just met her." It was true, but he felt as if it wasn't. If he were a believer, he'd think that they had been together in a past life.

"Then why put your career on the line like this?"

"I don't know." He frowned as he shook his head. "I just know I have to make sure she's safe until this is over. I have time coming. Or I can take unpaid leave. Or I can do this on my own." He shrugged. "Whichever way, I'm taking this case."

Trent stared at the chief, glad that he had a sizable nest egg. The chief stared back. Finally he sighed and pushed the badge and gun back to Trent. "I don't know how long I can do this."

"Thanks, chief." He turned to go.

"You don't bluff."

"Never have."

Trent didn't try to understand his own actions. He just went back to Angela.

Four

For the first time since she got to this unreal place, Angela looked around the drab room. It was taller than it was wide. If she stood with both arms outstretched, she could almost touch the side walls. She wrinkled her nose. When was the last time they painted this room? She swallowed the lump that had formed in her throat. Was a cell this small? She shivered. *I hope I never learn the answer to that question.*

She pushed that thought away. *Detective Stewart said he's not going to arrest me.* She frowned. *Was that before or after he found out that I worked for the mob?* She shook her head. *Not the mob. Somebody else.* The crease in her forehead deepened. *Who else was there? Somebody just as bad.* She let out a slow breath. *Don't think about that.* She forced herself to go back to examining the room.

Small and gray and dirty. It looked as if the only color the painters had was dirty grayish brown. Over the years real dirt had layered over the paint. How old was this building? She hadn't noticed what the outside looked like when she came in. She had been too busy trying to hold herself together. Fear tried to grow inside her, now, but she made it stay small enough for her to handle. *Concentrate on the room.*

She glanced at the ceiling. How did it get so dirty looking? This time it was only her head that shook. This room probably looked dirty when the paint was new. Was ugly paint cheaper? She took a deep breath and wrinkled her nose. Even the air was ugly.

She walked over to the mirror stretching across the wall opposite the table. *Was this one of those windows where they could see you, but you couldn't see them?* She once read an article that told about a way you could tell if glass was mirrored. She frowned. She couldn't remember how, though. She tapped her index fingernail on the glass, barely touching it. A mirror/window wasn't important to her. She didn't care who was watching her or how many were watching. Not in here where it was safe. The more people who saw her identify the killer, the more would be looking for him, and the better the chance of him being caught.

She closed her eyes. Please let it be soon. In spite of the close air, she took a deep breath. *What happens now?* Her stomach growled its hoped-for answer.

She paced around the table as if it were a miniature field and she was going around the track. By the time Trent opened the door, Angela felt as if she had completed enough circuits to make several laps around a real field. She looked at him as if seeing him for the first time.

Her glance had to move up as he got closer. *How tall is he?* He stopped when he reached the opposite side of the table. *Over six feet. Way over six feet,* she answered her own question. He had probably shaved this morning, but the shadow of a beard was forming beneath his full mouth. She blinked. *This morning was a long time ago.*

His white shirt contrasted with the caramel color of his face. What kind of detective wore a tuxedo? A shiver rippled through her. If she hadn't been in a police station, she would have questioned again whether he was really a police officer. Never mind the ID that he had shown her. If people could counterfeit money, identification would be easy.

She made herself calm down. She was in a police station and some of the uniformed officers had spoken to him as if they knew him. If he wasn't an officer, he wouldn't have brought her here. She sighed. *Enough of this.* She wanted it all over.

"Can I go now?"

He stared at her with eyes that looked as if somebody had colored them in with a black crayon. She started to repeat the question when he finally spoke.

"Sit down. Please."

That was not an answer to her yes-or-no question. She stared back at him. She felt as if she were back where she started from when she first came into this room. *Now what?*

"Why is it that nobody ever has good news when they say 'sit down'?" She crossed her arms and continued to stare at him. She did not sit down.

"We have a problem."

"What kind of problem could there be? You know who the killer is. I identified him. You pick him up. He goes to trial, a speedy trial. I testify. I'm out of this mess. How is that a problem?"

"The killer is a professional hitman."

"What does that mean?"

"That means that he gets paid for killing people."

"I know what 'professional hitman' means. I do read the paper and watch television. Sometimes. What *I* mean is what does what he is have to do with me? We still know who he is." She glared at him. "You do prosecute professionals no matter what their job when they break the law and when they've been identified, don't you?"

"Miss Baring, please sit down."

She stared at him a few seconds longer, then sat in the same chair where this part of her nightmare had started.

Trent stared back. *Where to start? How to put this so she didn't bolt or tumble over the edge?*

He shouldn't have asked for this case. He had felt himself pulled to her from the second he saw her. He couldn't afford to let his emotions get involved. *Any more than they already are,* his mind added. *It was too late.* Still, he should have let the chief assign somebody else to her—anybody else—so Trent could get her off his mind and move on to the next case and back to his controlled life. *Lonely life,* his mind added. *How do you make your mind shut up when it's telling you the truth?*

He shook his head slightly. No, he didn't mean just anybody else. A couple of his colleagues couldn't guard a turtle without losing it or fouling things up. If there were an award at the annual banquet for incompetence, Trent could name at least three people who would be in the running.

The image of the result of such a botched assignment by a former detective flashed through his mind as it had when he was going to see the chief. He hadn't been able to blink it away; that was why he insisted that the chief assign Angela Baring to him. *Not this time.* He couldn't let what happened that time happen to her. This time he was handling the witness. Lester Ford would have to go through him.

Trent wasn't the only competent detective in the department, but his record showed that he was up there with those who were. He wasn't going to lose her. They needed her. And he, he needed . . . . He frowned. He wanted. . . . He shook his head. *Don't go there, Trent. This is a job. And that's all it can ever be. Your needs and wants don't enter into this.*

"What now? What do you have to tell me?" Angela's words pulled him back to the present.

"Do you want some coffee?"

"No, I *still* don't want any coffee. It keeps me awake, remember?" She glanced at her watch. "You seem to be substituting for coffee tonight." She sighed and leaned back. "Just tell me, okay?"

"As I said, Lester Ford—that's the killer's name—is a hitman. Yes, we will prosecute him. We have an excellent case. But we've had him before and we could never make the charges stick." *Please don't let her ask me why.*

"Why?"

Trent took a deep breath and tried to sound casual. "Usually the jury didn't think we had enough evidence." Before she could ask about the times that weren't usual, he went on. "The only way we can nail him is with an eyewitness."

"Me."

"You."

"So? I'll be glad to testify. What's the problem?"

He hesitated. She waited. He couldn't think of a way around the answer. "We've lost witnesses before."

"What do you mean, you've 'lost witnesses before'?"

"These people are dangerous."

"They scared your witnesses off?"

"Sometimes."

"Sometimes? Isn't it against the law not to tell the truth when you're on the witness stand?"

"Yes."

"Well?" She stared at him for a few seconds, waiting for an answer. Then her eyes widened, telling him the second she found the answer on her own. "They killed them, didn't they? They killed the witnesses."

"It won't happen to you. I promise."

She kept staring at him. He could see it in her eyes as soon as trust replaced her fear. Right then he swore to himself that he'd do everything in his power to keep that trust.

She swallowed hard. "What—what do we do now?"

"We get your things from your place and get you to a safe house."

"Safe house? You think the killer knows where I live?"

Trent tried not to notice the panic that returned and made her eyes widen again. He tried not to feel guilty that he had put it there. Again. "I think he can find out. I *don't* think he knows yet. He was a little too preoccupied to search the employee records in Mr. Hunter's office. He'd have to get the info some other way."

"He can do that? How?"

"That's not important."

"But. . . ."

"We need to leave now."

"We? Are you going with me?"

"Yeah. The chief gave me this assignment."

"For how long?"

"As long as it takes."

She took a deep breath. "Okay. I'm ready." Her voice shivered, but determination filled her face. Angela took a deep breath and stood. "Let's get this over with."

Trent looked at her for a few seconds. He had to look closely to see the slight tremor in her hands. He wished he could do something to make it go away. But then, if he had his wishes granted, she wouldn't be involved in this at all even if it meant that he never met her.

He walked in front of her as if he expected something to happen here in the station. He let out a hard breath. May as well start now.

Angela sat in the back of his car as Trent had insisted. *I'm too tired to argue,* she thought, as she crawled into the backseat.

She leaned back and closed her eyes. *Wouldn't it be nice to wake up and find that this is all a nightmare? That Nick is at his desk and Mr. Hunter is wherever he goes when he leaves the office.* She sighed. *While I'm riding a flight of fancy, wouldn't it be nice to wake up and find myself with an MBA degree and a corner office at a Fortune 500 company?*

She would not think again of how she could have made this come out differently if she hadn't gone back up to the office—if she had remembered her folder the first time instead of thinking about Dwight. Dwight. They didn't have a set pattern, but she usually called him when she got home. How would she explain this to him? She blinked hard. She was having trouble understanding it herself.

None of what was happening to her was in her control, now, and she didn't like it. She was caught in the middle. She opened her eyes and stared out the window. Regardless of how it had happened and whether it was fair or not, she was still caught. She was grateful that she was still alive to think about it all.

Trent stopped the car in front of the duplex town house near the end of the small old building where she lived. He looked in the rearview mirror and the side mirrors. Then he checked the rearview mirror once more before he turned and looked at her. She was staring ahead even though the front seat was blocking much of her view. It didn't matter. For all of her awareness, the car could be weaving in and out of traffic on the Schuylkill Expressway doing ninety miles an hour and she wouldn't know it.

He frowned. She had shown a little spark a couple of times. He hoped she had more. She was going to need a huge supply before they were through with this mess.

"Do you have your keys?"

"Huh?"

"Your keys to your apartment."

"Oh." She came back from wherever her mind had taken her and looked out the window. "We're here."

"Yeah. Do you have your keys?" *No sign of anyone, but no sense in staying out here waiting for somebody to show up, either.*

"Yeah, I have them." She frowned and stared at her hand and opened it. A wad of keys large enough to be used as a paperweight spilled from her palm. He watched her take a deep breath. "Just a minute."

She dropped the keys into her lap twice before she held on to them. He watched as she separated one key from the rest so it stuck out, then she handed the bunch to him.

He took it and frowned. *What reason could she possibly have for carrying all of these keys? He had always thought that carrying a ton of keys was a man thing.* He shrugged. "Which one is for the back door?"

"The back door?"

"You do have a back door?"

"Yes."

"You do have a key for it, don't you?"

"Of course I do." She took the keys back, pulled up the one next to the front door key, and handed the bunch to him again.

He checked around outside once more. The street was still asleep. He hoped it stayed that way, at least until they got away from here. He frowned. *Leave her here in the car, or take her inside with me?*

"Come on." His instinct told him that her place was still safe. His jaw tightened. He hoped his instinct was right.

He got out of the car and opened the door for her. As soon as the car door was closed, he grabbed her hand and hurried around the building and into the narrow alley. He breathed a little easier when he saw that it was empty: no people, no cars. He knew he was going too fast for her, but he'd rather have her fuss about trying to keep up then have her not be able to fuss at all.

He glanced at the spindly bush in the tiny backyard. Too small for any harm. Still holding her hand, he dashed up the six steps leading to her door pulling her with him, jammed the key into the lock, and shoved open the door. She was still trying to catch her breath when he pushed her inside.

"Why did you . . . ?"

Trent put a finger to her lips. No other sound escaped; still he had to force his hand away when what he wanted to do was rub a thumb along her bottom lip. Twice? Three times? After that, he wanted to . . . He sighed. Maybe in another place. Definitely not at this time.

He motioned for her to stay in place beside the door. She nodded. He listened, but wasn't satisfied that the only sounds were the hum of the refrigerator and the heating unit. He peeked out the back window, then stole through the small kitchen.

He glanced back at Angela, nodded when he saw her still where he had put her, motioned for her to stay there, and disappeared into the hall.

Angela stood as if glued to the wall. If he hadn't come inside with her, she would have sworn that she was in the house alone. She took a deep breath. If she had been able to move as quietly in the office building as Detective Stewart was moving now, the killer—that Lester Ford person—wouldn't have known she was there. She sighed.

It wouldn't have mattered much. She still saw him kill Mr. Hunter and she still would have told the police. Of course, the killer wouldn't have known that she saw him until the trial. That would have given her more time. She could have finished her courses. She probably would have graduated before the trial began. Maybe she'd have a job where she could use her degree. She swallowed hard. Nick would still be dead. So would Mr. Hunter. She blinked. *Did their families know yet?*

The refrigerator clicked off, rested awhile, then clicked back on. Had it always been so loud? Still she waited.

The rooms in her first-floor one-bedroom apartment were small. What was taking him so long? What if somebody had been in the apartment when they got here? Just because she couldn't hear anyone else didn't mean somebody wasn't in here. She couldn't hear Detective Stewart and she *knew* he was here. What if something had happened to him? It would be her fault, all her fault.

She took a deep breath, grabbed the biggest knife from the rack on the counter, and pushed off from the wall.

Five

"Where do you think you're going?" Angela jumped when she turned the corner into the hall and bumped into Trent.

"I was . . ." She frowned. "I thought . . ." She took a deep breath. "You were gone for so long. . . ." Her words trailed off to nothing as he glared at her.

"I told you to stay there. Where were you going?"

"I-I was coming to find you." She glared. "I thought something had happened to you."

"And you were going to . . . ?" His face tightened. His glare gained strength. "You were going to save me? How? I have a gun. Anyone here would have had one, too. You do not have a gun. You have probably never touched a gun." He clenched his teeth. "You probably don't even carry a can of mace or pepper spray." He saw color redden her skin. He nodded. "That's what I thought." He'd lecture her about that later. "What did you plan to do? Talk the gun away from them?" He glanced at her hand and back to her face. "Or use that knife? Do you really think someone with a gun would let you get close enough to stab them? Maybe you planned to throw it at them. I'm sure you've practiced that trick so that you're as good as the men in the circus acts."

For a few seconds she felt foolish. Then she stood up straight, stretching her five-foot-four-inch height to at least five-six. It didn't matter that she deserved to feel like a fool. She was trying to help. "I thought something had happened to you. If so, it would have been my fault."

He stared a bit longer, then he shook his head. "Look. I'm

supposed to protect *you*. That's *my* job. *You* are supposed to keep yourself safe. That's *your* job. Anything happens to me is *my* fault. Clear?" She shrugged. "I'll take that as a yes. Come on. Let's get what you need and so we can get out of here." He shook his head again. "Give me that before you hurt yourself." He took the knife and tossed it to the hall table and stared at it. Then he took it into the kitchen and put it back in the rack. "Okay. Let's do this so we can leave."

Angela's glare hardened as she slipped past him. She'd be glad when this was all over and she didn't have to see him any more. He was too bossy.

She took a suitcase from the upstairs hall closet and went into the bedroom. Then she took out the smallest suitcase nestled inside the larger two.

"That's all you'll need? I never knew a woman to travel so light before."

"It will only be for a couple of days, right?" She opened a couple of dresser drawers.

"You better plan on more than a couple of days."

She stopped and clutched a handful of clothes to her. "How long will I be gone?"

"Use a bigger suitcase."

She stared at him. "How long will I have to be away? You know who you're looking for. If he's still in Philadelphia, you can get him. If he's not, he can't get me, right?"

"Pack a bigger suitcase."

"Fine." She lifted the largest suitcase to the bed, opened it, took out the middle-size one, and opened it, too.

He closed the largest bag and set it on the floor. "The two smaller ones should be okay."

She shrugged, opened the closet door, but didn't take any clothes out.

"What are you waiting for?"

"I have to decide what to take."

"Is that a variation of 'I don't have a thing to wear'?" He ignored her glare. "Take basic stuff. Pack whatever you're comfortable in. You're not going to any social functions and you're not going to work." He regretted his last words as soon as he said them. He watched as color fled from her face. He should have known what her reaction would be.

Her hand shook as she reached for a pair of jeans, but she didn't say anything. The trembling had almost stopped by the time she took out a second pair.

Trent put the largest suitcase back into the closet, then came back into the bedroom. He leaned against the wall and watched as she finished filling the two bags. She glanced at him and tried to block his view when she got to her underwear. In spite of the situation, he had trouble keeping a smile from his face when she had to turn his way. There was no way she could pack them without him seeing them. She probably referred to them as unmentionables. *Was she as innocent as she seemed?*

He watched as she hurriedly placed them in the corner of the suitcase and zipped it closed. *It didn't matter. This was business. Only business. I'll never find out.*

"Ready?"

Angela stared at the only photograph in the room, hesitated, and took it from the dresser. She wiped her hand across it and slipped it into the bigger suitcase before closing it, too.

"I'm ready." She slipped her purse strap over her shoulder and lifted the smallest bag from the bed. She never looked back. He couldn't tell her to say good-bye to this place—that she wouldn't be coming back. The chief would have somebody pack the rest of her things and put them in storage until after the trial, but she didn't have to know that right now.

"Wait." She stopped in the living room and picked up a backpack. She looked at him before she picked up the folders she had worked on tonight. When she got to the one she had gone back up to the office for, the one that had started this flight, she hesitated. He watched as she took a deep breath, wiped her hand on her slacks, and then slipped the folder into the pack. "My course work. I worked too hard to leave this. I only have one more paper to finish and hand in. It's due Monday. This coming Monday." She looked at him and waited, but when he didn't say anything about Monday, she continued, "After my finals I graduate. I'll have my degree."

"Ready?"

"Yes." She started toward the front door.

"Wait." He stopped her before she could open it and looked out the window. The only cars on the street were the ones that were there when they parked. Quiet still filled the street. He shielded her anyway as they went to the car. Being careful never hurt. He hurried her into the car, then put her luggage into the trunk. In less than a minute they were at the end of the street, and no one had known they had been there.

"Do you have any family to tell so they won't be worried?" Trent drove onto the expressway and blended into the traffic. He remembered the picture she had packed and glanced over at her.

"No. My parents and grandparents are dead. I come from a small family."

"Husband?" He hadn't seen any signs of a man living with her, but he hadn't been looking for any. She didn't wear a ring, but there could be several reasons for that.

"No. I'm not married."

Why did that make him feel good? "Boyfriend?" He tried to convince himself that he only wanted to know because of the case.

"I'm seeing someone."

Now he tried to convince himself that hearing that didn't bother him. He failed at that, too. "You should call him so he won't worry." He handed her his cell phone. "Just tell him that you'll be away for a while. Don't tell him why."

She took the phone.

"Hi, Dwight. Yeah, I know it's late. No, I haven't been working on an assignment all this time. I-I . . ." She frowned. "I have to go away for . . . ?" She looked at Trent, but he didn't help her with an answer. "I have to be away for a while. No, it doesn't have anything to do with school." She frowned. "I know we haven't. I was going to call you earlier, but . . ." She sighed. "I know I said that before, but this time I meant it. Look, I don't want to argue. I'll call you when I get back." Her frown deepened. "Is somebody with you?" Trent saw her eyes fill. "I know I don't own you. I thought we had something special. Evidently I was wrong."

She broke the connection and handed the phone back to Trent. She turned her head, but he saw her wipe her eyes anyway.

He was sorry that she was hurting. *What kind of fool was she seeing that he didn't see what a wonderful person she was?* He wanted to comfort her. He tried not to be relieved that things with the "someone" were shaky. He shook his head. It was a good thing that he was more successful at doing his job than he was at convincing himself to believe a lie.

She was in the car, but her thoughts were still on the conversation with Dwight. *How dare he. All the talking he did about how special I was to him, and he was with another woman. And he had the nerve to act as if it were my fault.* She glared at the back of the front seat. This time the shiver that rippled through her had nothing to do with the murders. She had thought he was special, but all she was to him was a challenge to his male ego. How long had he been running around on her? She shook her head. That wasn't important. He was running around. That's all that mattered. She frowned. *Why is my ego hurting more than my heart?*

They had been riding for about twenty minutes when she broke into the silence.

"Where are you taking me?"

"West Philly. I have to pick up a few things from my place."

"And after that?"

"There's a place we call a safe house. We'll go there."

"Oh."

She didn't want to know how safe the "safe house" was nor how he knew she'd be safe there. Right now the only thing she wanted to know was how long it would be before she could put this mess behind her. And, no matter how good he was at his job, she knew that he couldn't tell her that.

For the rest of the ride she huddled in the middle of the back-seat; she hugged her purse to her as if it gave her comfort or protection.

"This is it." He looked around before he got out.

Angela looked out at the row of old stone houses that were built way before row houses became town houses. She opened the door, but he pushed it shut.

"Wait a minute."

She watched as he slowly glanced up and down the street. Shivers tried to take over her again. If he wasn't sure his own house was safe, she must really be in danger.

"Okay." This time he walked closely behind her.

His hand on her back hurried her up the steps and onto the wide porch. Even though they were rushing, she felt safer with his hand on her. He unlocked the door and they went in.

"You can wait in here." He led her into the living room. "Sit there." He pointed to a chair against the wall when she headed for the couch under the window. She didn't want to think about the reason for that. She sat and closed her eyes. There was a lot she didn't want to think about.

He finished much faster than she had. Soon he came into the room with a small suitcase and a duffel bag. He went into the hall and came back with a couple of blankets and pillows. "Will you carry these?" She nodded as she reached for them. Her hands were steady. He smiled slightly. "We can go now."

He stopped her at the door and looked out.

"The street is full of parked cars. How do you know whether or not somebody is out there who . . . who . . ."

"I know my neighbors' cars." She was asking hard questions. That was a good sign.

They were almost out of Philadelphia when she spoke.

"I forgot something."

"What?"

"A book from my apartment. I need it to finish my report."

"You can't finish without it?"

"No. I-I'm sorry."

He glanced at her. Her warm brown eyes pleaded with him. He was a sucker for warm brown eyes. He left the express-way, turned around, and went back the way they had come.

He stopped at the corner of her street even though there was a spot in front of her house. "Where is the book?"

"I can get it. I know it when I see it."

"I'll get it. Where is it?"

"On the table. It's the book on the top of the pile to the right. Or is it the left? It's a statistics book. A library book. The one with a yellow and white cover. The only library book. You can tell by the pocket inside the back cover." She frowned. "I can't remember the exact title." She shrugged. "I looked at so many before I decided to check out that one."

"Why don't I bring all of the books on the table?"

"There are a lot." She let her gaze shift from his. "Okay. Bring them all. But if I come with you . . ."

"No. I'll bring all of them. Give me your keys. You stay here."

"Okay."

"I'll get the books."

"Okay."

"Don't get out of the car."

"Okay."

"I mean it, Angela."

"Okay. I'll wait here."

"No matter what."

"Okay, okay. I said I'll wait." When he stared at her without moving, she added, "I promise."

She watched him go. Everything was all right a little while ago when they were here. She didn't see why she couldn't go in and get the book herself. A minute. No more than two. That's all it would take. The one book that she needed was on top of a pile right on the table. It would have been a lot easier for her to go than for him to bring all the books. She sighed and leaned back. She said she'd wait and she would. At least for a while.

***

A book. He came all the way back here for a book. Big brown eyes were his weakness—*one* of his weaknesses. She had a few more of his weaknesses, too.

He drew his gun and held it at his side as he went around to the back. He stared at the windows of her apartment for a short while, but he didn't go up the steps. He went back to the corner, around to the front of the building and crossed the street.

He walked slowly down the sidewalk. He was just a brother coming home late. He stopped across the street from the house. He pretended to fumble in his pockets for something, but his gaze was on the house. Did a slight shadow cross in front of the living room curtain? He moved closer to a parked car and crouched out of sight. Then he watched and waited. Her apartment was dark. In another situation, he might think he had imagined the movement. The curtain at the small window in the door shifted slightly. It could be a draft from the heating/cooling vent. It was cool enough for the heat to click on and off. Or maybe it was the air from the refrigerator fan going off and on. The door was in a position for that to happen. He shook his head. He knew it wasn't either of those.

Damn. They had moved fast. He had been on the alert from the time he and Angela had left the station, but he was still surprised at the speed with which they got here. She must have really stumbled into something big.

For years the department had been hoping for a break like this. It was Angela's misfortune to be the one to provide it.

He stood slowly, brushed himself off, and continued to the end of the street.

Quietly he moved through the alley behind the houses, praying that a dog didn't give him away or that an edgy neighbor wouldn't call 911 and report a prowler. He didn't want to take time to explain what was going on. He had to get her away from here. He clenched his teeth. *She better still be waiting in the car.*

He slipped inside the car, glad she had listened to him. He didn't say anything, just started the motor and eased down the street.

"What happened? Where are the books? You couldn't find them? I know I left them on the table. Do you want me to go get them? They shouldn't have been hard to find. I know I left the table in a mess, but that's the way I work. Besides, I didn't cover up the books."

They were around the corner and a block away before he spoke. "You'll have to do the best you can without it."

"But I need it. I know the books were right there on the table. I don't understand. I'm sorry you had to come back for it, but you did. So why didn't you get it? Or let me come get it? I could have . . . Oh, no." She took in a sharp breath. "Somebody is in my apartment."

He didn't look back at her. "Finish your report without the book. Improvise." He wasn't going to tell her that finishing might be a waste of time. No way was she going back to school. Even if the chief handed in her report, she still couldn't take her finals. He shook his head. The chief would have to work something out with the school. It wasn't fair for her to come this far and not finish.

"I have to take that book back to the library. It's due on Tuesday. If I don't take it back I'll owe a fine." She took a deep breath, but it didn't steady her words. "Oh, man. Somebody is in my apartment. How did they find out where I live?"

"With the miracle of the Internet anybody can find anyone." He glanced back at her. "Unless the person takes steps to keep that from happening."

"How safe is the 'safe house'?"

"Like Harriet Tubman, I haven't lost anyone yet."

He wasn't using the safe house. If they found her apartment already, they might know where he was taking her. It wasn't pleasant to think about, but there were ways of discovering the locations of the safe houses, too.

Six

Trent hesitated, then headed for I-95. He waited until they were in Delaware County before he pulled over and made a call.

"A change of plans. We went back to her place but company was waiting for us." He shook his head. "No, no problem. We didn't go inside. No, they didn't see us." He glanced at Angela. "I'm not taking her to the safe house, though, too chancy." He nodded. "Thanks for your faith in me." A slight smile flitted across his face. "Yeah. Too bad you can't register 'gut feelings' as legitimate reasons for action." He chuckled. "Uh-huh. I'll keep you posted."

"Where are we going if we don't go to the safe house?" Angela waited until Trent hung up.

"I have a place in mind."

"How do you know it's safe if the police's so-called 'safe house' isn't?"

"Nobody knows about this place but me." He glanced back at her. "I mean nobody. Not even the chief and I trust him with my life." He glanced at her again. "Now, why don't you try to get some sleep?"

"You're kidding, right?"

"It's after two in the morning. We've got about a three-hour drive ahead of us."

"Oh, like a kid on a long trip, I should go to sleep so the time will go faster."

Nothing about her was kidlike; only a pervert would feel about a kid the way he was starting to feel about her. Of course he couldn't tell her how he felt.

"You've had a long, hard day. Try to get some rest." He glanced at her and smiled. "When we get there, you can stay awake if you want to while I get some sleep."

Trent continued south. Ten minutes later he glanced at her in the rearview mirror, hoping to see that she was asleep. She was sitting up straight. Her gaze was focused ahead, but he knew she wasn't seeing anything. He hoped exhaustion would overcome her. She had been through a lot. She'd be safe with him, but this wasn't over for her. It would get a lot worse before she was out of this.

A drizzle had started by the time he got to the Delaware state line. Rain was still coming down when Trent pulled off I-95 about an hour later, leaving the highway to the truckers and the few cars that must not have had a choice about stopping. He wondered how many of the truck drivers rolling past had gotten their training for going without sleep from the military, as he had. And how many truckers had grabbed a few hours sleep earlier this evening while the civilians crowded the road trying to get that last mile in?

He turned onto 301-13. Staying awake was harder without the distraction of a stream of other traffic. Another two hours. He only had to stay awake for about two more hours. He went over plans in his head: plans he might or might not use; plans he might not need to use.

He reviewed what had happened. And what most certainly would happen. And what he would not let happen. He thought about his passenger who had finally yielded to exhaustion about forty-five minutes ago. He shook his head.

She wasn't just a passenger—she was a witness: a vital witness in the most important case the police department had been working on in years. The feds were probably already involved but hadn't seen fit to tell them. Her testimony would help bring down one of the most powerful crime organizations in the country. He sighed. *Why couldn't the witness be an ugly old man? He'd be just as important and I would make the same effort to protect him, but no emotions would threaten to enter into the mix.*

What was there about her that made him wish for things

that could never be? He had dated women who were more beautiful. Carmen, his ex-wife, was an example. Another image, that of Lila, the cover model whom he had dated for a long while, sprang up in his mind. Her green eyes in her flawless face did nothing for him now. If he were honest with himself, he'd admit that it hadn't done much for him at the time they were seeing each other. He sighed. He felt no reaction to the memory, no regret that they had both decided that the relationship was going nowhere.

He glanced into his rearview mirror. Angela was still asleep, but the memory of her large brown eyes in a face that looked as if it had forgotten how to laugh shoved Carmen and Lila away.

Some men wouldn't bother to look at Angela a second time. She wasn't flashy or glamorous. Trent shook his head. Those men were fools who couldn't recognize something special when they stumbled across it.

He looked into the mirror again. Angela Baring was getting next to him. He shook his head slightly. He had to find a way to keep himself from getting next to her. His job was to protect her. That's all. If there were a way to carve that sentence into his mind, he'd do it. He forced his gaze back to the road, but his mind kept returning to Angela.

He turned onto a country road and drove past sleeping houses. He wasn't sure how he felt about having the road to himself. He drove slower, not just because of the lowered speed limit, but because he didn't want to miss the turnoff to the cabin.

Uncle Joe, Trent's last close relative, had left the property to Trent five years ago, but Trent hadn't been here since he took care of Uncle Joe's things after his funeral. Trent shrugged. Every so often he'd say he'd come down, but something always came up to change his mind. Maybe he just hadn't wanted to face the emptiness alone.

The mailbox marking the rutted, dirt pull-off road to the cabin was rusty and long forgotten, but it was the only sign that a cabin was at the end of the road. Trent straddled the hump left between the ruts. To call this a road or a driveway would have been too generous. If this were a couple of months later, weeds would have taken over and the only clue that this road had ever existed would be the abandoned mailbox.

Uncle Joe and Aunt Sadie called this their "get-away-from-the-world" cabin. Trent was counting on that.

He followed the car path as it wound its way toward the house, skirting the oaks and maples that had been full grown even before the cabin was built and that had no intention of giving up their places. Just when he reached the point where anybody who didn't know differently would have decided that this was a forgotten footpath and would have struggled to back out, the cabin came into view.

Trent stopped the car in front of the porch that spanned the whole cabin. Summers, he and Uncle Joe and Aunt Sadie would sit out here for hours; they in their matching woven split-wood rockers and he on the swing at the end of the porch, all three pretending that the citronella candles were keeping the mosquitoes hungry. Now the swing looked lonely, even with the rockers for company.

He turned and looked at Angela. She was still huddled in the corner, asleep. He hesitated, then he got out. She'd be safe out here while he checked out the house.

He unlocked the padlock on the door, relieved that it was still in place. Uncle Joe would have shaken his head at the idea of a lock.

"What do you think will happen?" Uncle Joe would have said. "Do you think the raccoons and 'possums would come in and steal our treasures?" Then he would have released one of the deep laughs that came from his generous belly. Trent sighed. That was the difference between city living and country living. The city teaches you that nothing is safe unless it's locked up, and sometimes not even then.

The outside of the weathered cabin made it look as if it had been abandoned decades ago and was just waiting to give the land back to nature. Trent knew the inside would tell the true story.

He stepped inside the cabin built to outlast the so-called

well-built buildings in the city, and allowed a slight smile to cross his face.

Sturdy but small. It wouldn't take long to check out the whole cabin. This room, a small kitchen, and the bedroom. That's all. The narrow, short hallway ended at the bathroom. Trent's smile widened. Aunt Sadie had said that she didn't mind the rough outside, but she had to have certain necessities inside and the bathroom topped her list.

Trent walked a path through the thick layer of dust. A chill rippled through him. He checked the firewood box beside the stone fireplace to make sure he had filled it the last time he was here. He looked at the stove against the wall. Uncle Joe had called the massive cast iron stove "Papa Bear." Trent chuckled. Uncle Joe liked the isolation, but he and Aunt Sadie also liked being comfortable. Trent was grateful for that. He peered inside the stove and his smile widened. He had once asked Uncle Joe why he laid paper and kindling for a new fire as soon as the ashes from the old one were cold. "When you're cold, you want to get warm as soon as you can," had been his answer. Trent shivered again. He had one more thing to be grateful to Uncle Joe for.

Trent got the box of matches from the wide oak mantel over the fireplace. He went back to the stove and hoped the matches were still good. He had been a boy scout growing up, but he had no idea of how to start a fire with two sticks unless one was a match.

In spite of the layer of dust, the yellowed paper peeking out between the wood lit with the second match. Trent had to force himself to wait until the kindling caught fire before he fed in bigger wood. When the log caught, he let out a breath that he hadn't been aware he was holding. Satisfied that the fire no longer needed him, he went through the narrow hallway and into the bedroom.

Cold filled this room, too. He turned on the lamp on one of the nightstands and smiled. How proud Aunt Sadie had been when she bought the lamps with the prize money she had won for her coconut cake at the county fair.

Trent carefully wiped the dust from the lamp. Aunt Sadie

never could tolerate dust. "Sign of a lazy housekeeper," she would say each time she handed him a dust rag and made him help her.

He looked around the room at the old, but still sturdy furniture. Dust covered it, too. *Boy, would Aunt Sadie be mad about the condition of this room.* Trent brushed a finger along the headboard. "Thick enough to plant seeds," another of Aunt Sadie's expressions, popped up in his mind. Dust floated down and joined that on the bed covering. It was a good thing that the mattress on the heavy mahogany bed was still wrapped with the plastic tarp he used when he was here last. Something else he had learned from Uncle Joe and Aunt Sadie. He examined the top and sides, slipped off the tarp that was still intact, lifted the mattress, and peeked under it. He nodded. No sign of any creatures taking up residency in the bed.

The thick coat of dust on the tall chest of drawers and dresser matched that on the floor. He hoped Angela wasn't allergic to dust. He frowned. He didn't know anything about her—nothing except that she was trying to finish her work for a degree and that she had been in the wrong place at the worse possible time. He knew one more thing: he was drawn to her like yellow jackets to sweets. He'd fight it because he had to, because he couldn't act on it. If he had the kind of luck on his side that didn't have anything to do with the case, she'd never know.

He lit the fire in the Baby Bear Stove in the bedroom, then left as soon as it caught. He refused to think about the fact that there was only one bed. He flipped on the electric heater in the bathroom and smiled as he was rewarded with a buzz. Neglecting to have the electricity turned off was in his favor.

The wall separating the kitchen from the main room was just long enough for the refrigerator. Dependent on heat from the stove in the living room when nobody was cooking, the kitchen had no door separating the two rooms. The only difference between the kitchen now and when he was last here was the coat of dust.

He flipped on the hot water heater and a hum joined that of the bathroom heater. Then, he plugged in the refrigerator without removing the mop handle propping the door open. He smiled when its hum joined that of the water heater.

He unplugged it until he could clean it. If the washer and dryer worked as well, cleaning clothes would be one less thing to worry about. Bless Aunt Sadie for insisting on convenience.

He fought a yawn as he went to check the pantry. His adrenaline supply was running out.

He noted the few cans of food, but didn't get excited. He had no idea how long canned goods lasted. He yawned again. Tomorrow he had to go food shopping.

"Are you in here?"

"Yeah." He allowed yet another yawn. "It's all right. Come on in." He went back to the living room.

"Where are we? What is this place?" Angela stood just inside the door.

"My cabin. We're on the Eastern Shore in Maryland in a little town called Lakeland."

"This is your cabin?"

"My Uncle Joe built it so he and Aunt Sadie could get away from everything. After she died, he sold their house in D.C. and moved down here permanently." He pointed around. "He brought this furniture with him. Said he felt closer to Aunt Sadie with these pieces." Trent shook his head. "Fifty years." He shook his head again. "They were married fifty years."

"You don't find many marriages lasting that long nowadays."

"No, you don't," he agreed.

His marriage had lasted only five years and that was two years too long. Carmen had divorced him after accusing him of being married to his job. Lila had said the same thing. He shrugged. Looking back, maybe they were right.

"Do you come here often?"

He smiled. She didn't even recognize that as a classic pickup line. He let out a deep breath. *Don't I wish that was how she meant it.* "Not as often as I'd like to. Work always seems to get in the way."

"Like now." Her voice was soft. Another of his weaknesses. He tried to ignore the stirring inside him.

"This is my choice, remember? Besides, it got me down here." He yawned again.

"You're sleepy. Why didn't you wake me and tell me to come in so you could get some sleep?"

"I wanted the cabin to warm up a little and to get rid of some of the dust first."

She shook her head slowly. "Why can't we get rid of some of the dust while the cabin is getting warm?"

He shrugged. *Smart, too.*

"Where are the bedrooms? We should only do the necessary dusting tonight." She glanced through the blue-and-white checked gingham curtains at the window. A thin gray streak of light was forming through the trees. "I should say this morning," she said.

"There's only one bedroom."

She stared at him.

"That's all Uncle Joe and Aunt Sadie needed."

She still stared.

"I'll take the couch," he said.

"And what will you do with your legs? Fold them up or put them in your pocket? You take the bed, I'll take the couch."

"The couch isn't comfortable."

"It looks okay to me." A crease in her forehead joined her stare. "I don't think that's your reason."

"I don't want you out here alone."

"Do you think he can find me here?" The panic was back in her eyes.

"No." He smiled. There had to be some way to make her panic disappear. "I've been accused more than once of being paranoid." His smile widened. "I think the people who said that were just out to get me."

After a few seconds her smile found its way out. "Let's get the bedroom ready. We can argue about who's sleeping where while we do."

Trent turned on the water and let it sputter its way back to life. Then he filled a pail with water and liquid soap and got a sponge from the cupboard. Cold water would have to do for tonight. He shook his head and corrected himself. *This morning*.

"Let me do that while you go get the bedding from the car. I'm sure you don't want me to go out there." *Another sign of her intelligence*.

"Sounds like a plan."

He went out to the car. When he got back, Angela had wiped down the headboard, footboard, and sides, and had just finished wiping off the tarp.

"That has to come off."

"There's no harm in wiping it off first. We can pull it off now." She glanced at him. "I already did the dresser, so you can put the bedding there."

"Okay." Trent did as she suggested, then came over to the bed, trying to ignore the fact that it was a bed.

They stood on opposite sides of the bed. Trent moved as quickly as possible so his mind wouldn't have too much to dwell on.

"We may as well make it while we're at it."

Trent didn't disagree. Putting it off wouldn't change things. He grabbed the bottom sheet and spread it over the bed.

It wasn't long before they were finished. Trent was grateful that he had something else to do.

He went back out and pulled the car around to the back of the cabin. He had to squeeze between overgrown brush, but he felt better with the car away from the front. No sense taking chances.

When he came back with two bags, she was finishing dusting off the chest.

"It's not perfect, but it will do for tonight." She glanced at him, then began mopping.

"I thought we were going to do that tomorrow."

"There will still be more than enough left to do then." She set the mop in the bucket. "You can put those things on the chest and dresser until I do the floor."

"Yes, ma'am." Aunt Sadie would have loved Angela. He smiled at her and went back for the rest of their things.

He yawned again as he got back inside. "Sorry."

"For what? For saving me? For letting me sleep while you drove for hours? I finished that corner." She pointed toward the spot beside one of the windows. "You can put those things there."

"Yes, ma'am."

"Stop calling me that. You make me feel like I'm taking over." He raised his eyebrows and stared at her.

"Okay, okay. Maybe I am taking over just a little. Let's fold the tarp so it won't take up so much space, and put it over there." She pointed to another corner. He continued to stare. "Okay. Maybe I'm taking over a lot, but it's temporary. Well? Are you going to help?"

"Yes, ma . . ."

"Don't you call me ma'am again." She put her hand on her hip. *Definitely a woman thing.*

"Okay."

His tiredness didn't keep a wide grin from his face. It stayed there while they folded the tarp. It disappeared when they finished and the bed seemed to loom larger than ever. *I've got to get out of here.* He turned to leave the room when her words stopped him.

"I don't see why we can't share the bed. Do you? The dust is thick on the couch; I haven't had a chance to wash it. Even if I did, it would be damp, so we couldn't use it even if we did agree on who would sleep there."

One reason reared up in his mind and stayed there as if planted in cement. *Was she really that innocent or did she see him as just a police officer and not a man?* He thought that if the latter was true, it should make this assignment easier for him. He closed his eyes. He wished she didn't, but she made sense. And it was too cold to sleep in the car.

She's an assignment. Only an assignment. Personal feelings between them would complicate the situation. Then why was he disappointed?

"No."

What could he say? *If I have to share a bed with you the temptation will be too much? Since the first time I saw you I wanted to hold you? That you're more than a case to me? That I want to see if you taste as delicious as you look?* He shook his head. *Nothing like having your weaknesses thrown at you to see if you can pass the test.*

"Which side do you want?"

"I'll take the side by the door." He was proud of the answer he gave when what he really wanted to say was, "the same side that you take."

Angela looked at him, sighed, then turned down the covers on her side. She removed a small bag from a suitcase and went to the bathroom. She didn't look at him again when she came back and took off her shoes.

"Good night." She slid into bed, still not glancing his way. Maybe she had thought of a reason for not sharing the bed. The same reason that he had at the beginning.

Trent took his toothbrush from his bag and went into the bathroom. Too bad the tub wasn't bigger. It was cold, but that would have been helpful. It was hard, too, but he wasn't going to think about that. He stared at it for a while longer. Finally he had to go back to the bedroom.

The bed looked as if it had shrunk. Why hadn't his aunt and uncle gotten a king-size or at least a queen-size bed?

He took a deep breath and got under the covers, working to stay on his crib-size half. He turned out the light. *I'm glad I'm tired.*

He let out the breath, took in another and closed his eyes. Gardenia perfume. He inched closer toward the edge, regretting that he reached it so soon. *I'd better be tired enough.*

He wasn't going to look ahead to tonight when he would be well rested.

He turned his back to her when what he wanted to do was gather her to him. He wanted to wrap his arms around her and fall asleep with her in his arms after they made sweet, thorough, complete love.

He kept his hands and arms to himself and waited for—hoped for—the tiredness to take over.

* * *

Angela stretched and opened her eyes. She closed them against the sunlight filtering through the curtains and frowned. Where was she and what was holding her? She turned her head and stared at the handsome face beside her; against her face. His five o'clock shadow was fast becoming a beard. She didn't satisfy her itch to touch it. Instead, she tried to shift away. His arm tightened around her middle. His hand started moving in small circles across her stomach, starting a warmth to spread inside her enough to make a heater envious. *Now what?*

She tried to ignore the fire that his hand was causing to build. The man was asleep. She could be anybody. What did she know of his personal life? Nothing. He was probably dreaming about his woman. Or women.

Carefully she lifted his hand from her and slipped from the bed. Then she gathered her shoes and small suitcase and tiptoed from the room.

Seven

"Good morning." Trent stood in the doorway, stretched, and glanced at the blue clock on the kitchen wall. "Or rather, good afternoon."

"Good afternoon."

Angela looked at the clean counter, at the freshly mopped kitchen floor, at the sponge in her hands that she continued to wring as if it were dripping wet instead of as dry as when it came from the store. She looked everywhere to keep from looking at Trent.

Did he know how he had held her while they slept, as if there were some feelings between them? As if they had made love last night? Was he aware of how his touch had stirred something inside her that she couldn't identify? Would he see it in her face? She took a deep breath. No. If he remembered it at all, he probably thought it was a dream with a beautiful woman— not her or somebody plain-looking like her. She took another deep breath and forced her gaze to center on him.

"Coffee?" Trent stood straight and his face lit up like a kid who just discovered a hidden treasure. "Do I smell coffee or is my imagination in gear?"

He didn't remember. Good. That had to be good. She felt the tension ease from her body. A smile found its way out. "Don't get too excited. I found a can of coffee in the pantry. It wasn't opened, but I'm not sure how long coffee stays fresh." She took a clean mug from the dish rack on the counter and filled it. "I also found an unopened jar of creamer and a canister of sugar. The canister was taped shut so no insects got in, but you'll have to chip some off; it's as solid as concrete." She handed him the mug. "I don't see how people dealt with it when that was the only way you could buy sugar." She tried not to notice when his fingers touched hers as he took the cup. She tried hard. "I'll bet somewhere there's a statue to the person who discovered how to grind sugar."

"Probably. But I don't have to thank him. Or her." He held up the cup. "I drink it just like this. But I do thank you." He took a sip. "The secret of life is coffee." He looked around. Flames had licked away most of a log in the living room stove and had started on another. "You've been busy. You even fed the fire. How long have you been up?"

"A while." No sense telling him that she was functioning on four hours of sleep.

"Did you sleep well?"

"The bed is very comfortable." She had slept well until she awoke with his hand on her, stroking her middle, making the stove unnecessary. She swallowed hard. She couldn't blame the stove for the warmth flooding through her right now. *Tonight, no matter what he says, I sleep on the couch.* "Did you?"

Trent stared at her as if he knew where her thoughts had taken her. "Did I what?"

"Sleep well?"

"Oh. Yeah." He stared at his cup. "As you said, the bed is very comfortable. I always sleep well down here."

Angela stared at him, but he didn't know it. He was staring at his cup as if waiting for a secret to float to the top.

"What did you find to cook?" He smiled. "Imagination doesn't include smell, does it?"

"I don't know. Smells can be pretty powerful." She smiled back. "But not concerning our breakfast. I already ate. I found a couple of cans of hash. I had to throw out the bag of grits. Even though it was in a tightly closed canister, a moth was lying on top when I opened it." She shuddered. "I don't want to think about how that could happen, or worse, when the moth eggs got in there." She put the rest of the hash on a plate and handed it to him.

"Thanks." He sat at the small kitchen table. "As soon as I finish, we have to go food shopping." He looked around. The refrigerator and the stove looked new. "You've been cleaning since you got up."

"It needed to be done." She blinked. "I had to stay busy. I had to try to keep my mind off. . . ." She shrugged. "Things."

"I doubt if they've caught Lester already, but I'll call the chief from town."

"No idea how long we'll be here, huh?" She stared into space.

"It's been awhile since we've had a case this important, so I don't know. If we're lucky, it won't be long."

"I'll go unpack my things while you finish breakfast."

Trent stared at the doorway even after she left the kitchen. She had bounced back. No one who didn't know would suspect what she had gone through and was still going through. Most civilians never saw one dead body until after the funeral director had finished with it. He shook his head. *She had seen one man murdered and another still oozing blood.* Yet her composure was back. *Angela was a strong woman.* He sighed. Another trait he liked in women.

He frowned and made his stare stop waiting for her to come back into the room. His stare left the doorway, but his thoughts were still on the woman who had gone through it.

How could a woman look so sexy in a big sweatshirt and loose pants? With her hair pulled back into a ponytail, she looked like a kid. He shifted in his chair. He was glad she wasn't a kid. If a kid stirred up these feelings in him, he'd fit the mold of a dirty young man.

When she had come close enough to hand him his coffee, he had caught a whiff of gardenias again. *Please let the perfume bottle be almost empty before it becomes my favorite.* He got another cup of coffee. Maybe the aroma would drown out the gardenias.

She had gone into the bedroom. The bedroom. She was probably smoothing out the bed. He should have done that. His mother had tried to get him into the habit of making the bed as soon as he got up, but after a few years she gave up.

His pants grew tight. The bed. He was in the middle of the bed when he woke up. Had she been there, too? Had her soft body been pressed against his hardness while they slept? He shook his head. *No.* He shook his head. *He couldn't have slept through that. He had been tired, but could he ever be that tired?* He let out a hard breath. Tonight he would be rested. Tonight he'd sleep on the couch. Or on the floor. Or in the car. Or in the bathtub.

He tried to derail his train of thought as he washed his dishes. One night and already he was struggling with his self-control. He didn't want to think about the many other nights they would have to share this cabin. He hung the dishcloth on the rack beside the sink.

Why hadn't Aunt Sadie insisted that Uncle Joe build a second bedroom? They could have afforded it and they certainly had enough land. Trent sighed. If he had known that he would be in this situation, he would have added another bedroom himself. Maybe two, with a long hallway between them and the main bedroom. He shook his head. *Don't think about bedrooms.*

Angela hung her outer clothes in the closet after dusting the rod and the walls. She put the rest into dresser drawers after she dusted all of them. Should she have left one side of the dresser for Trent or would he have used the chest? Was it fair for her to take the top two drawers of the dresser? Was there a set of rules for this? She shrugged.

She could always move the clothes. Drawer space wasn't the real problem here. She didn't want to think about what *was* the real problem. She took a deep breath and left the bedroom.

"Ready to go?" Trent met her in the living room. She nodded. "I'm sorry, but I think you should go with me. You'd probably be safe here, but I don't want to take that chance. Okay?" She nodded again and followed him out. Already she had learned to trust his judgment.

Angela stared out the window during the ride. This is what

she missed last night. She sighed. *Was it only last night?* She never would have imagined that so much could fit into one day.

They passed a pasture with several horses. Chickens scratched the ground in the next yard. Trent continued to pass similar yards on the way to town. Whether or not the yards had animals they all had boats; some were just rowboats, but some were almost as large as the houses.

"Does everybody down here have a boat?"

"Just about. This is the place for serious fishing, and these folks are serious about their fishing. And crabbing. A lot of the folks make their living from the water. For Uncle Joe, it was always a hobby. When he retired from the post office, he had more time for it. A lot of times Aunt Sadie went with him; she said that was the only way she would ever see him. I came down here a lot more then. I got to be pretty good at fishing, but not as good as they were." Trent swallowed hard. "When he died, Uncle Joe left his boat to one of his friends. That was fine with me."

Now and then a car passed going in the other direction, but they had the road pretty much to themselves.

After a while, Angela noticed that the houses were built closer together. A while later, the side yards were narrower and sidewalks appeared as if somebody had gotten tired of the dirt along the street.

They rounded a curve and the houses gave way to a few storefronts. Another curve and Trent slowed down. Near the far end of the curve, a sign announcing Delsey's Food Store and Bakery hung over a small building on the left. Several people were coming out of Jack's Hardware Store across the street. Two more buildings and only the sidewalk kept the street company. No more houses. If this side followed the other, the sidewalks would disappear on the other sides of the buildings and around the next curve.

Trent frowned. You didn't come to town on Saturday if you wanted to avoid people. There were parking places in front of the store, but he parked in the last spot at the far end of the side parking lot, glad that the building next door was empty.

"I think you should stay here." He turned to Angela. "Just keep down. Okay?"

"Okay." She scrunched down on the seat, away from the window. He knew she was thinking of why that was necessary.

"I'll try not to take too long."

Trent glanced back after he had gotten a few feet away and nodded. Good. He couldn't see her. There were enough other parking spaces near the front so nobody should park next to his car. He stared for a few seconds more, then he positioned a shopping cart into the middle of the space next to the car and nodded again. That should do it. Still, he had to hurry. If Miss Delsey got busy, somebody would move the cart and take it or the space. He looked back once more just before he turned the corner. Then he went inside.

"Hey, Miss Delsey."

"Well, bless my soul. Little June Bug. Where you been?" The small brown-skinned woman came around from behind the counter.

Trent had tried for years to get away from that silly nickname his father had given him when he was a baby. He shook his head, remembering the teasing he had gotten from the other kids. He smiled now, but it wasn't funny at the time.

"You know how it is, Miss Delsey."

She wasn't as tall as his shoulder, and she couldn't have weighed a hundred pounds, but she wrapped her arms around him as far as they would go. Trent hugged her back.

"We thought you dropped off the face of the earth. Or gone on even though you're too young to collect your Heavenly reward." She stepped back from him.

"I've just been working hard."

"It's rough coming to a place when the kinfolk you used to visit are gone. Ain't hardly no reason to come at all."

"Yes, ma'am. That's right."

"You here for long?"

"Not too long. I figured I'd get away for a while." He looked around. Then he stared at her. "I don't expect it, but if anyone comes asking for me, I'd appreciate if you don't tell them you saw me."

"I ain't laid eyes on you in years." She stared at him. "I just about forgot all about you."

"Thanks a lot." He kissed her cheek. "I need some supplies." He grabbed a cart from beside the door and went up and down the aisles as quickly as he could. He didn't want to take too long, but he didn't want to have to come back either.

He finished and took the heaping cart to the counter. Nobody that he remembered came into the store. As Miss Delsey rang up the order, she filled him in on the latest news about everybody he knew and some that he didn't. He hesitated, then grabbed a newspaper, hoping he wouldn't find anything of interest.

"Nice not seeing you." The old woman smiled as he wheeled the bags out of the store. He hurried across the lot, but not fast enough to attract attention.

Trent glanced into the car, was satisfied that Angela was still in place, then he put the supplies into the trunk. A minute later they were on their way back out of town.

Just before the street changed back to a road, he pulled over.

"Sit tight." He looked around before he went to the phone booth outside the gas station and made a quick call. The sidewalk was still deserted when he got back in and drove away.

"Did you call the chief? What did he say?"

"They have a few good leads. They expect to pick up Lester soon."

"Good. Then that means . . ."

"Angela, even after they find him, the trial won't take place for a long time, unless his attorney demands it. I don't see why he would." He glanced at her. "The term 'speedy trial' is a relative term. The feds are involved, so that will help. The murder was under our jurisdiction, but the drug angle is their territory. We cooperate. We're all on the same page." He tried not to notice that the hope had disappeared from her face. He started the car and headed back to the cabin. It seemed like everything he said disappointed her. He spent the rest of the way back hoping to figure out how to avoid doing it again.

* * *

"Why don't you work on your paper?" They had finished putting away the groceries.

"Why?" She shrugged. "I don't have any way to turn it in. Even if I did, I won't be able to take my finals."

"The chief can get you an extension. He's working on it. Even if you take incompletes, you'll be able to finish when this is over. If you finish the writing while you have the time, you won't have to bother with it later."

She sighed. "I guess you're right."

Trent put wood in the stoves then went into the kitchen. The coffee and hash were long gone from his stomach. He smiled when he glanced at her and saw her take out her file folders and start writing. His stomach rumbled, but he didn't start lunch right away. Instead, he poured a cup of coffee and he sat at the kitchen table, giving her time to work at the small dining room table without interruption.

She was still working when he finished his coffee, so he opened some soup, poured it into a pan, and made sandwiches. When she stopped, she'd be as hungry as he was. He stood in the doorway and allowed himself a long look at her.

He couldn't see her eyes, but he couldn't forget them. Too large for her face, warm dark chocolate in a lighter chocolate face. An almost too large mouth that begged to be kissed. Full lips that begged to be touched, sampled, tasted.

His body stirred to life, but his imagination rolled on. Her body was lost in her large shirt and baggy pants, but that didn't stop him from imagining. What would it be like to ease them from her body? To feel her smooth chocolate skin beneath his hands? To fill his hands with her two mounds of sweet chocolate? To taste dark chocolate tips? Whatever the size of her breasts, they would fit in his hands perfectly—as perfectly as he would fit inside her body.

He pushed off from the doorway and went to the back door. He stepped onto the back porch, hoping a breeze would come along so Angela wouldn't see what his thoughts had done to his body. *Think about something else. Anything else.*

It was a long time before he went back inside. This time he stayed away from the doorway leading to the dining room, leading to temptation.

When Angela closed the folders a short while later, Trent had regained control. He turned on the soup and grilled the cheese sandwiches he had prepared.

"Lunch time. I should say, 'soup's on' since that's what we'll start with." Trent leaned against the doorway again, hoping it was safe now. She rewarded him with a smile. *What could he do to earn another?* An image formed in his mind but if this were reality, what he was thinking wouldn't bring smiles. Pleasure, satisfaction, an easing of tension, but not smiles. At least not at first. Later . . .

He went back into the kitchen, wishing he hadn't already made the sandwiches, hoping that putting the things on the tray would give him enough time for his body to cool off to normal. Too bad he didn't have a turkey to roast. Would that have given him enough time, knowing she would still be here when he finished?

He took a deep breath and swore that he'd get better control of himself. After all, he was a grown man. He should be able to do this. He let out a deep breath. The fact that he was a grown man was a big part of the problem. The fact that she was so beautiful was another. He picked up the tray and went back to face his temptation.

Eight

"Tell me about your paper." He sat across from her trying not to notice that, yes, she was just as sexy as he had thought.

"It's boring."

"Try me."

"I'm doing a paper on bookkeeping and the various ways to create a database and how to determine which approach is best for each specific business. I'm trying to show that, whatever the approach, the results are the same."

"You're using the distributorship as your example."

"No, I made up a dummy beer distributing corporation."

"You made it up?"

"Practically. From some of the data I got from Mr. Hunter's company." Her face clouded over. "How can they have a funeral without his family making the arrangements? I know that Nick has family to take care of him. What will happen to Mr. Hunter if they don't find any relatives?"

"I'm sure they can locate somebody who will make the arrangements. Don't worry about it."

She swallowed hard. "Sometimes Mr. Hunter wasn't easy to work for, but he paid well and the work wasn't hard." She frowned. "Sometimes I wondered why I was there at all. Some days no one came to the office, but other times we had a steady flow of people." She frowned. "I never knew why they were there. Mr. Hunter gave me his list of appointments in the morning and I let him know when the people were there." She looked at Trent. "I did a lot of straightening desk drawers and supply closet shelves. A lot of the time he wasn't even there. Sometimes he snapped at me even though I hadn't done anything wrong." She sighed. "No matter what, he didn't deserve to die like that."

Her face tightened and Trent knew she was reliving what had happened. The pain on her face was his fault. Again. He had started this conversation. If he was right, he was probably about to deepen her pain.

"Mr. Hunter gave you the information that you used for your paper?"

"Not exactly. I did the payroll every two weeks, so I had those figures. I ordered office supplies, so I had part of the business expense. I also had a running list of the inventory in the warehouses, as well as at each distributorship. When I straightened up his desk one time I found some papers with information that I knew would be helpful when I had to write my paper." She shrugged. "The rest I made up."

"Mr. Hunter didn't mind you using what you found?"

"I didn't tell him. I wasn't dealing with anything important and a lot of what I wrote was fictitious. I didn't even use the company name. What harm was there?"

Trent slowly shifted his plate an inch to the side. He straightened the spoon beside it. "Did you finish your paper?"

"I ran into some trouble with the figures that I found the last day I was at work; the day Mr. Hunter was—was . . ."

"On Friday."

"Yes." Trent saw her swallow hard as she nodded slowly. "On Friday. I worked the math over so many times that I was afraid my brain would disintegrate, but I still couldn't get the bottom line to come out right."

Trent stilled his hand. "What was the problem?"

"My calculations were way off. The figures didn't add up. It looked as if we had three times as many employees as I know we had. And there's no way we could have turned the profit that was showing on paper—not with the inventory we were moving and the inventory still in the warehouses. The inventory listed as in the warehouses wasn't even right." She frowned at the memory. "The papers in Mr. Hunter's office even showed an extra warehouse." She turned her frown on

Trent. "His accountant is doing a lousy job of keeping the books. I could do better and I'm not even certified yet."

"What did you do about it?" Trent looked at her and hoped his face didn't show what he was thinking. No sense scaring her again, at least not right now.

"I didn't have time to do anything." She hesitated as if waiting for Friday to leave again. Then she sighed and continued. "I wouldn't have done anything anyway. I figured that I must have copied some numbers wrong." She shrugged. "I don't know how, but it happens. After so long, sometimes the figures blur together and you can't make two and three equal five." She sighed. "I worked backward and changed the glitches until the numbers came out right." She shrugged again. "It was supposed to be a dummy corporation, anyway. The purpose of the paper was to prove that I could handle the books for a company, and I did. My paper is finished. I was going to tell Mr. Hunter about the mistake on Monday so he could check the figures for himself. He needed to know about the accountant's miscalculations."

"You still have the information that you were working from?"

"Sure. Of course, I don't have the original papers from Mr. Hunter's office, but I made copies of them and I have the rough work that I did for my paper. I also have all of it on a disk." She shrugged. "It's a lot of paper, but my professor might question something and I would have to check my work." She shook her head. "I learned the hard way not to throw away my research until I get my graded paper back. In my freshman year I did exactly that and I had to start over from scratch. It took forever and I had to pull an all-nighter, but I . . ." She stared at him and frowned. "What?" Her eyes widened and she leaned back in her chair. "I didn't make a mistake, did I?" She shook her head. "You think my figures were right; you think I stumbled across something, don't you? Something about the—the money laundering."

"It's a strong possibility." He kept his words soft and hoped his calmness would rub off on her.

"It just keeps coming, doesn't it?" She opened her hands

in a plea. "I start out with an ordinary job with what seemed like an ordinary business. Then I witness my boss getting murdered and some stranger tries to kill me because I saw him do it. Then I find out that the business isn't ordinary after all; that Mr. Hunter is involved with. . . ." She shook her head. "He *was* involved with the mob. *Then* I find out that it's not just murder; the company was laundering money and what I saw was a hit. Now you think I accidentally uncovered evidence of the laundering." She frowned at him. "I'm not doing anything and I keep getting pulled deeper and deeper into something that I didn't even know about."

Trent laid his hand on hers. He wanted to calm her. He left his hand there; never mind what it was doing to him.

"Everything is the same as it was. Just because we uncovered something new, doesn't make the situation any worse."

"Things can't get any worse." She pulled her hand away from him and stood. "I can't go home. I can't turn in my assignment. I can't take my final. I can't graduate. I don't have a job. And more importantly, not one, but two men are dead. The only way things could be worse is if Lester Ford found me."

She pulled his plate from in front of him and stacked it with hers. Trent noticed the tremor in her hands.

He stood and touched her hand again. "That won't happen. I promise you." He held her hand until she looked at him. Then he squeezed it. "You have to believe that. I'm good at my job. I swear that I'll keep you safe." Her tremor slowed but didn't disappear. "Look at me."

She continued to stare at the stack of dirty dishes. He continued to hold her hand. Finally she gave in. She sighed and let her stare meet his. He nodded at her. "Good. You will be safe with me. Do you believe that?" She hesitated before she nodded. Only a small piece of the tremor hung on to her. Trent continued to talk. He felt rewarded when the panic almost left her eyes. "I will protect you for as long as it takes. Do you believe that?"

She hesitated again, then she nodded again.

"Good. Now let's clean up and I'll show you the best fishing hole in the state of Virginia." He smiled and her smile in return, though slight, eased away some of his concern about her. He picked up the dirty dishes. "The fish won't be biting tonight, but we'll try to outsmart them tomorrow morning. If I'm a quarter as good as Uncle Joe was, tomorrow night we'll have fresh fish for dinner. Okay?"

Trent watched the end of the tension leave her. She sighed away the last bit. "Okay, but I'll wash the dishes. It's only fair since you cooked."

"It's a deal. I never did like doing dishes."

"Woman's work?"

"No such thing as woman's work." He smiled. "Mama and Daddy taught us that from an early age."

"Good answer." This time her smile was full. So was Trent's lower body.

He loaded the tray and led the way into the kitchen hoping the short distance would give him enough time to regain control of his body.

"That's it." Trent looked around the kitchen as he hung up the dish towel. Aunt Sadie wouldn't have complained if she were here. He was back in control. Then he looked at Angela and realized that his self-control was fragile and in danger of being overrun by his need. "I think I need to go outside—maybe chop some wood." *What he needed had nothing to do with wood, although a part of his body was doing a realistic imitation of its hardness.* He didn't look at her. "I have to check the shed for the fishing gear, too. I'll probably be out there for a long while."

"Okay. I'll find something to read." Her smile almost made him forget his rule about business and pleasure and not mixing the two. He was glad she walked away; he didn't think he could.

He watched her go over to the bookshelves along one wall of the living room. Her sweatpants were so roomy that he had to imagine her hips swaying as she walked. His body tightened. Unfortunately for him, he had an excellent imagination.

He pulled himself away from the doorway before he gave

in to the temptation to check on how much of a sway she had without her sweatpants on; with just her . . . He frowned. Cotton? Or satin and lace underwear? *None of your business*, the sensible part of his mind said, but the other part caused his body to tighten even more as he thought about learning the answer. He went outside while he could still walk.

Angela tried to keep busy looking at the books. She tried to read the titles, but an image of a strong brown face kept getting in her way. His stare always seemed to see right through her, into her mind, reading her thoughts. How long before it discovered her attraction to him?

She frowned. A day ago she was sure that she was in love with Dwight. She had been planning to make love with him. Now, after a few hours with Trent, she could barely remember what Dwight looked like. Instead, she found herself wondering what Trent's arms would feel like if she were in them. She shook her head. She knew what it felt like to have one of his arms holding her. Her breath caught in her throat as she remembered the feel of his hand when she woke up.

One hand was just a tease. She could almost feel again the small circles he had traced on her middle; the circles had spread wider, dipped lower. She breathed in, trying to take in enough air to cool her thoughts, to change direction of her imagination. It didn't work.

What if she had stayed in bed? What if she had waited until he woke up? What would have happened between them? She had no experience in that department, but that didn't stop her mind from making something up.

She closed her eyes and took a deep breath. Then she opened them and went back to the kitchen. Maybe if she did something physical it would keep her mind off something else physical.

She filled a bucket with water, got some rags, and went back to the bookshelf. Maybe busy hands would help keep her thoughts on something neutral, acceptable. Something that didn't involve her and Trent getting closer than she had ever been with anyone.

She took the books from the top shelf and stacked them on the floor. Then she washed and dried the shelf, dusted the first book, and put it back in place. She took a deep breath and wiped the second one. Maybe by the time she finished, her common sense would be back in charge. Hopefully by then she would have remembered that she was business to him— a witness, just the answer to an important case. *A few days after the trial, he will have forgotten me and moved on to the next case.*

She stared at the bookcases stretched along the wall and wished Trent's uncle and aunt had left more books here. She sighed. She could always start reading them when she finished dusting.

Angela put down the book she was reading and finally gave in to her curiosity. She had been hearing a strange noise for a while, but the hold of the Ralph Ellison book she had found was stronger than her curiosity once she got into it. She finally reached a place where she could stop.

The noise sounded as if somebody was slamming something, but she wasn't worried. If it were something to be concerned about, Trent would tell her.

She opened the door and stared out just as Trent lifted an ax and brought it down on a thick log. The log split evenly in two as if he had measured to find the exact middle. He set one piece on the chopping block and cut the piece in two. Then he did the same to the other piece.

A pile of logs lay waiting on one side of the block and split wood was stacked on the side closest to the door. She tried not to notice the sweat glistening on Trent's bare back. She never was good at purposely not noticing anything.

His muscles rippled as he positioned another piece of wood on the block and raised the ax. His shoulder muscles stood out as if waiting for her to use them for an anatomy lesson. Or in some other way. As if she could shove aside what the

sight was doing to her insides, heating them hotter than the
wood would be in the iron stove. As if teaching an anatomy
lesson was what was in the front of her mind.

She clinched her hands behind her to keep from doing
something stupid like going over to him and stroking her
hands along the muscles glistening in the sunlight as if they
were waiting for her, beckoning to her.

She felt sweat trickle down her own back. In sympathy? Or
in anticipation? Suddenly she was overdressed for the temperature. Or the temperature had changed drastically. She
swallowed hard.

She should go back inside. She had discovered what was
causing the noise. Her curiosity was satisfied. She sighed. One
of her curiosities. Another had replaced it: a stronger one.
Would his muscles feel as hard as they looked? Would the
tight skin over them be as soft as the brown velvet that it re-
sembled? She shook her head, but she never took her gaze
from him. There wasn't anything soft about Trent Stewart. She
had to pull her attention away from his bare back before her
impulse overruled her good sense. She shifted her gaze lower.

The backs of his thighs strained against his worn jeans. As
Trent raised the ax, the muscles of his behind tightened and
molded the fabric to his body. Just as bad. Her body tightened
in response to the sight. *Worse.* She had heard that wood
warms twice: once when the person chops it and again when
the wood burns. She took in a deep breath, hoping it would
help her gain control. *Whoever said that would have to add a
third time: when a person watches somebody chopping it.*

He had to work out in a gym; his body couldn't look like
that unless he did. A bead of sweat ran down from between
his shoulder blades and stopped at the waistband of his jeans,
as if reluctant to explore below his waist. But her imagination
kept going.

He raised the ax again. *Nobody could accuse him of having
love handles. There was nothing to wrap your hands around
and hold onto when. . . .* She shook her head. Self-torture had
never been her thing. Until now. She should leave the doorway.
The "should" was not in charge.

She looked for shade so she could shift into it only to discover that she was already covered by it. Sunshine had nothing to do with her body heat. Her hormones, long dormant, were making up for missed time.

She watched as two new pieces of wood fell from the block. How much more would he cut? How much more could she take?

Finally Trent released her from his hold. He turned to pick up a piece of cut wood and saw her.

He said, "Did I disturb you?"

Angela managed a slight smile. *If you only knew.* Responses played tag with each other in her mind. *"You're kidding, right?"* Or *"It was a sweet disturbance."* Or *"Not as much as I'd like to be disturbed by you."* Or how about *"I'd have to be dead not to be disturbed."* Or maybe *"Let me show you exactly how much."*

Her possible answers chickened out and left a safe one. She met his stare. "It was time for a break anyway."

He picked up the towel draped over a bush and began to wipe his chest. Slowly. Too slowly.

Angela bit her tongue to keep from offering to do that for him. Instead, she let her gaze follow the movements of the towel and just wished that her hands could replace it.

"It must not have been exciting if you can't remember the title."

"Huh?"

"I asked what you're reading."

"Oh." She was still in the shade, but she felt her face flush. "I was rereading an oldie: *Invisible Man.* Ralph Ellison had it right. I've felt like that more times than I want to remember."

"I know what you mean. That's what I said when I read it in school. We had a heavy discussion about it. My teacher let us vent. We never did agree on whether or not what he did was right."

"That character and Nat Turner showed what happens when your anger gets control over you."

"Yeah." He stared toward the woods as if there were something of interest to see. "Now, I don't need books to show me.

I see it every day, especially in our young men. I wouldn't mind if it disappeared so much that I'd be out of a job. Anger is so self-destructive." He frowned and shifted his stare to a bare spot near the new wood pile. "I wouldn't mind one bit."

His face looked as if he was seeing the horror that went with his job. She wanted to make it go away, to ease his pain. "Your aunt and uncle had a lot of books."

"Uncle Joe always said that books are inexpensive treasures. 'Once you transfer the knowledge from books to your brain, nobody can take them away from you,' he used to say. He and Aunt Sadie spent many hours every day reading." Trent laughed. "Notice there's no television here? 'Devil's invention to go along with the idle minds', Aunt Sadie used to say. The books in the house are just the ones they couldn't make themselves part with. I know half of the books in the local library were donated by them. They also gave some to the high school. Uncle Joe said that reading was his addiction." Trent sighed. "I guess I should go through them and see if there are any of these that the school could use. Uncle Joe also said that a book on the shelf might as well be blank; that it just takes up space that could be used by knickknacks." Trent draped the towel back over the bush.

"What's that?" Angela pointed to front of his shoulder.

"That is evidence of my stupidity."

"A tattoo?" She leaned closer. "Of a rose?"

"We were celebrating the conviction of my first big arrest. It took years, but we finally got him. Evidently I drank enough for my common sense to lose control. I don't remember the conversation, but I do know that I took a dare." He pointed to his chest. "Here's the proof. We ended up in the tattoo parlor a few doors from the bar." Trent shook his head. "Lucky for me his needles were clean. Ever since then, one drink is my limit. Now I always volunteer to be the designated driver."

"Why a rose? Was that your girlfriend's name?" *If not that, then what? And did she want to know about the woman in his life?*

"No." He laughed. "The guys wanted me to get a dragon. I

wanted to show that I was still rational so I picked something as far away from macho as I could." He laughed again. "Of course, if I had been rational, I wouldn't have gotten a tattoo at all."

"You were young."

"I won't use that as an excuse. I was just stupid."

His stare found and held Angela. A bird sang. She didn't know how far away it was, but her heartbeat was louder than the song.

The look on Trent's face was the way she felt: hungry, wanting, needing. Trent blinked. His chest swelled as he took a deep breath. She felt her breasts harden in response.

"I'd—I'd better go get cleaned up."

"Yeah." Her answer rasped out. Her mouth felt as if she had swallowed a bucket of sand, as if she were dying of thirst and only he could quench it.

Neither moved until a slight rustling in the dead leaves under the trees reached them, releasing him, but left something still holding her in place.

He moved toward her and she wondered what would happen when he got there; she knew what she wanted to happen. He was taking too long.

She swallowed hard and licked her dry lips. Surrounded by the whole outdoors and she still couldn't find enough air to breathe.

Nine

Trent took as long as he could to reach her. He wished he had decided to chop the wood farther off, maybe a mile or two into the woods. Maybe then he'd have enough time to strengthen his resolve to keep his hands off her.

He wished her eyes weren't so brown, so warm, that her skin wasn't so soft looking that it was making his hands ache to touch her. He wished that she wasn't so sexy. That her mouth didn't look so much like sweet chocolate waiting for him to take a taste; to sample what was waiting inside like the inside of the world's sweetest chocolate. He wished that she didn't have the same hot hunger in her eyes that he was feeling inside himself and that she didn't look as needy as he felt. Most of all he wished that she wasn't part of his job so that his other wishes weren't necessary.

He didn't expect it to work, but he took one more deep breath to try to help him gain control and he used one more impossible wish to want more steps leading up to her.

Too soon, he was standing in front of her. He should have brought the towel with him. Or even a piece of wood. Then he'd have something to hold, something to make it harder for him to reach out to her, to touch her, to pull her to him, to press her against his body; his body that was aching to feel her softness against his increasing hardness. Anything to add strength to his resolve to keep his hungry hands to himself.

The new sweat forming on his chest had nothing to do with chopping wood and everything to do with wanting her.

"Trent . . ."

His name whispered from her tempting mouth. He steeled

himself against the offer that he saw in her eyes. He took in another deep breath and wished for some of the cold of January—for anything to cool his desire.

"I-I have to get cleaned up." His words sounded as if he had swallowed a bucket of damp soil before he shoved them out. "Then we have to talk." He tried not to see the frustration in her face; he knew his was showing the same thing. Just a few more steps. It was the hardest part, but just a few more steps and he'd be clear. He eased past her, forcing himself not to touch her. If he did . . .

He walked into the cabin with only his regrets for company. Leaving her was the hardest thing he had ever done in his life.

"Fool," Angela muttered after Trent left her standing in the doorway too filled with her frustrations to be embarrassed by his rebuff. She stood there aching for his touch even as she tried to convince herself that it was better that they not complicate matters by getting involved emotionally. She shook her head. *It was too late for that, at least for her. Her emotions were already tangled with his.* She closed her eyes and corrected her assessment of reality. It was better that they not get involved *physically.* She sighed.

She wasn't having any more luck convincing herself of that than Mr. Hunter had had convincing Lester not to kill him.

She shuddered as the scene replayed in her head. She had seen it happen and still she was having trouble believing it had not been a nightmare.

She stepped off the porch. Maybe a walk would help her come to her senses and accept the reason why it was not a good idea to get physical with Trent. In her mind she knew this was best; it was her body that needed to be convinced. Maybe Trent left a bucket of reason out there waiting for her.

She followed the path to the woodpile, hesitated, and then walked around it without looking back. The image of Trent chopping wood was still with her as if it was determined to keep her common sense away.

She stepped under the canopy made by the trees, and put distance between herself and temptation, hoping that time and space would make it easier to cope. A soft, cool breeze brushed over her. Maybe that would help, too; she needed all the help she could get. She kept walking. She had no idea where she was going and that was all right. She was only out here to put more distance between herself and Trent.

"Where did you go?" Trent was standing on the porch with his arms folded when Angela got back.

"I went for a walk." She stared at him. *Should I thank him for putting on a shirt? For covering his magnificent chest?* She sighed. It was too late—like wrapping a gift after the recipient already saw it. Her recent memory of the scene in the yard was with her to stay, at least until a better one came along. She sighed again. *Did such a thing exist?* She took a deep breath as an image tried to answer her question. Slowly she walked up the steps. *Why only six? How much time before the new image quit trying?*

"You were gone for over an hour." He scowled at her as he gripped the railing. "Do you know how worried I was?"

"I hadn't realized that I was gone that long." She frowned as she stepped onto the porch. "Why were you worried?" Her eyes widened. "Did something happen? Did somebody call with news? You said I'd be safe here. Is that true?"

"You are safe. Nothing happened, nobody called. I was just. . . ." He shook his head. "Look. Next time you decide to go off, let me know. Okay? Better still, don't go without me. You don't know these woods. Something might happen and I wouldn't know it."

"I have been in the woods before, you know. I'm not a kid and the woods aren't all that deep." She glared at him. "Besides, you were taking a shower. How could I let you know?"

Trent stared at her. He didn't answer out loud, but a response ambled through his mind anyway. It was followed by a different kind of response from his body. *Another time, under different circumstances, I would definitely have known where you were; you'd have been with me. We would have . . .* He shoved the thought away and hoped his body would forget her question and return to normal. "We have to talk."

He moved back into the cabin, out of the doorway, giving her plenty of room to get past him. The last thing he needed was for her to come close enough for him to touch. She walked a wide path around him, but not wide enough. *Just once, why couldn't she forget her perfume?*

He sat in the chair instead of on the couch; he still had enough sense to know not to sit on the couch. He didn't need for her to sit beside him with her thigh against his. He let out a hard breath. *That* was the last thing he needed. He tried not to think of the first thing he needed.

She sat huddled in the corner of the couch, still looking shaken at the careless way he had made her remember why they were here, and he almost forgot that he shouldn't touch her. She looked so vulnerable as she stared at her fingers in her lap.

A frown worried Trent's face. He wanted to smooth his hand over her forehead. He wanted to lift her chin, to caress her face. He wanted to do a lot of other things instead of say what he had to say. His want for her was still with him. He shook his head. Nothing to do but to come right out with it.

"Look, Angela, you *are* safe here. That's not what I want to talk about. We need to talk about us." Her head came up and the desire smoldering again. . . . still? . . . in her eyes almost made him change his words, his mind. "I can't think of an easy way to say this, so I'll come right out with it. We can't. . . ." His frown deepened. "We can't get involved. I never get involved with my cases; it complicates things." He stared at her. "Maybe I'm wrong anyway. Maybe I'm imagining things. Maybe this pull is one-sided on my part."

He waited. He didn't know for what, but she didn't respond so he went on. "I'm attracted to you, but nothing can happen between us, okay? It just wouldn't be right. You're vulnerable right now. A lot has happened to you in a short span of time.

Your life has been upended and we don't know when it will be back to normal." She still didn't say anything, but her eyes widened. "But it will get back to normal," he added hurriedly. "I promise you that you will have a normal life again. Meanwhile, I have to concentrate on doing my job. There can only be business between us, no matter how we feel. . . ." He shook his head. "No matter how *I* feel, it's got to be business only. Carelessness is dangerous."

He stared at her and she stared back. He tried to think of something else to say—anything to fill the heavy space between them.

"Okay." Her voice was flat, as if a weight were keeping her emotions penned inside, squashed down. She blinked hard.

He thought that maybe he saw moisture in her eyes, but he wasn't sure and he didn't dare look close enough to find out. He didn't want to know. He noticed the shift in her as she sat taller. He said, "I . . ."

"Will you show me the fishing hole now or should we wait until tomorrow morning?"

"Now. Right now." He looked away from her to something safe but it wasn't able to make him forget what he had seen. "Before it gets too late." Better the big outdoors with her than this small cabin.

Why was he disappointed that she accepted what he said without arguing with him? Why didn't he say "tomorrow" and use the time now to continue trying to convince himself that his "hands-off" policy was best?

"Okay." She stood. The light had gone out of her eyes again. Trent tried to convince himself that this was a good thing.

"Get a sweater. It's always cooler beside the water."

"Okay."

He watched as she left the room. He should have turned away instead. He felt like a kid looking at a candy display, hungering for a candy bar when he only had a dime in his pocket. He shook his head. *Quit thinking about kids. Kids don't have hungers like this.*

He got his navy blue sweatshirt from the rack beside the

door and pulled it on even though, right now, the last thing he needed was something to hold in his heat.

He waited by the door for her, needing to see her again even though she had just left the room, yet wanting her to take long enough for him to get himself together. *Again.* He let out a harsh breath. There wasn't that much time in the world.

The red sweatshirt that she wore when she came back barely touched her body. That didn't stop Trent's imagination from making up what he couldn't see. If he was lucky, the temperature outside would be in the low forties and his excess heat would disappear. He shook his head slightly. It would take more than luck to make his hunger for her go away; nothing short of a miracle could do that.

"Let's go." He stepped outside first, trying not to let her see that he was checking the surroundings. Then he moved aside so she could come out. Neither mentioned the reason for caution.

He led her through the brush at the back of the cabin. "There used to be a path here, but it hasn't been used in years. Now all that's left is a slight difference between the walking place and the rest of the woods. By fall, the woods probably won't have left a trace of it."

They stepped around a massive, decaying log blocking their way. Thick shelf fungus grew along what was left of the crumbling wood. The damp smell of decaying wood and leaves and toadstools hovered in the air, weighting it down with their dank scents.

"Careful with that moss." Trent pointed to a thick rich patch growing in the shelter of another decaying log. "I found out the hard way how slippery moss is." He held her hand as she climbed over the log. Then he forced himself to let her go after she was back on even ground.

As they walked, he told her about how he had explored the woods during his childhood years. "I spent many summers here. There were never many other kids around. Mostly older people lived along here but that was all right. I enjoyed my own company and these woods were better than any playground. Sometimes I was a pirate going to hide my treasure and other times I was looking for treasure. A few times I was

even a space traveler exploring a new planet." He smiled.
"Whatever the subject of the last movie or video that I saw,
that became my world out here." He pointed to the left. "I
used to climb that oak tree." He laughed. "Of course, it wasn't
that tall or thick then. Still, I could see all the way to the shore
on the other side and way downstream. I'd sit up there for
hours watching the boats moving up and down along the wa-
terway; I was fascinated that I could see them, but they didn't
even know I was there." He looked up at the canopy of
branches with small new leaves. "Other times I took a book
up there with me." He pointed to a sturdy crook where a large
branch met the trunk. "I'd lean with my back against the trunk
and lose myself in the book. Sometimes I didn't realize how
long I had been up there until it got too dark for me to read."

"Sounds like you had fun."

"Fun isn't a strong enough word." He glanced at her. "I had
a friend back home who always complained that he didn't
have any brothers or sisters to play with. I never understood
him. I have two brothers and two sisters, but they never
wanted to come down here; they said it was too boring, that
they didn't have anything to do. I had a great time alone. I
loved spending summers here." He held back a low branch
spread across what used to be the path. "Just a little farther."

A songbird announced his presence and chipmunks scampered in the piles of last year's leaves still blanketing the
ground. The soft fall of Trent and Angela's footsteps on the
thick leaf bed was the only sound not made by nature. Angela
felt as if Friday night had happened to someone else. She
breathed in the cool, late afternoon air and felt her tension go
when she exhaled. A real smile, hiding for too long, found its
way to her face.

"Here we are."

Trent stepped to the side and let Angela step beside him.

"Oh." She moved forward as if she had forgotten how to
walk. Her gaze grabbed the view and held it. "It's—it's so
beautiful." She couldn't pull her stare away.

Part of the Chesapeake Bay widened here as if reluctant to
give up its waters to the ocean. Angela glanced at the tiny island

opposite her. It was the only thing keeping the side of this
branch of water from joining with the rest of the bay. Tiny
waves slapped at the edges of the bank playing tag with it.

She leaned against the trunk of the willow bending over the
water. A bird dipped down, scooped its dinner from the water,
and disappeared around the bend.

Trent stood beside her and rested his hand on her shoulder.
The smell of saltwater mixed with fresh rode the breeze
that met them. The rustle of shore grasses sounded like dry
hands rubbing together. An animal plopped into the water,
getting away from the humans who disturbed its domain.

"I remember the first time Uncle Joe brought me here."
Trent gazed at the island. "I was fascinated by the idea of a
deserted island, no matter how small. Then, when I was about
ten, I was determined to swim over there. I had read *Treasure
Island* and I was convinced that some pirate had buried his
treasure over there. Never mind that this section of the water
is much too shallow for a large ship." He shook his head. "I
had already searched this side." He laughed. "I made a list
of how I would spend the money." He laughed again. "A
horse was high on that list." He glanced at her. "Not a pony,
mind you—a full-grown horse. A stallion. Don't ask me
where I intended to keep a horse, but I read an old book
named *King of the Wind* and I just had to have a horse."

"What happened?"

Trent shook his head. "When Uncle Joe couldn't talk me
out of swimming over so I could search the island, he said I
could try, but only if he rowed alongside me. I was still reluctant to have him go, until he pointed out that I couldn't
swim and carry a shovel, too, and 'how was I going to dig for
treasure without a shovel?' I was kind of relieved that he decided to come with me."

"Did you make it?"

"I swear somebody kept pushing the island away while I
was in the water. The pull of the water is stronger than it
looks. I was so tired that I thought my arms would drop off.
It took longer than the twenty minutes I had expected—a lot
longer—but, yeah, I made it."

"What did you find?"

"Nothing that wasn't over here. Only less of it." He laughed again. "I searched every inch of the island. In many places the brush was too thick to dig, although I did try. Uncle Joe waited for me in the boat; he said he didn't want me to think he was trying to claim any treasure that I might find." Trent nodded at the memory. "Somebody else might have teased me when I came back empty-handed, but not Uncle Joe. He said that we never know what we might find until we look for it." He sighed. "I miss him."

"Yeah." Her voice was soft. "But each memory is like a little part of him is still with you."

Trent nodded slowly. "That's exactly right." He looked at her. "You sound like you know what I mean."

"I do. I feel the same about my grandmother. My parents died when I was three, so I don't remember anything except the love they had shown me. Grandma James raised me. She died when I was twenty. It took awhile for me to realize that I had part of her in each memory of our years together and that I'd have my memories forever."

They both stared out to the island, but neither was thinking about it. They were each back in a different past.

Ten

"I guess we'd better head back." Trent was suddenly aware that his hand was still resting on her shoulder. He wanted to touch more than her shoulder—much more—but he forced himself to push off from the tree, severing even that little contact.

"Yes. It's getting dark." Angela shifted away as if she, too, were suddenly aware of the contact between them.

"And chilly." Trent stared at her for a few seconds before he turned away.

"Very." Angela followed him silently as if as eager to get away as he was.

Shadows had already formed under the willow, settling in for the night. Shadows of other trees touched each other.

If it were a month later, the full branches overhead would have made it difficult for the two to find their way back to the cabin. As it was, several times Trent had to stop to get his bearings. He frowned. Angela couldn't see it, but that was okay. He wasn't frowning at her; this frown was just for himself.

If he had been thinking straight, he would have brought a flashlight as Uncle Joe had taught him to do whenever he came into the woods—even in full daylight. Trent sighed. If he could think straight, his mind wouldn't have been on other things in the first place and he could have waited until tomorrow morning to come out here.

Finally the brush wasn't quite as dense. Then, suddenly, nothing was in front of them except tall grass and not quite an uneven dark.

"Wait here." Trent stopped before they stepped from the

last of the woods. The cabin loomed as a darker rectangular shadow. The moon had taken the night off.

Angela grabbed his arm. "Wait." She held on as if he would leave her here forever if she let go. "Do you—do you think someone is in there?"

"No." He put his hand on top of hers. "I think I'd better turn on a lamp so you can find your way. No sense in both of us stumbling in the dark." He waited for her to let go. He couldn't see her face in the country darkness, but he felt her uncertainty in the way she held his arm. He waited until she trusted him again.

"Okay." Her hand still on his arm didn't agree with her answer.

"We would have heard if anyone drove up here. Not even my friends know about this place." He could barely make out the outline of her face. Not that it mattered. He could picture her with his eyes closed. His mind had proven that. "It's okay. Really it is. Angela, we need to get inside because the cold is moving in. That's the only reason."

"All right." Slowly she removed her hand.

Trent squeezed her arm. "Be right back. Don't run off and leave me, now."

She tapped his arm. "You just hurry back."

"Yes, ma'am."

Angela felt him leave her. Before she had time to worry, a light came on in the cabin and he jogged back to her.

"Come on. Let's go get warm." He took her hand and led her to the cabin. She went, but his touch was doing a better job of warming her than any fire a stove would hold.

"My turn to cook," she said after they were inside. "I know it's kind of late, but I'm hungry."

"Me, too." He stared at her. "Do you want any help?"

"No. I got it covered. You can find something to do." She glanced at the floor, the wall, the chair—any place but at him.

"Yeah. I have to put more wood in the stoves."

At the mention of the word "wood," Angela's gaze flew to his face. His stare met hers. She remembered the sight of him chopping wood earlier, and suddenly she didn't feel cool at all. His stare looked as if he could see what she was remembering.

"I'll—I'll just go get started." Angela forgot to move.

"Good idea." Trent did, too.

"I'd better go now." Angela looked as if she forgot where the kitchen was.

"Me, too." Trent couldn't find the stove a few feet from where he stood.

Finally he broke the stare, turned his back on her, and moved to the firewood box. That freed Angela. She walked into the kitchen as if that was the last thing she wanted to do.

It was hard being noble. Trent heard, rather than saw Angela leave the room. He didn't dare look at her again. He couldn't, not if he wanted to keep his hands off her.

He stirred up the embers and then put a piece of wood on them. He corrected himself. He didn't *want* to keep his hands off her. He *had* to. He closed the stove door and backed away. He didn't need heat from any other source. His body was providing enough all by itself. He thought of the way Angela's shoulder felt when he wrapped his hand around it. His body tightened in anticipation of a repeat. *Man, Trent. Her shoulder. The memory of touching just her shoulder does this to you.* He tried not to think of how it would feel to hold her body against his. How her breasts would touch his chest. How he would explore the taste of . . .

His lower body tightened even more. He was way past uncomfortable. He had reached agony. He tried times tables, but they were too easy to occupy his mind. He moved on to square roots, but he didn't know enough about them for it to help. He went back outside, welcoming the chill, hoping it would get cold enough to help him gain control.

"Trent?" Angela stood at the screen door. "What are you doing out here in the cold? Are you crazy?"

The answer to her last question must be "yes." Why else would he be thinking about impossible things?

"Dinner is ready," she said, when he didn't answer. She stepped back from the door, holding it open.

He went inside still without answering.

The smell of chicken reached Trent as soon as he stepped inside. His stomach rumbled. He almost forgot the other hunger camped out inside him. Angela had placed their dinner on the table in the dining area.

"I'll go wash my hands." *So far so good,* he thought, as he went to the bathroom. His body was back to a normal state. *Got to keep it neutral. Just keep it neutral.* He sighed before he went back to the living room. If it was as simple as saying a few words, he wouldn't be in this fix.

"Absolutely delicious." Trent put his napkin beside his empty plate.

"It wasn't anything fancy. Chicken and rice and green peas will never win a cooking award."

"Fancy is highly overrated. This was the best dinner that I remember ever having."

"The fact that we walked so far, and it's so late, and lunch was so long ago might have had something to do with it, but thank you."

"I'll clean since you cooked. It's only fair."

"Okay, but these things are all that's left. I cleaned up as I went along. I hate to look around after I finish cooking and see dirty dishes and pots and pans everywhere. It's enough to take your appetite away."

Trent made a mental note. *Next time you cook, clean up as you go.* He stacked the dishes and went into the kitchen. Angela followed with the serving bowls.

"Okay. Go back to your book. I got this covered."

"Yes, sir." Angela smiled and Trent felt that he might have to go stand outside in the cold again.

"Go ahead. You cooked. Your turn to relax."

He watched Angela go. *What does she sleep in?*

The dish pan overflowed, taking the suds with it. Trent emptied it and started over. *Please let the chief tell me next*

time I call that they caught Lester and that we can leave here.
He picked up a glass and rubbed it as though stuck-on food
had found a home. Much more and the pattern would have
disappeared.

Trent returned to the living room after he couldn't find
anything else to clean in the kitchen. Angela was standing beside the made-up couch.

"Thank you for fixing this for me."

"I'm sleeping out here. You said we're safe. Besides, if anybody comes, they won't expect anyone to be sleeping in the
living room." She pointed to the door where she had propped
a chair under the knob. "Also, my handy-dandy security
alarm will work fine." She looked at him. "Last of all, you're
too tall for the couch. How can you protect me if you're half
asleep?"

"Maybe you should have majored in law instead of business." He stared at her. "Okay. You can take the couch, but
don't fuss tomorrow about it being uncomfortable."

"I won't. I have to get my things from the bedroom. I'll just
be a minute."

She left the room and Trent tried not to be disappointed
that tonight would be nothing like last night. He checked the
windows and doors once more. When he heard her go into the
bathroom, he went into the bedroom. No sense facing temptation again tonight.

Trent made it a point not to see Angela again before they
went to bed. When she came out of the bathroom he waited
until she had time to go into the living room before he left the
bedroom. *Why was forbidden fruit so sweet?*

The living room was dark and quiet when Trent left the
bathroom. He tried not to think of who was tucked in on the
couch.

He slipped between the sheets and lay with his hands behind his head. How could he miss sharing a bed with
someone. . . . He released a heavy breath . . . with *her*, after
only one night? He shifted positions, but he left the blanket

folded at the bottom of the bed. The way his thoughts were working tonight, he wouldn't need a cover.

Angela tried not to, but she heard Trent leave the bathroom. She knew he didn't have any reason to come back to the living room, but she was still disappointed when he didn't.

She punched her pillow, lay her head on it, then punched it again. Morning was hours away, but already she was missing his hand on her middle like it was this morning. She turned onto her other side. Then she turned back. The comfort of the couch had nothing to do with her not being able to sleep.

An owl hooted. She smiled. It sounded just as she had imagined. Another night bird called, but she had no idea what it was. Insects, she guessed they were crickets, threw their sounds into the night quiet. She didn't miss the city noises at all.

She turned over again. She thought about warming some milk, but she doubted it would help. She didn't want to think about what would. She had never been close to a man, but here she was thinking about Trent, about sharing his bed, sharing her body with him. Her love.

She sat up. Oh, no. This couldn't be love. She must be suffering from that syndrome where the victim fixates on . . . She shook her head. No, that couldn't be it. That involved the victim with her captor. Trent wasn't her captor; he was her protector. She frowned. Maybe it was like when women fall in love with their doctors.

She shook her head harder this time. No. She was not in love with Trent. She had just met him. Love didn't come that quickly. She just wasn't used to being this close to a man.

For the next hour she tried to convince herself of that. She thought about Dwight. Comparing what she had felt for him to this was like comparing a searchlight to a night-light.

Then she gave up and went to stand on the porch. She had once heard that night air helps you sleep. She hoped so. She sighed. Another hope to add to the pile. She closed her eyes and tried to let the night air soothe her body.

"I thought you were asleep." Trent let the door shut behind him and went to stand beside her.

"I thought you were, too." Angela opened her eyes, but she didn't look at him. She wished she could find a way to forget he was so close. She frowned into the night. *Didn't she?*

"I had trouble falling asleep."

His voice was too close. *He* was too close. "There's a lot of that going around tonight."

She tried not to notice his body heat. She tried not to lean closer to see if he felt as solid as he looked in the daylight. When he was chopping wood. She swallowed hard. She didn't want to close her eyes; it would only make the vision stronger. She tried her best not to turn toward him. If this were a test, her score would be zero and she wouldn't care.

She sighed and eased toward him; knowing she shouldn't; knowing she wanted to; knowing she would.

"Trent?" Her hand found his chest. The T-shirt didn't hide his strength, his heat. His chest was as solid as a slab of steel. Only warmer, much warmer, She brushed her hand across his flat nipples and felt his heartbeat increase as if it were behind in a race and trying to catch up. She had never been so bold before; she had never had the want or the need to be before.

"Angela." Her name groaned from him as he wrapped his hands around her shoulders and drew her body against the length of him.

She raised her face toward his, waiting. He didn't make her wait long. His mouth found hers in the thick darkness as if they were standing in full sunlight. She felt as if she were. She felt hungry; she felt him. She felt as if, after a long search, she had found her home.

"We can't."

The words rasped from Trent's own mouth, but he didn't pay them any mind. His mouth feathered kisses along her jawline. How could contact so light start a fire so strong? His lips found her neck. His tongue tasted her skin and a bolt of heat flew from her neck to her private center as if a line connected them. Her hands tightened around his shoulders. He kissed his way to the place where the top edge of her nightshirt ended. Then he kissed a slow line along the top. She wished she had worn a low-cut nightgown. He paused at the hollow in the middle and her heart speeded up. She heard a moan and realized it came from her. She gasped as his body tightened against hers. She tried to get closer.

"No." Trent pulled his mouth away from her. He rested his chin on her head. It hadn't been enough—not nearly enough. "This . . ." His words stopped as if the rest of the sentence got lost. Then he eased away from her but kept his hands on her shoulders. *Definitely not enough.*

"Angela." He eased her chin up with his finger. She stared at him, but she could barely make out his face in the darkness. "We can't do this." He removed his hands from her and she felt as if the most vital part of her was missing.

He took a step away from her and it might as well have been miles between them instead of inches for the way he felt. He touched the side of her face, then, without saying another word, he left the porch and melted into the night.

He was right; Angela knew he was right. Then why did her body ache for him to come back and finish what they had started?

She felt her face get even warmer. She had behaved disgracefully: throwing herself at him, offering him something that he didn't want. She wrapped her arms around herself. *How could she?* Suddenly she was aware of the cold filling the night air.

She went inside and sat on her couch bed. How could she have acted like that? What must he think of her? How would she face him in the morning?

Cold settled in the room for the night. Angela put a couple of logs on the fire, then scurried back to the couch. She lay down and wrapped the covers around her to try to get warm. She wasn't going to think of the better way to get warm. That was not an option. Trent had made that clear. She sighed. The way feelings were churning through her, she didn't expect to sleep.

* * *

Cold overrode Trent's good judgment and forced him from the car. Hopefully Angela would be asleep. He hoped so. He had used up all of his resistance a couple of hours ago. If she even looked at him again tonight, not to mention called his name, he would lose what little control he had left. He tried not to remember how her body felt pressed against his, how he knew it would be a perfect fit, and how he knew they could give each other such pleasure if only. . . .

He stopped in the middle of the front yard. His body tightened so hard that he wasn't sure he could walk. He took more deep breaths than he had ever taken at one time, hoping it would work, but not expecting it to. Maybe the cold air would help.

He stood at the edge of the clearing until shivering took over. Still, the main part of his body that needed cooling remained hard.

He needed a run. Maybe if he ran to town and back it would get his body back to normal. But he didn't dare leave her. He believed she was safe here, but he wouldn't take chances with her life because of his libido. Besides, the state he was in, even if he *could* manage to run, he could run across the country and back and it wouldn't help. He needed to get away from her. He frowned. No. That wasn't what he needed. He *had* to get away from her as soon as he could because of his need.

He stepped quietly back onto the porch and opened the door. He should have gone out the back door. That way he wouldn't have gotten anywhere near her when he left and he wouldn't have to get near her again when he went inside.

He closed his eyes and took one more deep breath before he went into the cabin. *Please let her be asleep. If not, please let her pretend to be asleep.*

He eased the door shut and slipped the bolt into place. Then he silently made his way across the room. He paused when he got beside the couch. Angela's even breathing tickled the air. Trent continued past, refusing to decide if he was happy or disappointed that she was asleep.

He stared at the low fire in the stove in the bedroom. He tried to decide whether to put more wood on it. Common sense finally appeared. If he did manage to get to sleep, he didn't need for the cold to wake him.

He placed two logs on the fire and poked the embers. When he finished he stood for too long, staring at the closed door.

Then he did what he knew he had to do—he turned his back on the door and walked to the bed.

He got between the covers, grateful for the chill on the sheets. Maybe by the time the air in the room got warm, his body would have returned to its normal state. He closed his eyes.

Please let fish jump on our lines tomorrow so we won't have time to think about tonight. Let us be so busy that I won't have time to think about what almost happened and what I might not be able to keep from happening the next time. Please, when I call him tomorrow, let the chief tell me it's safe for us to go back.

Eleven

A small sound nudged Trent and he pulled himself from sleep. Still not fully awake, his instincts took over. He kept his eyes closed, turned slowly to his stomach, and slid his hand under his pillow. His finger positioned itself on the trigger of his gun. All the years and this was the first time he needed to use the weapon that was part of his bedding. *How had they found the cabin?*

He forced himself to lie quietly, pretending to be still asleep. The reason for the sound identified itself and he allowed himself to relax. *Water running in the bathroom.* He pulled his hand from under the pillow and relaxed it on top of the covers. Then he allowed a big breath to fill his lungs. Angela was up. And she was all right. He stared at the ceiling. *Had she slept any better than he had?* He pushed himself to a sitting position and allowed a full breath.

Daylight had pushed the night aside when he had finally drifted to sleep. He glanced at the bed and shook his head. The way the covers were tangled and hanging off the bed, it must have been a fitful sleep. The bed looked like something other than sleep had taken place in it. It looked as if two people had enjoyed something other than sleep. As if he and Angela had . . . *Don't even think of going there, Trent.*

He got out of the bed before his thoughts could continue on that path. The bathroom door opened and closed, but he waited a few more seconds to make sure she had gone back to the living room. *I'm not prepared to face her yet; I'm not sure I will be later, either, for that matter.*

He went into the bathroom and took a comfortably warm

shower. Cold showers didn't work. He had proof of that. He sighed and got dressed. Then he made the bed, unmade it, and made it again. He shook his head. The day was too long to spend in the bedroom, especially since he would be alone. If Angela. . . . *Cut it out.* He sighed again as he left the bedroom. Maybe things would be different today. Maybe control would come easier. *Yeah, and maybe Lester Ford would surrender and bring all of his buddies with him.*

He grabbed what he hoped was a soothing breath and entered the living room.

"Good morning."

"Good morning." Angela couldn't look at him. How could she after the way she had acted last night? She swallowed hard. Last night. She had heard him come in late and she had wanted to curl up and disappear at the memory of how she had behaved earlier. Instead, she had made herself breathe the way she hoped a sleeping person sounded until he had gone to the bedroom.

She chewed at her lower lip. She had just spent the longest night of her life. She sighed. But today and tonight would be longer.

"I see you made coffee."

"Yeah." She filled a mug and set in on the counter for him. "Do you want eggs this morning?" *Did he want what she wanted?*

"No, thank you. I'll just have cereal."

"Are we still going fishing?"

She stared at the lower wall behind him as if something of interest were there.

"Why not? It might not be as easy since it's so late, but something will probably be biting." He stared over her shoulder as if something were there besides plain wall.

He's still uneasy about the way I behaved. "Good," she said. "I mean good that we'll probably catch something." *Good that she didn't have to spend today doing nothing with Trent, when she wanted . . . No. Stop it.*

She took two bowls from the cupboard and tried to hold them steady. When the dish rattle continued, she shifted one to her other hand. *Too bad my problem can't be so easily solved.*

Neither found words during breakfast to mix with the soft sounds of the spoons. Finally the bowls were empty.

"Ready?" Trent took his bowl to the sink and rinsed it.

"Sure." Angela waited for him to move aside before she did the same.

"Okay." Trent caught her stare and held it.

"Let's go," he said, but he didn't move.

"Okay." She didn't move either, at first. Then she blinked loose and moved from the sink.

"We have to go outside." He stated the obvious, but she didn't point it out. Instead, she followed him out of the cabin.

"First we get some worms." He started to the backyard.

"What? Wait a minute. Worms? You didn't say anything about worms."

"Bait."

She followed as he got the shovel from the shed. "Why can't we use bread? I heard that bread makes good bait."

"This isn't a kid's story where we make a trail." He stared at her. "Besides, it didn't work in the story, either. Fish like worms."

"You're going to pick up the worms?"

"They won't jump into the can."

"You're going to touch them."

"That's the easiest way to do it. It would take forever waiting for them to crawl in."

She glared at him. "I guess then you'll have to put them on a hook."

"They won't jump on the hook by themselves. I haven't found a kamikaze worm yet and I've seen a lot of worms. Come on and try it. They won't bite."

"I'll eat peanut butter and jelly for dinner."

"The worms won't hurt you."

"I'm not touching them. They're slimy."

"How do you know? Ever touch one?"

"Once. When I was too young to know better. That was more than enough." She crossed her arms. "I'll just watch you fish."

"Chicken."

"Cluck, cluck."

The cell phone rang and they both jumped.

"Yeah?" The fisherman had disappeared and the detective was there. "Okay. Yeah." Trent nodded. "Sure." He hung up and looked at Angela.

"They caught Lester late last night. A few minutes ago he agreed to cut a deal."

"You mean it's over? I can go home?" The lightness in her voice kindled a heaviness in Trent. He was going to have to watch it disappear.

"Let's go inside and talk about it." He managed a slight smile, but his gaze avoided hers. "Looks like the fish got a reprieve."

"There you go with that 'let's go inside' stuff. Why aren't you as happy as I am? What aren't you telling me this time?" She frowned. "What's the problem, now? They caught Lester. He confessed. He cut a deal. That should make your case simple. He'll testify. I won't have to. I get on with my life. What's to discuss?"

He exhaled sharply and stared at her. "Angela, you're still in danger." More than they had thought at first, but he wouldn't tell her that. "We have two cases going here. It's not just Lester. Seems like, besides killing your boss, Lester's assignment was to pick up the set of books from Mr. Hunter's office."

"You mean the information I found when I was writing my paper? The figures that didn't jibe?"

"That's it. Lester admitted that he destroyed the books. His bosses have no idea that the information still exists and Lester can't testify about them since he doesn't know what was in them. He says he just glanced at them to make sure they were what he was after."

"He didn't destroy anything. He was too busy chasing and trying to kill me."

"He said that after he left the building, he checked into a motel and burned the papers in the bathtub. He was supposed to take the books to his boss, but he was afraid we were close because of you and he didn't want anything to link him to the murder." He stared at her. "They didn't find the books when they searched the office."

"Well, maybe he's lying about looking at them. Maybe he knows what was in them."

"Lester isn't smart enough."

"I have it all on a disk. Remember? I also have copies of some of the papers." Her face brightened with her idea. "We can give them to the chief."

Trent nodded. "We will."

"But?"

"I'll explain when we get inside."

"That bad, huh?"

"Angela, please. Let's go inside."

"Okay. And then I pack to go home." Her glare dared him to disagree.

She went into the house without looking at him. As soon as she got inside, she turned to face him. "What?"

"We have a relocation program called the Witness Protection Program. It . . ."

"I've read a little about it. It's for people involved with the mob."

"It's for witnesses," he corrected her, trying to prepare her.

"So you're talking about relocation for Lester? After what he did he gets to go free?"

"I'm sure that will be part of the deal after he testifies."

"What about Mr. Hunter? He was killed and his killer gets off? What kind of justice is that? How will his family feel when they hear that?" She glared. "How many killers are out there that you guys let off? How many people got away with murder?" She shook her head. "People don't have a clue. How can you talk about justice and do this?"

"If Lester talks, we bring down a whole organization responsible for a lot more than one murder outright without even considering the deaths they caused because of their drug trade. The books are another case all together. That's when the feds go after the drug trade."

"But Lester will be free by then. And it was two murders."

Trent didn't expect her to agree with the policy. He still had trouble with it himself. He hated that there was a way to get away with murder even after the government had you.

"I'll bet Mr. Hunter's family wouldn't think that's a good trade-off."

"Look. Don't think about that. We don't have anything to do with that." He let out a deep breath. "There's more that I have to tell you." He held her with his stare. "As I said, the program is for witnesses, not just criminals."

He watched as her glare changed to a frown which changed to a wide-eyed stare as she realized what his words meant. He continued anyway.

"Without you as a witness against him, Lester won't roll over. He'll never talk about the organization because the government would never be able to prove the murder charge without you. Lester knows it and his bosses know it or they will know it. He'd walk unless you testify."

"He's going to walk anyway."

"He'll testify first and we'll get his bosses for ordering the murders. Meanwhile, the feds build their case on the information you have."

"So what does that have to do with me?"

"The program isn't just for criminals." He repeated. His voice softened as if that could ease the impact his words would have on her. "It's for any witness who may be in danger, Angela."

"Me? You mean me?" She shook her head. "No. I know that I'm a witness, but, no. You can't mean me."

"I'm sorry, Angela. I wish there were another way."

"You mean . . ." She stared at him. "I have to move? I have to move forever? I have to give up my life? I don't know anybody anywhere else. Where will I go? What about my things? My degree?" She struggled for air.

"The chief is already working on it. There are some variations, but the basics are the same for all such programs. Do you have any preference as to where you go?"

"I don't know any place else. Just the Philadelphia area." She shook her head. "I just found out about this and you expect me to be able to make a decision that will change the rest of my life? Just like that? This is happening too fast."

"It has to. You can let the chief decide for you, if you want. He's working on several possibilities already."

"I'm supposed to let a stranger decide where I'll spend the rest of my life?"

"Unless you have any suggestions. We have to move quickly."

"I told you I don't know about any other place."

His gaze softened. "Trust the chief. He'll pick a city not too different from what you're used to. You'll adjust." He smiled for her sake. "You're good at that. You'll be okay as long as worms and baiting hooks aren't involved in the move."

Trent watched as Angela blinked hard and swallowed just as hard as if trying to keep her tears inside. Still, a tear slid down her face.

"Oh, Angela." Trent gathered her to him. He wrapped his arms around her wishing that he could protect her from all danger. He held her close, feeling his heart tear apart at the sound of the sobs escaping from her. "Let it out. It is unfair to you. I know. I'd give everything if I could change things for you."

He brushed his hand over her hair, trying to soothe her, knowing he couldn't. He let her cry while he mourned the loss of something that had never been allowed to develop between them. Finally her crying eased, then stopped. It was almost impossible, but he eased her away from him. He wiped the tears from her eyes with his hands, wishing he could take away her misery as well.

"You can do this. It's easier than what you already went through." He smiled at her even though it was the last thing he wanted to do. "The chief will call me back as soon as everything is set."

He let his stare rest on her as if to store her image away for after she left him. As if he could ever forget her.

"Now we . . ." She swallowed hard as if to keep her words from escaping. She wiped her eyes. Trent was glad that no new tears fell. "We pack?"

"We pack."

She swallowed hard. "That quickly."

"If things go the way they're supposed to, yeah, we'll be out of here way before dark." *We can't give them a chance to regroup,* he thought, but he didn't say it to her.

He went into the kitchen and took out a grocery bag. He was proud that he had learned to mask his feelings so well. He stared at the counter. He wished he knew how to hide them from himself.

Two hours later the cabin looked as if they had never been there. Angela looked around the living room. The only difference was the lack of the layer of dust, now, but a new one would form and cover every trace of her and Trent. She hadn't been here long enough to make her mark. So why were tears forming at the thought of leaving?

"Ready?"

She nodded, went outside, hesitated, then climbed into the backseat. Her part of the chief's plan was about to start.

Before they reached the highway, the cell phone rang. Trent pulled over to answer.

Angela tried to block out the part of the conversation she could hear. As long as she could put off the future, she would.

"Have you ever been to Chicago?"

"No. I . . . Is that where I'm going?"

"That's one of the places the chief mentioned. Do you have any objections?"

She shook her head. *What did I learn about Chicago in school?* She frowned. *Gateway to the West. DuSable. Stockyards? It was so long ago.* She always thought she'd die an old woman in Philadelphia. She sighed. *If I stay, I'll probably die a young woman there.*

"What do you think?"

"About Chicago?"

"Yes. Any objections? It's not much different from Philly."

"How can I object? I don't know anything about it."

Trent pulled back onto the road. "An apartment will be leased for you in a complex used by business people whose jobs have transferred them. It's temporary. You'll move to another place in a couple of months. Your things will be shipped to you." This wasn't the first time he did this. But it was the first time that his heart was involved. "I'll take the papers you've been working on for your classes to the chief and he'll handle that part of it. I'll stop at a copy place and give him a call. He'll fax your new resume to us." He glanced at her in the rearview mirror. "Any questions?"

"I'll have to lose my name, won't I?"

"That's the only way relocation works."

"I feel as if I'm dying."

"You'll still be the same person."

"I'll never be the same person again."

Trent didn't disagree. Neither did he tell her that if she had to testify, she'd have to move again. She already had enough to handle today without thinking about what might happen to upset her new world in the future.

When they reached Baltimore, Trent made two stops. Angela stayed in the car and tried not to think about losing her identity. She didn't even look to see where Trent was going. It didn't matter. She couldn't change what was happening to her. She chewed on her lip. *I always thought I was so much in control.* She blinked.

"Here." He handed her three big boxes.

"What's this?"

"One is your identity that will take you to Chicago. The other two are decoys."

"Decoys?"

"Just in case." *Please don't let her ask "Just in case what."* "Use the top one."

Angela lifted the top. She pulled out the yards and yards of black fabric that made the outfit that a Muslim woman would wear.

A woman who dressed like this had been in several of her classes. Angela had asked her about it out of curiosity. She had never dreamed that she herself would one day wear the dresslike garment called the *hijab.*

"I'm supposed to wear this?"

"Only on the plane. The phrase is 'hide in plain sight.'

You'll change when you get to BWI. Then change back to plain clothes when you get to O'Hare."

"Gloves?" Angela held up a pair of black cotton gloves.

"The less anyone sees of you the better."

He drove a little longer and pulled into the far corner of a shopping center parking lot. There he called the chief and gave him their location.

"The fax will be in that shop in a few minutes." Trent pointed to a copy store across the lot. "Be right back."

Angela leaned back against the seat and closed her eyes. *If only it would all just go away.*

"Here." Trent got in and handed her a sheet of paper without looking at it before she had time to think more about her situation. "Don't tell me what it says. Chicago is a huge place, so that part isn't as important. The fewer people know everything, the better for you."

"And the better for the federal government."

"I don't give a damn about their case." He waited long enough to make sure that she understood. "Don't tell me what it says, okay?"

"But you wouldn't tell."

"Never."

Their stares held for several minutes before he broke contact and headed for the airport.

Angela read the sheet of paper that held the plan for her new life, then reread it when she realized that she had no idea what she had read. Finally she gave up and folded it and put it into her purse. Reading it now wouldn't make a bit of difference.

"What if I have to testify?"

Trent sighed. "Then we bring you back."

"Then I'll have to move again."

"The chances are slim that you'll have to testify in this case. We expect that just knowing that you *could* testify against him will make Lester talk."

"But I'll have to come back for the other case." She took a deep breath. "The chances were slim that I'd witness my boss's murder, too."

"Angela, don't worry about what might happen." *His*

thoughts flew to what might have happened between them if things had been different.

He continued in the direction that would separate them forever. Finally, when he didn't think he could stand it any longer, he arrived at the airport.

"Here we are. I don't know what airline you need, so this is the middle."

He stared at her. There was so much that he wanted to say, but nothing he could say that would make any difference. She was leaving. She had to. He got out and opened the trunk.

"Trent . . . I-I . . ." This time she didn't bother to wipe her eyes. New tears would just come to replace the ones that were falling.

"Angela . . ."

He pulled her into his arms for the last time. He would never forget how perfectly she fit against him. He would always regret that this was as close as they would ever get. He struggled for control. "You have to go, sweetheart. Don't make it harder. Take care."

His words stopped coming. It had been years since he had cried. Not even at Aunt Sadie nor Uncle Joe's funeral had he allowed tears to surface. This time was worse and no death was involved. He swallowed down his emotions. None except for the death of something that was never allowed to exist.

He handed her the small suitcase that held her link to her old life. He watched as she walked away, carrying the boxes containing her new temporary identity and taking his heart with her.

She never looked back and he was glad. If she did, in spite of the danger, he might do something foolish like go get her and bring her back to him. Or go with her.

Twelve

Trent had lied. Chicago was not like Philadelphia. Chicago was cold. In May. The end of May. After two years, Angela was just about used to her new name: Jane Johnson. She frowned. *Will I ever get used to the Chicago climate?*

She adjusted her jacket as if that would help her get warmer. True, she lived in Glenwood, not Chicago, but if Chicago got snow, Glenwood was covered by the same blanket.

The wind blew and Jane hunched over as if she could avoid it. She must have been out of her mind when she decided to take the long way home today. A sudden gust gave further proof to her lack of common sense.

Trent had mentioned the wind and she knew Chicago was called the Windy City, but she had thought they meant breezes like in Philadelphia—nothing like this. This is what she imagined a hurricane to be like.

The trees would be just about full with leaves by now, at home, and the weather would make you look for an excuse to be outside. Philadelphia. She sighed. She never thought she would miss it. A handsome brown face floated up in her memory the way it did so often, too often since it wasn't reinforced by the real man.

Trent. Two years later and pain still knifed through her heart when she thought of him. She was Jane Johnson, now. Angela Baring had been left in the airport two years ago, but it didn't matter who she was called. Her feelings for Trent were the same.

She waited at the corner for the light to change. Funny, but she wasn't laughing. Nothing had happened between her and

Trent except a couple of kisses, but she still felt as if she had missed what was supposed to be her future. She had never believed in the idea of soul mates and past lives, but looking back on her experience with Trent changed her thinking.

Once she had recovered from the initial shock of the murder she had witnessed, she had felt drawn to Trent. She sighed. *Being together at the cabin hadn't help cool things off.*

She still got warm. . . . She shook her head—no, hot— thinking about him. Maybe that was the answer to fighting the Chicago cold. Think about Trent and imagine what could have been. She blinked hard. Maybe so, but that solution was too painful. She could stand the cold better than the ache of remembrance. Twice she had been in his arms. Neither time was enough. Set to music, their story could be a modern opera; it had the same kind of unhappy ending.

"No! Come back here, Kim!"

Jane turned toward the voice and saw a little girl run into the street nearby. Jane's purse fell and the briefcase she was carrying hit the ground. Papers spilled out and scattered as she darted after the child, ignoring the car barreling toward the girl. She was not going to witness another death.

As she grabbed the child, the car bumped against Jane, knocking her down, but she held on to the girl. Pain exploded as her head hit the ground. She closed her eyes to try to make it go away.

It was still there when she opened her eyes.

"Are you all right, Miss?"

Jane frowned up at the woman on her knees asking the question. *Maybe if I just am quiet for a while the pain will go away and things will be back to normal.* She stared at the woman, trying to make the picture clear, but wanting to keep her eyes closed and wanting to block out the pain in her head, her shoulder, her side. Her frown deepened as she tried to figure out what happened.

"I'm—I'm so sorry." The woman looked closer at Jane as if that would help. "The little girl just ran out to the street, right in front of me." She pointed to the car pulled sideways a short distance off. The motor was still on and the door was open. "If you hadn't grabbed her. . . ." She took a deep breath as if she were the one who needed to gain control.

"What's your name?" A man stuck a microphone in front of the woman. Another, holding a camcorder, was focused on Jane, who had managed to sit up, but was still on the ground and still holding the now screaming child.

"Thank you, thank you. I can't thank you enough." Another young woman, tears running down face, grabbed the child and clutched her close, rocking back and forth. "You saved my baby." The child had quieted to a whimper.

Jane sat up further and tried to shake off the headache. She frowned again. "Do I know you?" The woman looked familiar, but she wasn't a client.

"Are you hurt?" The driver straightened, but took a step closer and bent down. "My name is—my name is Felicia Wayne. I have my insurance information." She fumbled in her purse, pulled out a wallet, dropped it, picked it up, and dropped it again. "Are you okay? Can you talk?" She retrieved her wallet and managed to pull out a card. "It's all here." Her hand shook so hard that Jane couldn't have read it even if her head hadn't been throbbing. "Maybe somebody can copy the information for her? I can't . . ." She shook her head. "I . . ."

"I'll do it." An older woman in the crowd took the card and got a notepad from her own purse. "You need to slow down, Miss." She glared at the driver.

"Yes, ma'am."

The woman copied the information as she continued with her lecture. "Makes no sense to go tearing around like that. Leave fifteen minutes earlier." She glared at the driver as she returned her insurance card. "This is not a highway. This is a residential area. You need to learn to be more careful."

"Yes, ma'am. I'm sorry."

"Sorry don't do a bit of good."

"Yes, ma'am. I'll be more careful." Felicia Wayne's hands still shook as she took the card back, but not quite as much as before.

"Here you go, baby." The older woman tucked the paper into Jane's purse and set it on her lap. "You all right?"

Jane looked up at the woman and nodded. The pounding in her head got harder at the movement.

"Back off. Give the child some room," the older woman said.

For the first time Jane noticed the wide circle of strangers surrounding her.

"What hurts? We don't want to move you if it will make your injuries worse." A man knelt down and stared at her.

Jane shook her head again. "I have a headache, that's all. I think I'm all right. Please help me up."

"I think you should wait for the ambulance. You might have a back injury," said another woman holding a different child.

"Or a head injury." A short balding man peered closely at her as if he could see inside her head. "Concussions are common in accidents."

"I don't need an ambulance." Jane struggled to stand up. Her head hurt worse when she moved, but she wasn't going to say so. She wasn't going to consider the possibility that she had a serious injury.

"You need to be sure. You don't want to make your condition worse."

"I don't have a 'condition.' Just a headache."

As if to solve the argument, an ambulance pulled up and stopped nearby. A woman carrying a black case came over.

"What's your name?" The technician knelt and proceeded with the examination without waiting for an answer.

"I-I'm Jane." She frowned. "Jane Johnson."

"Here." A woman separated from the crowd and brought Jane the briefcase. "I'm not sure if the papers are in the right order, but I put them inside and closed the zipper. I'll just put it here."

"Thank you." Jane laid it on the ground beside her.

"Miss Johnson, do you know Delores Dixon?" A man leaned over her. "Are you part of K-O-C-S?" The microphone was close enough for her to take a bite, if she wanted to. Jane frowned and pulled back.

"K-O-C-S?" Her frown deepened as a camera pointed down at her and the cameraman moved around to get different angles. Other cameras appeared like sharks to food in the program that she had seen on television.

"K-O-C-S. Keep Our Children Safe. The pickets," another reporter said as he pointed to the crowd.

For the first time Jane noticed that many of the people surrounding her held large signs. That's where she had seen the woman. She had been interviewed several times on the news about the group protest for an additional traffic light before the new playground opened.

Jane glanced at the rest of the people. Many of them held cameras or microphones. A few looked as if they had just happened to come past at that time. All were staring at her as if she were someone famous.

"Is that why you were the one who grabbed her? Are you part of them? Were you helping the protesters make a point?" Another microphone nudged against the first one. "Is this a setup to prove the need for a traffic light now that the new playground is open?"

"Setup?" Jane rubbed her head and looked around. "I grabbed her because a car was about to hit her." The crowd had grown. More cameras helped form a ring holding her in.

"How dare you imply that I would purposely place my child in danger." The woman holding the little girl took a step toward the reporter who had asked the question.

"Come on, Delores," another woman said. "Don't play into their hands. They want something negative to happen to take the focus off the fact that we need a traffic light at this corner even if there is one at the next intersection." She pulled on Delores's arm.

"You folks want to take it somewhere else?" The emergency technician never looked at the others. She finished examining Jane's head and placed a large bandage over the scrape on the side of her forehead. "Your vitals are normal. I don't think you have a concussion, but you should get checked out. Do you want us to take you to the emergency room?"

"No. I don't want to go to the hospital."

"We need for you to sign this release then." She handed Jane a paper and pen and waited for her to sign it. "Okay, then. We're through here. You should still get checked out by your doctor to make sure." She stood. "It's okay to stand now." She put her hand under Jane's elbow and helped her up.

"Can't I just take a couple of aspirin when I get home?"

The technician shrugged. "I'm supposed to advise you to see your doctor." She packed the equipment into the ambulance.

When the ambulance pulled away from the curb, the reporters came back to Jane more like sharks attracted to blood than before.

"Miss Johnson, You never answered. Are you part of this group?"

"I'm not part of any group. I just decided to take a different way home today."

"You're coming from work? You work around here? Where?" One microphone moved forward in front of the others.

"And you live around here, too?" A man elbowed his way forward. "Nearby?" He looked around as if expecting to see a sign announcing "Jane Johnson lives here."

"I . . ." Jane swallowed hard, suddenly aware that cameras meant television. This wasn't Philadelphia, but still. . . . "I have to go. Excuse me."

"Wait." Delores shifted Kim to her other hip. The child had quieted to sniffles. "I have to do something more. Thank you isn't enough for saving my daughter's life." She wiped her eyes. "How can I get in touch with you?"

"That's not necessary."

Jane eased away. The crowd moved with her as if attached like parts of a child's pull toy. She tried to turn away from the cameras, but they moved when she did. "Anybody would have done the same." She remembered why she had come to Chicago. She had to get away from this attention.

She didn't wait for any other response. Instead, she jogged away from the crowd, glad she had spent the time since she got to Chicago getting in shape. The jarring of running didn't help her headache, but she kept the pace until she turned the corner and got to the end of the next block. Before she turned yet again, she glanced back. No one was following her. She eased into a walk.

Two years had passed. No one had gotten in touch with her, but surely the danger was over by now. Besides, Chicago was a long way from Philadelphia and this was local news related to a very local situation. She frowned.

Had she given her address? She couldn't remember if the medical technicians had asked. They probably had. Even so, it was a medical record, wasn't it? Medical records were confidential, weren't they? A lot of people had heard her name, but she was sure that it was okay. There must be tons of Johnsons in the phone book, and she had an unlisted number, anyway.

She doubled back toward her house. No matter how she fought against them, memories of another flight flooded her mind.

A tightness gripped her chest that had nothing to do with the accident or her jogging. *What's Trent doing now?* She sighed. Probably married. He hadn't felt the pull between them as much as she had. He couldn't have. If so, he never would have let her leave. She felt her eyes fill. How could it still hurt so much after two years? More importantly, when would it stop?

Kisses. The only thing between them had been kisses. What would her pain be like if more had happened between them? *Worse. Much, much worse.* She sighed. *Then why do I regret that we never made love?*

She wiped her eyes, looked around one last time, and walked slowly up her driveway and into her house. The quiet greeted her as it always did, but today it seemed heavier and her small house felt as large as a mansion. Maybe she should have moved to another apartment instead of buying a house. Or at least a town house instead of a three-bedroom single.

She set her things on the hall table and went into the kitchen. She had to find a way to move her life forward. Looking back never changed anything.

A viewer in Philadelphia was watching the end of the six o'clock news—not really paying attention, just waiting for the game show that would follow.

"Now for a good news story for a change." The newscaster smiled into the camera. "This is from our sister station in Chicago." The screen went blank for a split second before another reporter appeared.

"The opening of a new playground in Glenwood, a Chicago suburb, was saved from a tragedy when a woman passing by risked her life to save a a child from getting hit by a car. Since the playground construction was announced, it has been the site of numerous protests demanding a traffic light. Officials have been reluctant to add one since there is already a light at the next corner. This incident may make them reconsider."

A news clip appeared of the accident and its aftermath. Everyone involved had a turn in front of the camera, but the most attention was given to the woman.

The viewer leaned close to the television and smiled, the game show no longer of interest. This story might not be about Philadelphia, but there was a tie-in.

Everything else was forgotten as the film ran several times as if to make sure that the so-called heroine was identified. And she was. Then the Chicago reporter reappeared.

"Regardless of what happens as far as the traffic light is concerned, Jane Johnson happened to be in the right place today and little Kim Dixon is alive because of her. Miss Johnson brushed off the accolades and continued on her way without telling us anything about her except her name. I guess her actions spoke for her. This is Ann Darby of WLCS, Chicago. Back to you, Jim."

The local newscaster continued, but he could have ended there for all the attention he now received from this viewer.

"So. Chicago. I knew if I waited long enough, Little Miss Witness Protection would surface. I don't care if she didn't testify, it's her fault that I'm alone. If she hadn't threatened to talk, everybody would have dummied up and Big Tic would still be alive and with me." A frown marred what could have been a pleasant face. "She still looks like her old high school picture from that one news story. The stupid woman didn't even try to change her appearance. I guess she's smug enough to figure that she's safe."

Narrowed eyes stared at the television after the news went off. An angry fist swiped at the lone tear that dared to escape. No more fell. "I haven't gotten Lester yet, but I've got her. I think she's due for a blast from the past. I'm not talking about old songs, but it *is* time for her to face the music." The laugh that followed held no humor. *Road trip. Never been to The Windy City.*

The television droned on even though the living room was now empty.

"Damn." Trent frowned at the television. "That woman is a magnet for trouble." He stared at the news film clip the way a thirsty man would stare at a glass of water. Two years and she looked even better than he remembered.

His pain was still as sharp. It couldn't be more intense, but he had learned to accept it and live with it. Whoever said "time heals all wounds" had lied. An ache tinged with regret welled up in him as it did each time he thought of her. He should be comfortable with the feeling by now.

What would have happened if he had gone against his better judgment and kept her with him? Or what if he had gone with her? He sighed. He hadn't had a choice. He could have been traced since they hadn't planned for him to leave. A short while with her wasn't worth her life. His, maybe, but not hers.

The phone in the hall rang and rescued him.

"Yeah, I saw it, chief." It had been over a year since he had chosen to leave the department rather than take a desk job, but the chief would always be the chief. It wasn't his fault that Trent had been wounded while on duty.

Trent stretched his left leg to ease the stiffness. In the year since it had happened, the action had become automatic. His jaw tightened. His leg still didn't stop him from operating his private investigating business successfully— even the physical part.

He didn't need the money. When he was on the force, a

portion of his pay had gone into investments that others had said were foolish. The returns proved them wrong. He'd even have trouble spending all the interest. He'd learned that he had a knack for knowing when to jump on a stock and when to sell. He had stayed on the force then for the same reason he had formed his own company: he'd climb the walls if he didn't have something to do.

"What?" The chief's voice pulled him back. "Yeah, I'm catching the first flight that I can get." The hum of his empty apartment filled the space until he dared to ask the question: "Do you think she's still in danger?" He pushed the speaker phone button, put down the receiver, and rubbed his old wound. Then he moved to a runner's stretch. In a few seconds his leg was almost normal.

"I doubt it," the chief said. "The old organization is dead. Since Big Tic died in prison, the others have regrouped. If they came in contact with Angela—or rather Jane—now, they'd probably want to reward her for allowing them to move up." The chief's sharp laugh reached Trent. "Still, it wouldn't hurt to go. You know the feds haven't done anything with their case. I don't know when, or even if, they will. They don't see fit to tell the lowly local forces about their plans."

"Yeah. I remember."

"Your calendar free?"

"Yeah." *If it wasn't, he'd have cleared it.*

"I always felt there had been something between you two. For a few months after she went into the program, you were worse than impossible to be around. If the guys weren't so honest and didn't like you so much, they would have taken up a collection to hire a hit man to take care of you and put them out of your misery."

"I know. I still feel bad about that."

"They got over it."

Trent closed his eyes, but his ache for Angela only intensified. *He was glad somebody had.* "There wasn't anything between us. You know I don't mix personal with business. *But he had wanted to, oh, how badly he had wanted to.*

"I know, but there could have been."

"Yeah, there could have been." Again silence pressed in on him. "I got to get ready to go. Thanks for remembering."

"I'll make a few calls and see if I can open a few doors for you. I have no idea where she is now, but an old army buddy is the chief of the Third District in Chicago. I haven't talked to him in a good while, but I'll see what I can do. Glenwood will have its own force, but maybe Bruce can steer you to somebody who can help you there."

"I'd appreciate it."

"Good luck. Give me a call when you can and let me know how you made out."

Trent broke the connection and got out the yellow pages. If he was lucky, the first airline he called would have a flight that he could take.

An hour later he was climbing into a cab. Two hours later he was on a flight to his second chance. Only a few others had boarded with him and that was fine. Trent stretched his legs out, grateful for his bulkhead seat and that no other passengers sat beside him, not just because of the extra room, but because he didn't want distractions. He needed the time to plan his actions more than he needed the space. Even with the chief's help, she wouldn't be easy to find. He chewed on his lower lip. But he *would* find her.

Somebody else on the flight had the same goal as Trent, but not for the same reason. Somebody else would be just as glad to see Jane Johnson as Trent would be.

Near the back of the plane, determination filled the other passenger on the same quest as Trent. *It doesn't matter what she calls herself now, in a little while the only thing she will be called is dead.*

Thirteen

"Now what?" Angela turned off the television but stared at the dark screen. After she had seen the story about her on her usual news channel, she had surfed through the others. Every television news broadcast had featured the story.

Her face—with a confused look, but definitely her face—had been thrown from the television to viewers of every local station. There must have been something more interesting to report. Why pick this story?

She hadn't even been aware that there was a battle between the neighbors and the city over a traffic light. Then, just because she had decided to take the long way home, she had ended up right in the middle of the battle. And on television.

A chill went through her, but the temperature didn't have anything to do with it; her house was warm.

Was she still in danger? Two years had passed. Was everything really over back home?

Angela closed her eyes. She hadn't wanted to know what was going on, but during the trial every evening the local television news programs made room for updates from Philadelphia. Each day it had seemed as if more murders were revealed. When the witnesses testified, they sounded as if they were talking about purse snatching rather than killings. The trial had gone on forever.

She swallowed hard. If she had realized how much danger she had been in at the time her boss had been killed, she probably would have dropped dead from fright and saved them from trying to kill her.

The trial had finally ended a long time ago. When it was

over, Lester had gone into protection, others had made deals just as he had, and the top three in the crime organization had been convicted. The story had died out until a few weeks after the sentencing when one of the leaders had died in prison.

Angela still checked the Philadelphia papers on-line from time to time. The prison murder was the last thing she saw about the case. Since then, nothing.

Did that mean she was safe? What about the federal case based on the information she had stumbled upon? Had they decided not to pursue it? If so, why hadn't they told her? If not, would she have to relocate again when they did? She curled her legs under her. She was still adjusting to this move, still trying to fit in. What if she had to start over somewhere else?

After the chief had sent her diploma to her by mail, she had established her own accounting firm, keeping the books for area businesses too small for larger accounting firms to want to bother with. She was making a comfortable living and had money in the bank. She sighed. But she had few friends.

She got up to shut the drapes and checked the street as she always did. She had fought him on it, but Trent had been right about her having to leave Philadelphia. She sighed. *Trent.*

Her memory pulled up his image. Piercing black eyes dominated his strong features. She still remembered the intensity when he was taking her to safety. And the desire that flared up inside her when she stood close to him. And the kisses. She closed her eyes. And the kisses.

Her body tingled with the memory and ached for the memory to be replaced by reality. It didn't take much effort to relive the time she spent in Trent's arms. The time hadn't been long—not nearly long enough—but what there was kept her memory strong.

She grew warm and her body tightened in some places and moistened in others as if he were there and she would finally fulfill her longings. They had never had a chance to tell their love, to show their love. She had never felt him inside her, her center closed around him tightly; she had never shown him how she felt.

Funny. One time in his arms and her longing would be with her for the rest of her life. What might have been, would always be with her.

What if she went back? She'd be safe, wouldn't she? She could find him. She shook her head. *Then what?* If he felt about her what she felt about him, he would have come to her. If she was safe. If he was interested.

What was he doing? Had he moved on? Had he found somebody? Had he forgotten all about Angela? When Jane Johnson appeared, had Angela Baring disappeared for him, too?

She would be a fool if she didn't believe that was possible. Some other woman would have found him, captivated him, claimed him for her own. Angela couldn't blame her. She would have done the same if she could have.

She should work on the accounts that were due tomorrow. Instead she turned on the television again. Any work she did right now would have to be done over.

She tuned to the rerun of a sitcom that she didn't want to watch, but she needed something to drown out her loud thoughts. Maybe later she could concentrate on the present and shove the past back where it belonged. Maybe.

Even though it was late, Trent went directly to the Third Precinct. He knew what would happen, but he was still disappointed when he was told to come back in the morning.

He tried to tamp down his impatience as he followed the desk sergeant's directions to the closest hotel. After all, he knew Angela was here. That was more than he had known for the past two years. By this time tomorrow, he'd be drinking his fill of her beautiful face. A slight smile softened his features. *Angela.*

His arms tingled at the thought of holding her. He didn't want to consider that she might have somebody else to do that now. Against his desires, reality eased in and made his smile leave. Even if she did, he had to make sure she was still safe. She had no way of knowing that her story had been broadcast in Philadelphia. If she had found somebody else, he'd make sure she was safe and then leave. He hoped he would be noble enough to wish her well, but he wasn't sure that he could go that far.

He parked in the driveway of the motel six blocks away and checked in, but he didn't expect to get much rest. Tomorrow was too far away and what it would bring was too uncertain.

Trent checked in quickly and hoped the night would pass just as fast. He stretched out on the bed, grateful for the relaxation techniques he had learned after he was shot. He had to get some rest. If somebody *was* after Angela, he had to be alert enough to keep her safe.

Early daylight reached through the crack around the drapes and jabbed him awake. He got up and glanced at the bed. It looked as if he had fought a battle in his sleep or as if somebody had done more than sleep last night. He sighed. Unfortunately a battle was the reality.

He took his shower and checked out. He was not going to accept the possibility that by tonight he wouldn't be any closer to finding Angela. He went back to the station. It was too early to expect the police chief, but he didn't have anywhere else to go. Besides, if he was there when the chief came in, maybe he would give Trent some time before the day got busy.

"Is the chief in?" Trent knew the answer, but he asked anyway. He went through the same routine of introducing himself and showing his ID to this sergeant as he had done with the other one last night.

"He won't be in until late. He has a press conference and a couple of other events on his schedule."

"Any way I can reach him?"

"He'll be moving around a lot. Your best bet is to wait here for him."

Frustration made Trent pace the floor as if that would help. The only thing that kept him there was knowing that this was still the best way of finding Angela. His only contact was here.

After he had walked miles back and forth, he sat in the waiting area. Walking hadn't eased his frustration one bit.

He leaned back in the hard plastic chair. The same person must have worked out a plan that every police station in the country followed. The chairs were identical to the ones at home. Even the paint color was the same. Did some company submit low bids on furniture and paint for police stations all over the country?

He leaned forward, checking his watch as he changed positions. Ten minutes had passed; only ten minutes. Life buzzed around him: phones ringing, people passing by, others sitting in chairs just like his. Every so often a uniformed officer paused to stare at him as if trying to place him from a wanted poster. Had he done the same when he was on the force? He shrugged. Probably so. You didn't survive as a police officer if you weren't alert and a little suspicious about strangers.

He stood and paced again as if that would hurry time along. The chief had a press conference. And after that there was what the watch captain called a media event. What event? Why today of all days?

He walked to the window and glanced through the thick bars as if that would help him find Angela. He shook his head. She was Jane, now, not Angela.

He left the windows and paced to the door. It didn't matter what her name was now, she was still the same person. His body tightened at the memory of her. He hoped it wasn't obvious to the others unfortunate enough to have to be in this room. He wanted her. Still. More than he had that day on the porch. Or when he took her to the airport. If his need for her had been as great then as it was now, there was no way he could have let her go.

He frowned as he paced to the side. She might still be in danger. Probably not, but maybe. He turned and went the other way.

Even if he knew for certain that she was safe, once he had learned where she was, he was determined to find her—to see if she remembered him. He stopped when he reached the wall.

He wanted more than remembering from her; he wanted to learn that she had ached for him every night for the past two years as much as he had ached for her.

An Important Message From The ARABESQUE Publisher

Dear Arabesque Reader,

I have some exciting news to share....

Available now is a four-part special series **AT YOUR SERVICE** written by bestselling Arabesque Authors.

Bold, sweeping and passionate as America itself—these superb romances feature military heroes you are destined to love. They confront their unpredictable futures along-side women of equal courage, who will inspire you!

The **AT YOUR SERVICE** series* can be specially ordered by calling 1-888-345-BOOK, or purchased wherever books are sold.

Enjoy them and let us know your feedback by commenting on our website.

Linda Gill, Publisher
Arabesque Romance Novels

BOOKS

Check out our website at www.BET.com

ARABESQUE

* The AT YOUR SERVICE novels are a special series that are not included in your regular book club subscription.

A SPECIAL "THANK YOU"
FROM ARABESQUE JUST FOR YOU!

Send this card back and you'll receive 4 FREE Arabesque Novels—a $25.96 value—absolutely FREE!

The introductory 4 Arabesque Romance books are yours FREE (plus $1.99 shipping & handling). If you wish to continue to receive 4 books every month, do nothing. Each month, we will send you 4 New Arabesque Romance Novels for your free examination. If you wish to keep them, pay just $16* (plus, $1.99 shipping & handling). If you decide not to continue, you owe nothing!

- Send no money now.
- Never an obligation.
- Books delivered to your door!

We hope that after receiving your FREE books you'll want to remain an Arabesque subscriber, but the choice is yours! So why not take advantage of this Arabesque offer, with no risk of any kind. You'll be glad you did!

In fact, we're so sure you will love your Arabesque novels, that we will send you an Arabesque Tote Bag FREE with your first paid shipment.

Call Us TOLL-FREE At
1-888-345-BOOK

* Prices subject to change

THE "THANK YOU" GIFT INCLUDES:

- 4 books absolutely FREE (plus $1.99 for shipping and handling).
- A FREE newsletter, *Arabesque Romance News*, filled with author interviews, book previews, special offers, and more!
- No risks or obligations.

INTRODUCTORY OFFER CERTIFICATE

Yes! Please send me 4 FREE Arabesque novels (plus $1.99 for shipping & handling). I understand I am under no obligation to purchase any books, as explained on the back of this card. Send my **FREE Tote Bag** after my first regular paid shipment.

NAME _____

ADDRESS _____ APT. _____

CITY _____ STATE _____ ZIP _____

TELEPHONE ( ) _____

E-MAIL _____

SIGNATURE _____

Offer limited to one per household and not valid to current subscribers. All orders subject to approval. Terms, offer, & price subject to change. Tote bags available while supplies last.

Thank You!

AN063A

ARABESQUE

Accepting the four introductory books for FREE (plus $1.99 to offset the cost of shipping & handling) places you under no obligation to buy anything. You may keep the books and return the shipping statement marked "cancelled". If you do not cancel, about a month later we will send 4 additional Arabesque novels, and you will be billed the preferred subscriber's price of just $4.00 per title. That's $16.00* for all 4 books for a savings of almost 40% off the cover price (Plus $1.99 for shipping and handling). You may cancel at any time, but if you choose to continue, every month we'll send you 4 more books, which you may either purchase at the preferred discount price. . . or return to us and cancel your subscription.

* PRICES SUBJECT TO CHANGE

THE ARABESQUE ROMANCE CLUB: HERE'S HOW IT WORKS

THE ARABESQUE ROMANCE BOOK CLUB
P.O. BOX 5214
CLIFTON NJ 07015-5214

PLACE
STAMP
HERE

What if she had found somebody else? What if she was involved with somebody and he was just someone from an unpleasant part of her past life? He shook his head. That wasn't possible. No way could his feelings be this strong and hers nonexistent. Fate couldn't be that cruel. He couldn't even consider that.

He looked at his watch again. Time was playing games with him, moving in slow motion when he wasn't looking. Another fifteen minutes had crawled past. At this rate, if he didn't get rid of some of his stress, they'd have to peel him off the wall when the chief finally came.

For a few seconds he considered going to the Glenwood Station and asking for their help. Maybe they'd believe that he was still a Philadelphia police officer. He frowned. Probably not. He wouldn't if the situation were reversed. Then he'd never get their help. He sighed. He couldn't afford to take a chance on antagonizing them.

He walked back to a chair and stretched his legs out. Maybe the district chief would be back in time to keep him from going off the deep end.

Afraid to leave the station, Trent had made lunch and dinner from the stuff in the vending machines. It all tasted the same, but that wasn't important. The only thing that mattered was finding Angela and he still hadn't done that. He looked at his watch then checked it against the clock on the wall. They both agreed. How much longer?

"Hey, Buddy." Trent looked around. He was the only one left in the room. He looked back at the officer behind the desk, afraid to believe that he was talking to him. The man nodded and Trent walked over to the desk. "The chief just called. Because it's so late, he won't be in until tomorrow. Sorry."

Trent glanced at his watch. After six. "Isn't there some way I can talk to him tonight?"

The officer shook his head. "Sorry."

Trent stared at him. No, he wasn't sorry. If he were, he'd tell Trent how to get in touch with him now. "This is important."

"It doesn't matter, anyway." The man shrugged. "I told him about you. He said he didn't get any phone call from Philadelphia. He said he doesn't know anybody in Philly, anyway."

"He and my chief were in the army together."

"Chief Williams wasn't in the army. He was in the navy." The man stared at Trent as if he had caught in him in a lie. "Maybe you're at the wrong station."

"This is the Third Precinct, isn't it?"

"Yeah."

Trent frowned and shook his head slowly. "How long has he been chief?"

"He was appointed yesterday. That's the reason for the news conference and all of his other appearances today. He's playing catch-up."

Trent groaned. "What happened to the former chief? How can I reach him?"

"He retired as of yesterday. He said he was going fishing to try to get rid of thirty years of tension."

"Did he say where he was going?"

"Nope."

Trent fought the frustration that threatened to overwhelm him. He had wasted a valuable day sitting around because he had failed to ask a few simple questions. Why hadn't he checked with the chief back home when he got here? Why hadn't he at least asked the chief's name when he got here? Why had he made assumptions that cost so much time? He wouldn't have made a mistake like this if he were still on the force. He headed for the door.

"Hey. What you going to do?"

"I'm not sure." He left the station, got into the rented car, and never looked back.

He sat behind the wheel and allowed himself a few minutes to rail at his own stupidity; at his chief for not being up to date, and at fate. Then he opened the map of Chicago and the surrounding suburbs.

He'd make up a Plan B as he drove to Glenwood.

* * *

Trent parked outside the Glenwood Police Station thirty minutes later. His plan wasn't really a plan, but it was all he had: the truth. He tightened his jaw and walked into the building.

"I'm a former police officer from Philadelphia and I need to speak with your chief." He held out his old ID.

The desk sergeant stared at Trent for a while before he made a call. For a few nods and several "yes sirs," he stared at Trent. Finally he hung up. "Captain Ellers said for you to come on back. Last office on the left." He pointed to a hall behind him.

Trent sent up a prayer, took a deep breath, and went down the hall. This had to work. He didn't have a Plan C.

"Thanks for seeing me," Trent said, after he had introduced himself. Then he told the short version about Angela.

Captain Ellers stared at him for a few seconds. "How can I reach your chief?"

Trent gave him the station number and the chief's home number and hoped the chief was at one of those places. He forced himself to be patient.

"Why don't you go back to the waiting room? I'll come get you when I have something."

Logic said that he should appreciate the precautions the captain was taking, but his heart was impatient, not logical. It had been too long. He didn't want to do it, but he went back to the waiting room that was just like the other one; he felt as if he were regressing instead of making progress.

He prayed that this delay wouldn't put her in jeopardy. He hoped that, if anyone was after her, they were running into the same problem. He had the help of the police. He hoped. That meant that he would find her ahead of anybody else looking, didn't it?

He paced across the small room. How many more police stations would he have to pace before he found Angela? He hoped the answer was zero, but if not, he'd wear paths in every police station in the state, the country, even the world, if it came to that; if in the end he'd have Angela back.

When Trent felt as if he would burst from the frustration of waiting, Captain Ellers walked over to him.

"I talked to your chief. We're trying to get that information for you. We're working from voter registration, street residences, and drivers' license lists. We're bound to find her on one of those." He stared at Trent. "Wouldn't it have been simpler to notify us of the details of the problems and let us handle it from here?" His stare intensified. "Why is a private eye involved and not the feds?"

"We don't have any proof that anyone's after her. The main players are dead or in jail. I don't have anything concrete to give you yet."

"You know your license doesn't mean anything here."

"I know."

And even if you were still on the Philadelphia police force, you're way out of your jurisdiction here."

Trent nodded. "I know that, too. If I had anything except a maybe, I'd give it to you. I was never one to refuse help." Trent hesitated. "She's more than an old case to me." He hesitated again. "I couldn't let anything come of my feelings for her before, and I thought I had lost her forever. This is like fate felt sorry for me and gave me a second chance." He stared at Captain Ellers. "Do you believe in fate?"

Captain Ellers pinned him with a stare. Then he shrugged. "Never thought that much about it. I guess everybody has something happen that can be credited. . . ." He frowned and said, ". . . or blamed on fate." Then he added, "I don't suppose you want to go back to your motel and wait for me to call you?"

"I'll wait here."

He didn't tell Captain Ellers that he had given up his room. It didn't matter. He wouldn't leave even if he hadn't.

"I thought you would." He nodded. "I'll let you know as soon as I have something."

Trent watched him leave the room. He hoped the lists were in the computers so the search would go faster. And he hoped she was on at least one of the lists. And he hoped the computers wouldn't crash. He sighed. He wished his future was pinned on something more substantial than hope.

He began to pace again. If he were a smoker, he would have gone through several packs of cigarettes by now. He didn't think she was in danger. Now that he was so close, he was just anxious to see her.

While Trent waited for his Plan B to work, somebody else had a different Plan A in operation.

"Bingo." Hard eyes lit up at the sign beside the door. The name matched the one that had been on the ambulance in the news story. A smile found it's way to the face and fastened itself in place as the doors swished open.

"Hi there, Miss . . ." Eyes peered closer at the ID badge of the woman behind the desk. "Miss Coburn. I'm Sara Willis. I'm a member of the Citizen Appreciation Association." A wide smile accompanied the card handed to the receptionist. "We plan to give an award to Miss Jane Johnson. You know, the brave young woman who risked her life for that little girl? I'm sure you saw the story. It was in the papers and all of the television stations carried it."

The plan was simple, really. A few business cards made at a machine in a mall. Machines didn't ask for an ID when you typed in a name, and human nature made people—most people—want to help somebody win recognition. Another requirement was the guts to pull it off. A killer smile helped. The smile widened even more at this last thought.

"Oh, yes. I remember." Miss Coburn's head bobbed up and down like one of those dolls people put in the back window of their cars. A wide smile lit her face, matching the one she was looking at. "I saw the story. Wasn't she brave to do something like that?"

"Yes she was." *I could think of another word to describe her, but you don't need to know that.* "It's so seldom we hear of good deeds that our organization wants to recognize them when we do. Maybe it will inspire others." The smile was forced to soften. "The problem is, we have no way to get in touch with Ms. Johnson. We're hoping the EMT recorded her address or phone number."

The receptionist stared at the business card again. "I just started working here today. I'm not sure if I should . . ."

"You can call that number to verify me, if you want. *I hope you're as trusting as you look.* Sara pushed on. "I can understand your reluctance. I assure you, we only want to see that Ms. Johnson gets what she deserves." Hesitation in the receptionist's eyes gave hope for success. "We feel that if we give recognition while the story is still fresh, it might inspire someone else to put the needs of others first." It was a struggle, but the smile stayed in place.

"Wait a minute. I'll call the team and see what I can find out for you, Miss Willis." Miss Coburn left the counter and went to the desk against the far wall, smiled at Sara, and picked up the phone. "This shouldn't take long. Just wait right there."

As if she would go anywhere else when she was so close.

Karen Weston—temporarily Sara Willis—forced herself to look relaxed, not to tap on the counter, and to keep the smile in place. Finally Miss Coburn hung up. When she returned to the counter her look spoke before a word left her mouth.

"I'm so sorry, Miss Willis. They said we can't give out that information to anyone no matter what the reason. I told them what you wanted it for, but they still said 'no'." She looked sorry, but not as sorry as Karen felt. "I'm so sorry. I do want Miss Johnson to get what she deserves."

"Not as much as I do."

"What will you do now? How will you find her?"

"I'll have to find another way."

"You think I might still hear about this on the news?"

"If things go according to my plans."

Miss Coburn was still apologizing as Karen left the office.

This was a setback, only a setback, Karen thought. *I'll find her.*

Fourteen

Daylight was still making its appearance when Jane stepped onto her front porch. It had been a long week and what she really wanted to do was go back to sleep. Between deadlines on some clients' accounts and her neighbors who saw her on the news and stopped by to compliment her for what she did, she needed to unwind.

She took several deep breaths. She didn't feel like it, but she was going for a run. She jogged in place for about five minutes, trying to hype herself up. Then she stretched. She ended with several more deep breaths.

She still wanted to go back inside, but she forced herself to walk down to the sidewalk where she hesitated again. She did not want to go anywhere near that playground. Or any other one.

She popped a tape into her portable player, positioned the headphones on her head, and took off in a different direction.

Very few people were out this early and she liked it that way. The tape shifted to a faster tempo. She found her groove and jogged her favorite route past the warehouse two miles from her home. She was the only one out in this section. The quiet more than compensated for the lack of sidewalks.

She turned the corner and was back on a street where houses, with their neat little yards, took the place of the warehouse. She continued her run, looking forward to completing the large rectangle that would end at her house. She smiled. When she got home, she wasn't going anywhere for the rest of the day. She would get her latest book and a cup of Earl Grey tea and . . .

"Watch out! Watch out!"

Jane looked toward the street. She hoped another child wasn't in danger. She didn't know if she could do the Superwoman thing again.

A dark car sped toward her as if she were a magnet. Jane stared like a deer pinned in place by headlights. Just as the car reached her, she roused herself and jumped to the side, landing on her shoulder and hip, rolling up the slight grade onto the lawn, and ending in a flower bed.

"Are you all right, Miss?"

Jane looked at the woman standing over her. She looked old enough to be Jane's grandmother. "I'm okay."

Her shoulder and hip burned and her whole side ached, but the woman's face was covered with concern and Jane didn't want to worry her any further.

"You sure you're all right?" She looked closely at Jane's arm. "You got a bad scrape there and you hit the ground real hard. Maybe I should call an ambulance."

"No, please. I'm all right." Jane stood and slowly moved her shoulder around. It still hurt like crazy, but nothing felt broken. She rubbed her upper arm, but stopped when a spot screamed at her touch. She kept her face from showing how much it hurt. She was not going to end up on the news again.

"Come sit on my porch." The woman put her hand on Jane's other arm.

Jane followed her only because she knew her legs wouldn't take her very far if she didn't. She felt like a magnet made just to attract cars.

"You sit right there, baby." The woman patted Jane's arm and pointed to the glider against the brick wall. "I'm Louise Dalton. As you can guess, this is my house. Is there anyone I can call to come get you?"

"No, thank you. I'm all right."

"That man looked like he was aiming right for you. Probably talking on one of those cell phones 'stead of paying attention to his driving." She shuddered. "I don't want to think of what would have happened if I hadn't stepped outside to get my morning newspaper when I did." She shook her head. "I'm sorry I didn't get the license number. I was so busy looking at you. . . ." She took a deep breath and let it out slowly. "Are you sure you're all right?

"Yes, ma'am." Her pain had eased a bit and Jane believed what she told Mrs. Dalton.

"You don't look so good."

"I'll be okay. Thank you for what you did." She stood. Pain shot through her hip. She forced herself to ignore it. "I'd better get home."

"I can clean up your arm. That's a bad scrape." She leaned forward and looked at it again.

"Thank you, Mrs. Dalton, but it's not much. It will wait until I get home."

"You just sit right here as long as you want. Can I get you something? A cup of tea? A glass of cold water?"

"No, thank you. You're very kind, but I'm ready to go home."

"You live around here? How far is home?"

"Not too far." Angela looked out to the spot where she had landed. Every flower that had started to poke through in that section of the large flower bed was flattened. "Look what I did to your flowers. I'm so sorry."

"Child, they're just flowers." Louise shook her head. "I can carry you home in my car, if you want. Won't be any trouble."

"Thank you for offering, but it's only a few blocks. I think the walk will do me good. Help prevent stiffness." She didn't believe that, but she hoped at least it wouldn't make it worse.

"Good thing you're young. I don't want to think about what condition I'd be in if it were me dodging that car instead of you."

"I'm glad it wasn't you, Mrs. Dalton. Thanks again." Jane forced herself to move even though her muscles were screaming for her to be still.

"Wait a minute. Don't I know you?" A puzzled look replaced the older woman's frown.

"I don't think so."

"I've seen you some place before. What's your name?"

"I jog along here a lot."

"No." Louise shook her head. "That's not it." She frowned as she stared at Jane for a few seconds. "What's your name?"

"Jane. I'd better . . ."

"I know." Mrs. Dalton beamed. "You're that woman who saved that child from being hit by a car at the new playground, aren't you?"

"I . . ."

"Of course you are." Her face brightened. "Don't know why I didn't recognize you before. For a few days, you were all over the news broadcasts. They made you out to be a woman of mystery. They said they didn't give much information about you because they didn't have it, but it was you all right. I recognize your pretty face." Her frown returned. "Child, you do have a way of attracting moving cars, don't you?"

"I guess so." Jane stood and stretched her leg. "I'd better go soak in a hot tub."

"I hope it helps you. Rub yourself with some alcohol afterward. We used to use liniment, but I'm not sure they even make it any more. You sure I can't drive you home?"

"I'm sure. I can make it by myself."

"Well, if you're sure, then. You take care and take it slow. After you get home, you just take it easy."

"Yes, ma'am, I will." She wouldn't have any trouble doing that. Her body wouldn't let her do anything else.

Jane walked down the five steps, working hard to keep her legs from trembling and trying not to show the ache in her shoulder and the worse one in her hip. If she did show her pain, Mrs. Dalton was sure to call an ambulance and Jane didn't want that. Not again. Not the first time, either.

She turned and headed home. Something must have distracted the driver. *Was he related to the woman who almost hit Kim? It had to have been an accident.* She frowned. *Didn't it?*

She looked both ways twice before she crossed the street.

By the time she reached her block, her shoulder felt almost normal as long as she remembered not to swing her arms, but her hip reminded her with each step what had happened. A soak in hot water and a heating pad should get the soreness the rest of the way out. She increased her speed only to slow back down when her hip protested. Just a few more houses before she reached hers.

"Angela."

She stopped halfway up her walk, forgetting her aches, forgetting the present altogether, as she stared at the past standing on her porch.

"Trent? Trent. Is it really you?" She prayed that she hadn't hit her head hard enough to be hallucinating.

"Yeah, it's me." He hurried down the steps toward her. "You don't know how much I've missed you."

"Yes, I do." She rushed to him, the ache in her hip forgotten. "It's almost as much as I've missed you."

They stared at each other as if they could make up for the two-year drought.

"I've dreamed of this so many times," she said.

He opened his arms to her and she walked in as if that was where she belonged.

"I thought I had lost you forever." He closed his arms around her, but released her when she flinched. "What is it?" He frowned. "What's the matter?"

"Nothing." Reluctantly she eased away from him. "I fell."

"Fell?"

"I was almost hit by a car."

"That's still bothering you? Did you go to the doctor? What did he say? Did you break something?" He brushed a hand over her shoulder where he had touched her. "That was long enough ago so it shouldn't still be bothering you."

"How did you know about that?"

"You made the news back home. You were the 'feel good' story of the day. That's how I knew you were here."

"Let's go inside." She glanced around as she grabbed his hand. "Come on." She pulled his hand, not waiting for him to follow on his own. Her hand shook so much as she tried to put the key into the lock that she handed him the key.

"What's wrong, Angela? You've got me worried. Should I call a doctor? Take you to the emergency room?"

"No. Just hurry up and open the door. Please?"

"Sure." Trent took his gaze from her and did as she asked. He frowned as he followed her inside.

"I'm not talking about that time." Her words sounded as scared as she felt.

She locked the door as soon as they were inside and then peeped out the small window at the top of the door. Satisfied at the quiet coming from the street and the lack of traffic, she led him into the living room and then turned to face him. "I'm talking about just now."

"A car almost hit you just now?"

She nodded even though it was hard to move her head up and down when her whole body wanted to shake. It was still easier than trying to talk.

"What happened? How did it happen? Where did it happen? Are you all right?" He ran his hand slowly over her shoulder blade, but stopped when she flinched. "Let me see."

Without hesitation she pulled her T-shirt over her head. Trent's fingers gently inched over the side and back of her shoulder. He stopped near the top and eased her bra strap aside. "Here. Right?" He moved his hand to her shoulder blade. "And here."

"Yes." In spite of his gentleness, she bit her lip. "What do you see?"

"It's red. You'll probably have a couple of bruises before this is finished." Then he noticed the scrape on her arm. "Here, too?"

"Yes."

"That must have been some fall. We need to clean this up. Where's the bathroom?"

She led the way, then took the first aid kit from a vanity drawer.

"Sit." He pointed to the edge of the tub.

"Yes, sir." It was a lot more than a tickle as he cleaned her arm, but she smiled. Trent had found her. She didn't think she'd ever see him again, but here he was. Her smile widened. For a few seconds she refused to think about anything except right now.

"There." He patted a large bandage into place. "Now tell me what happened."

"There's not much to tell." She shrugged. "I was jogging. I had my headphones on and was lost in the zone." She looked sheepish. "You know how it is. I guess I wasn't paying attention." *That's all it was—carelessness on her part.* She continued, "Mrs. Dalton, the woman who lived in the house right there, yelled a warning and I jumped out of the way. I crushed her flowers when I landed in her flower bed. I'm going to plant some more for her." She smiled. "I'm okay. Really. Especially now that you're here."

His hand stopped in place when he saw her smile. "You're sure that's all it was? Carelessness."

"I'm sure."

"Then why the rush to get inside and why check the street afterward?"

"Silliness, I guess. Stop worrying. You're here. Everything is all right, now."

Trent's face eased into a smile of his own. "I've missed you."

"You said that before." Her words felt as if they had brushed across coarse sandpaper on their way out.

"It's still true." He traced a finger down the side of her face, stopping at her jaw. Then his hand cupped her chin.

She felt her pulse jump as if trying to move closer to his hand, just like she wanted to move closer to him.

"I was afraid that I'd never see you again." She touched the side of his face as if to make sure that he was really with her.

"I would have found you. I've been searching carefully so as not to blow your cover. I would have kept looking until I had you right here where you belong." Carefully avoiding touching her shoulder, he eased her into his arms. "In my arms."

"I feel as if I've been on hold, waiting for you to come back into my life." She pressed her lips against his chest.

His heartbeat raced as if it were late for something important. She was aware that her shirt was off when his hands brushed over her skin beneath her bra. He wrapped his hands around the sides of her waist. The heat built there and shared itself with the rest of her body. Chicago suddenly felt like a tropical island. She closed her eyes and lost herself in the moment.

"Angela." Her old name whispered from him and the past two years faded.

They were back on that cabin porch, finishing what they had started. His lips found hers. The kiss was sweeter than the one in her memory. She unbuttoned the top of his shirt and let her hands find the flat buttons hidden by the hair on his chest. He groaned and his kiss deepened. Her tongue mated with his, as a preview of what was to come.

His hand brushed across her fullness contained by black lace. Then his fingers found the hard tip waiting for him. He stroked across it, was rewarded with a moan from her, then stroked his way back. He tugged gently and Angela clung to him as if that was the only way she could keep from falling. She pressed against him, her soft parts welcoming his hardness. He wanted her. She moved her hips, trying to get closer, knowing that there was only one way to do that, wanting it as she had never wanted anything before.

His hands skimmed down her sides and found a stopping place when they reached her hips.

Her fingers worked the rest of his shirt buttons loose and pushed the shirt out of her way. His mouth mapped a trail down her chest, stopping when he reached the edge of her bra. Angela protested and shifted her body, needing his mouth to go further. She leaned against the wall, pulling him with her, impatient for him to continue. He didn't make her wait long.

His mouth continued it's exploring. *Too slow,* she thought, as his tongue skimmed the top of her fullness. She moved her hands to his neck and urged his mouth lower. He followed her urging.

Finally his mouth found the hard tip waiting, aching for him, only him. He tugged through the lace and Angela tightened her hold on him as fire shot through her, heating her, readying her body for his. His hands found her shoulders again and brushed back and forth over her back. Angela flinched and his hands stilled.

"Don't stop." She didn't recognize her own voice. She had never pleaded for something so unfamiliar before, something so life changing, as she did now. "It's okay."

Trent pulled back and stared down at her. She watched as his desire pulled back until it was barely there. Concern had taken it's place.

"Tell me. . . ." The huskiness of desire filled his voice. *That's where it went when it left his face,* she thought. He cleared his throat. "Sweetheart, tell me exactly what happened today."

He groped the floor for her shirt, found it, and handed it to her, never letting his gaze leave hers. Angela fumbled with the shirt before she managed to pull it on. Her breasts ached when the fabric slid over them, as if they had expected Trent's hand or mouth instead.

She frowned and took a few deep breaths, trying to find her way back to the coolness of reality.

"I told you. I went for a run."

"Tell me every detail from the time you left the house."

She told him the rest of the story. From time to time he interrupted with a question. As she talked, uneasiness returned and rippled through her as it had while she was on her way home. Trent tried to hide the depth of his concern, but Angela saw it flicker in his eyes.

"Get a few things together."

"You don't think it was an accident."

"No sense taking a chance."

"I'm tired of running away."

"I know. We'll discuss this later, okay? But for now, how about humoring me? Okay?"

Angela hesitated, then she went upstairs. She knew he was right. It wouldn't hurt to be careful.

Trent watched her go. If *he* had found her, why not somebody else? He frowned. But who? Who would still care enough? The major players were dead or behind bars. The only ones left who were connected to the organization had moved up the chain of command. If they found her, they would be more likely to reward her than harm her. At the least, they wouldn't care about her one way or another.

He hadn't been completely convinced that she needed to go into the program in the first place; it was just a precaution. No word ever came from the department sources after the trial that anybody cared about her. The only one who had an interest was Lester and he had gone into the program himself. Lester would never jeopardize his own position for something like this. After the way he botched things and then ratted the bosses out, he'd be busy watching his own back.

The feds had evidently decided to go after the organization on more serious charges than the ones involved in the information that Angela had uncovered. He sighed.

Maybe this *was* an accident. His jaw tightened. And maybe not. Just because he didn't know the player didn't mean there wasn't one.

He went to the door, but he didn't open it. Instead, he looked out the little window at the top, just as Angela had. Still not satisfied, he went to the living room and checked the street from there. He frowned. This was too much like that other time.

He let the white lace curtain fall back into place and was about to leave the window when a car came into view. His stare stayed glued on the car as he eased his gun from his shoulder holster.

Fifteen

Trent was back. Angela held a T-shirt close to her. She didn't believe she'd ever see him again, but now he was back. In spite of the situation, she smiled. Fingers of desire moved through her. Her breasts tingled, her body ached for an end to what they had just started downstairs. She shook her head. Her fall must have cracked open her head and allowed her common sense to escape. Her life might be in danger, yet she wanted nothing more than to stay here and finish what she and Trent had begun.

She got her suitcase from the hall closet. One day, when she had time, she was going to do a study on what happens to hormones when they are allowed to build up. She knew they didn't give up and dissipate over time. She was proof of that. Even now, with her life in danger, she was focusing on making love with Trent instead of on the best way to get to safety once and for all.

She forced her mind to concentrate on packing. This time, so different from the last, it wasn't her fear of a killer that messed with her concentration. It was Trent Stewart. Handsome, sexy Trent Stewart.

She took a pair of jeans from the closet, and lyrics of an old Luther Vandross song came to mind as if they had been hidden in the pocket. A blouse released words to another song. It seemed as if, along with her clothes, she had hung up songs, and not just any songs: words to every love song she had ever heard played back in her head.

She sighed and sped up her packing. She should be thinking about getaway songs.

* * *

Trent eased his gun back into the holster. Two cars had gone past. Both had moved slowly, but as this was a residential area, that was the way traffic *should* move. Maybe people obeyed speed limits better here than they did at home. *Was only one person after her?*

He watched as a car pulled to the curb. He was getting a lot of practice drawing his gun, but not much using it. That was fine with him. He wouldn't mind if he never pulled a trigger again except at shooting practice.

He aimed at the car and held his position.

A white-haired woman got out. "Thanks for the ride, Millie," drifted into the house. Trent watched as she took out a bag from the back seat with a chuckle. "See you next week, same time, same station." She laughed again and went up the sidewalk of the house next door.

"What are you doing?" Trent whirled around and faced Angela at the sound of her voice. Her eyes widened at the sight of the gun in his hand, but she rushed past him and looked out the window. "That's my neighbor, Mrs. Young. I recognized her voice from the bedroom. She and Mrs. Brown go shopping together every week at this time." She stared at him. "She's harmless. She always brings me dessert when she bakes, for goodness' sake. If she wanted to hurt me, she could have done it a long time ago."

"I'm just being careful." Trent slid his gun back in place. He smiled at Angela. "I can take her without the gun, anyway."

"Trent." Angela frowned at him.

"Just kidding. Sometimes that's the only way to break the tension."

He stared at her as another kind of tension replaced the first. This was the first time in a long time that she wasn't just an image formed by his memories. He fought the urge to take her in his arms and kiss away two years of being apart; to prove to himself that she was flesh and blood and finally with him. He took a deep breath. Just because it was two older women this time didn't mean there still wasn't a threat to her life.

He walked to her slowly, trying to give himself enough time to find his self-control again. It didn't help that she just stood there waiting; waiting for him. He took another deep breath and hoped self-control came with it.

Despite promising himself that he wouldn't, determined that this was foolishness at this time, he reached out to her. *I'll only touch her face, that's all. Just her face to make sure that she's really with me and not another agonizing dream.*

He brushed a finger down the side of her face. The hunger in her eyes was his undoing. His silent promises disappeared like water on a desert. That's where he was: on a desert and she was the oasis.

"Trent."

She licked her lips. He took it as an invitation. Then he took her into his arms. His mouth found hers and he tasted her sweetness. Her arms wrapped around him, trying to pull him closer. She pressed her body against his. Trent's hands found her hips and moved her closer still. Only their clothes were in the way. The kiss deepened, intensified, heated them both to the steaming point.

It took all of Trent's self-control to pull back from her. He saw regret rear up in Angela's eyes. His own regret filled him. "We have to go. Now." He brushed his lips across hers once more. "Later we'll finish this." His kiss was hard, but quick. Then he lifted his head and stared into her eyes. "Later, but soon."

"Yes."

The promise in her word gave him the strength to move another step away. He lifted her suitcases from the floor beside her, glad to have something for his hands to do so he wouldn't wrap them around her again, so he wouldn't take her upstairs to her bed and show her how much he had missed her, so he wouldn't take her right here on the rug in her hallway.

Soon her things, including her laptop computer and printer, and business records and supplies, were in the trunk. No matter what the situation, she still had clients and accounts to take care of. He watched her get into the car before he got behind the wheel.

"Where are we going?"

"Captain Ellers, at the district police headquarters, suggested the Ambassador Suites. It's large enough so our every move won't attract attention."

"How long will we stay?"

"I don't know."

"How will we know when it's safe for me to come back to my house?" She turned to look at him.

"I don't know that either, right now. The chief is digging into things at home. I'll give him a call tomorrow to see how he made out. Captain Ellers is checking with his informants on this end. Maybe we'll know something by tomorrow."

"I appreciate everybody's effort on my behalf, but I am not moving again. Two years and I'm still trying to get used to Chicago. If I go anywhere it will be back to Philadelphia." She sighed. "I still have trouble accepting how much I miss that city after all the times I complained about it."

"We'll talk."

"We can talk, but I'm not relocating anywhere else." She frowned. "Hey." She stared at him. "How did you get permission to come here? Are they looking for somebody who fled here from another case? The old case can't be a concern of the Philadelphia police department any more. I thought everyone involved in Mr. Hunter's case had been accounted for. Is there still a connected case that's open and that I don't know about?" The crease in her forehead deepened. "Even if there is, how would it involve the Philadelphia police? If anybody is interested in this at all, wouldn't it be the federal government?"

"I don't need permission."

"So you're your own boss, now, huh?" She smiled.

"You got it." He glanced at her and then back to the street ahead.

"I was kidding. What do you mean?" She frowned. "You're not with the police department anymore? Did you get fired because you spent so much time with me the last time?"

"That time I spent with you had nothing to do with me leaving the force. I had clearance for that. When I dropped you off that day, I went back home and started my next assignment." He glanced at her. "I didn't leave the department until about seven months ago." He drove onto the highway and merged with the late morning traffic.

"I thought you loved working with the police department. What happened to make you leave?"

"I refused to take a desk job."

"A desk job? You're their best. Why did they try to get you to take a desk job?"

"Thanks for the vote of confidence." Trent sighed. "I got hurt and they didn't think I was fit for active duty any more."

"Hurt? Badly? It must have been if they wanted to put you behind a desk. How? What happened?"

He shook his head. *May as well tell it all.* "I was shot while working on a case. My last case, it turns out."

"Shot?" Concern flooded her voice. She turned toward him and grabbed his arm. "What happened? How did it happen? You're so careful and thorough."

"I was assigned a partner—a rookie. We were after a suspect and we underestimated him. Kevin, my partner, almost got killed. I got shot in the leg." His jaw tightened. "But I got the suspect. Nobody will have trouble with him anymore." He switched lanes. "I'm all right now."

"If you were all right, you'd still be on the force." Angela chewed on her lower lip.

"My leg stiffens up on me from time to time, but I'm working on it and it's getting better. In spite of what the doctors said, I expect to get back to one hundred per cent soon." He tightened his hand on the steering wheel. "I got rid of the cane a month ago."

"Trent, I know how much the force meant to you. I also know firsthand how good you were at your job, but I'm glad you don't do it anymore. It's dangerous. What happened to you proves that."

She remembered how she was ready to go in after him when he took a long time to come back for her in her house in Philly. She didn't want to think of him in that kind of danger every day.

"What do you do now?" she asked.

He moved the car to the outside lane to pass a slow-moving truck. "I'm a private detective." He glanced at her to see her reaction. It was exactly what he expected.

"No, you're not." She shook her head. "A private detective? Are you crazy? You almost got killed while you were with the police force—with all that backup, with a partner, yet you decided to do the same work on your own? With no backup? No support? Have you lost your mind?"

"I have been accused of that."

"What if something happens to you? What if you get shot again? The next time you could get. . . ." She swallowed hard. "You could get. . . ."

He sighed. "Look Angela, it's what I do."

"Then find something else to do." She shook her head. "I don't understand. How can you go out on a case without worrying about the danger?" Her face brightened. "You work on divorce cases, missing persons, that kind of thing. That's it. Right?"

"Angela, I work on all types of cases." He hesitated. "I get a lot of referrals from the police when people need somebody and it doesn't come under police jurisdiction." He didn't look at her. "Sometimes I act as a bodyguard."

Angela thought of what a good job he had done protecting her. She blinked hard. She also remembered how much danger he had put himself in. She shook her head. *And he did this kind of assignment on a regular basis?* "It's—It's dangerous."

"Sometimes it is."

"I still don't understand." She chewed on her lip again. "How can you put your life in danger on purpose? You don't know what you'll come up against when you take a case. Even now. You're here putting your life on the line for me. Again. We don't know who might be after me or what they'll do next. I appreciate you protecting me, I really do, but it's dangerous for you. It is every time you take a case. How can you do it voluntarily?" Her frowned deepened. "There must be something else that you can do to make a decent living."

"It's not the money. I invested well."

"Then what is it? What makes you *want* to do this kind of

work? Want to take a gamble with your life every time you go to work?"

"You're exaggerating. Most of my cases are boring."

"But not all of them. Not this one."

"This isn't a case for me. You should know that. Besides, I'm good at what I do."

"So were the gunslingers in the Old West. How many died. . . ." Her words faltered. "How many of them died of natural causes?"

"Things are different, now. Besides, I'm trained for what I do. I know my job."

"Of course you do, but what happens when you run up against a criminal who knows his job just as well? What if . . ."

"Sugar, in this business, we don't deal with 'what ifs.' I prepare for my cases thoroughly. I do the research. You know how careful I am."

Angela sighed. *The Lord didn't make mistakes, but in her humble opinion, men and testosterone should never have been put together.* "You came here on your own to protect me."

"Since that day two years ago when I took you to the airport, I've been wondering where you were, but I was afraid to look for you; I didn't want to take a chance of putting you in danger. I had decided to wait and see where the federal case was going." He shook his head. "They sure move slowly. Then what do you do? You make the television news. National news, yet." He glanced at her. "You do have a way of making your presence known, don't you?" He smiled. "I saw the story, but the chief called me about it, too. We agreed that it would be best if I come to you, just in case." He looked at her. "I was coming whether he agreed with me or not. In fact, I had already started packing." His voice got husky. "You don't know how much I've missed you. You and I have unfinished business."

"Yes." She had trouble pushing out just that one word. She was more than happy that he had found her; she felt as if a missing piece of her heart had been put back into place. She thought about their unfinished business.

They had started something two years ago. It was past time to finish it. Her breath caught in her throat. She wanted him as much now as she had long ago. Then it had been a new hunger; now it was old, but, instead of weakening, it had grown stronger.

She swallowed hard several times and shifted in her seat, trying to find a cooler spot. If she had been with Trent these past two years, the weather would have seemed at least twenty degrees warmer year round. That would have been welcome in winter, but down right uncomfortable in summer. She smiled. She'd take the hottest heat wave if Trent were with her. If he were, he'd *cause* the hottest heat wave.

Her smile disappeared as she tried to dismiss the fingers of worry that poked at her happiness. Private detective, of all things.

Fifteen minutes later Trent parked away from the door of the office of the large hotel building. He shrugged. "No sense in taking unnecessary chances." He smiled at her. "Be right back. I made reservations over the phone so I won't be long."

Angela watched him go. The slight limp that had revealed itself in his left leg when he got out of the car disappeared by the time he took his third step. She sighed. Still, it had been there. Why couldn't he have decided to take the desk job? Why not be an insurance salesman? Why not any job where he was guaranteed to be safe? She refused to think about how safe her safe job in Philadelphia had been and focused on Trent instead.

She swallowed hard as she watched him. He looked better than she imagined possible, and he definitely felt better than she remembered from the brief times she had been in his arms. She smiled. The man could warm her without being there.

If it wasn't so painful, she could have used her memories and turned the thermostat in her house down to just above freezing during her winter months.

He went into the building, but that didn't stop her mind

from going on. Tonight she'd have more than memories.
Tonight she'd have Trent. They hadn't discussed it; neither
had mentioned it. It wasn't often possible to predict the future, but this time she was one hundred percent sure. Tonight.
She'd be safe. They could concentrate on building something
between them. She grinned. No, they could concentrate on
what had been building between them since they first met.

Her body warmed, ached. *How could she ache for something she had never known?*

If Trent had left the keys in the car, she would have opened
all four windows as far down as they could go. *Maybe women
and estrogen were a dangerous combination, too.* She smiled.
Two years of hormones were tired of being hidden and were
racing through her as if escaping from a prison. She swallowed
hard.

She was not going to think about prison. She would not
think about how someone behind bars might have a reach
long enough to get to her even here. She refused to think
about that.

Satisfied that that train of thought had been put to rest, she
put her head back and closed her eyes.

Desire for Trent mixed with apprehension about the un-
known and pushed all other thoughts from her mind. Tonight
she would be with Trent in every sense of the word. It would
be a new experience for her, but she wasn't afraid. She loved
him. She didn't understand how she could, after so little contact, but she would not question the miracle of love. If she had
found a man that she was interested in enough before now,
her first time would have been over.

Dwight's name drifted up, but his face was unclear. She
wouldn't have really gone through it with him; she had realized that before she knew that she loved Trent. She smiled.
She was glad that she had waited.

Sixteen

Trent waited for his turn in the reception area. Why were they so busy this time of day? He shrugged. It didn't matter. Angela was safe in the car. His common sense told him that what had happened to Angela had been a terrible coincidence. His gut instinct told him something else. He tried to remember how many times his gut had been wrong. Two times came to mind. Hopefully this would be number three.

He signed for his suite, lied and said that he was alone, and got his key. Then he went back to Angela. "Fifth floor, around back," was all he said. Angela shrugged as he started the car.

"Here we are." Trent parked near the entrance for residents only, gave Angela the key, and got the bags. Between them, they managed to carry everything in one trip. If it was not for the hum of the elevator, the air would be filled with silence.

Angela avoided eye contact as they rode up to the fifth floor. She was taking this one minute at a time. She was still having a hard time believing that she was in danger again. She hoped Trent was mistaken. She frowned. Had he ever been wrong about something like this? She wasn't sure she wanted to know the answer.

"I had to get a one-bedroom since I told them that I'm alone," Trent said, as he led Angela to the bedroom. He set the bags on the floor. "The couch is a sofabed, a real bed, not like the one at the cabin." At the mention of the cabin, Angela's gaze flew to his face. Her stare held his. The cabin came back to her, especially the porch. She saw the same memory flare up in Trent's face, showing his desire, causing her desire to show itself, too.

"I'm going to get us some food. Any preference?"

"Whatever you decide is okay with me." She frowned. "I mean food. I like just about everything. Not peas, though. They call them sweet, but they're not. Sweet, I mean. I don't like asparagus, either. Nor artichokes. They're like fat cacti. Those probably won't be choices anyway. I do like . . ." She finally noticed Trent's stare. "I'm rambling. I do that when I'm nervous."

"You don't have to be nervous. You'll be safe here. Nobody, not even the management, knows that you're here. As far as they know, I'm a single guy waiting for permanent housing after a job transfer."

"Okay." She couldn't tell him that that wasn't what she was nervous about; it *should* have been.

"Be back in a while, okay?" He smiled, meaning to reassure her, but it changed to something different by the time it reached his face.

Still avoiding eye contact, Angela nodded. "Okay."

She returned his smile and looked at him. He stared at her. Her stare got hung up with his and her breath got caught somewhere between her lungs and her mouth, but she was still disappointed when he broke the connection.

"See you later." He stood looking at her a little longer, then pressed his lips to her cheek. It was fast, but not so fast that it didn't kindle heat inside her. She felt like a wood stove in December, only hotter. She tried not to think about later. She failed.

He had been gone long enough to reach the car, when she finally managed to leave the hall.

"This is like that other time," she muttered. But right away she shook her head. *No, it wasn't. That other time I didn't know Trent, and we knew somebody was after me then. I had been numb and full of fear. This time . . .* She shook her head in an effort to keep the rest of the thought away.

She placed her suitcase on the bed, tried to pretend that it wasn't a bed, and unpacked her things. She used the top two drawers just like she had done at the cabin. She glanced at

Trent's suitcase, but left it untouched. They weren't at the point where she would unpack his things.

She leaned against the wall instead of leaving the room. Her gaze snagged on the bed, but she didn't try to free it.

One bedroom, one bed. There was the sofa bed, but she closed her eyes and imagined sharing this bed with Trent tonight. *Why wasn't she more afraid? Where had her assertiveness come from?* She had always been shy around boys—then men. When had that changed? She sighed. She knew the answer: *when Trent had come into her life.*

What would it be like? How would it feel to make love? Her friends had told her how they felt about their experiences, but they hadn't been able to tell her how it felt *physically*. When she pushed her friend, Lydia, she had finally told her with a voice full of exasperation, "I can't find the right words. You'll have to experience it for yourself."

Angela sighed. She would. Tonight. She smiled. She felt like the guy singing that song from *Westside Story*. She took one last look around, and went to the kitchen to see what kind of equipment they had. She was going to fix dinner for Trent. She had no idea what he would bring back, but she finally appreciated her grandmother making her learn to cook. "You eat, you should know how to put a decent meal together," Grandma James had said each time she taught Angela how to fix something new.

Angela's smile widened. She appreciated it after she got older. She'd appreciate it even more tonight. Tonight. She wrapped her arms around herself and danced around the small kitchen.

"Food, glorious food." Trent sang as he set three bags on the counter.

"You sound hungry." Angela smiled as she unpacked the grocery bags.

"My last meal was so long ago that my stomach is launching a protest." He patted his middle. "I guess I should have gotten something already cooked."

Angela laughed. "No. Grab an apple while I see what I can do about that." She took a package of chicken from a grocery bag. "You go unpack your things. You have done your part: the hunting and gathering. Now it's time for my part: preparing the food."

"Yes, ma'am." His smile widened.

A dimple. He has a dimple in his left cheek. What else don't I know about him?

She took the rest of the food from the bags and formed a mental menu. Then she began preparing. When had she cooked like she planned to do now? She smiled. When had she had someone this special to cook for? The answer was easy: never. She pulled out pots and pans and got started.

"My stomach made me come out here." Trent stepped into the kitchen an hour later. "I tried to keep out of your way, but my stomach overruled me." The dimple was back.

"Tell your stomach that it got you into trouble. Since you're here, you can set the table."

"That I can do."

In a few minutes the table was ready. Trent held Angela's hand and gave thanks for the meal before he held her chair out for her. She smiled at him. *I could get used to this.*

"Do you realize how little we know about each other?" Trent put a piece of baked chicken onto his plate. "Although, if this tastes as good as it looks and smells, I've just learned something new about you: you are a fantastic cook."

"I hope it lives up to your expectations."

"I'm sure it will." His stare intensified. "Everything about you will live up to my expectations. Or surpass them." His voice lowered. "I hope you allow me to test my theory later, just a little later."

Angela stared back. How could she still be conscious when she couldn't breathe?

The food waited in the serving bowls. The coffee cooled. The bread that Angela had taken pains to keep warm lost it's heat. Angela knew where it went. It had found her most private place and had settled in. Her stare refused to move. She imagined what the test would be. She felt enough heat to give back to the bread and still have too much left over.

She shifted her gaze to his hands at rest beside his plate. His fingers looked strong. She blinked rapidly. How would those hands, those fingers, feel on her body? What would he do first? Was there a certain order to be followed? Her breasts tingled in anticipation and tension spread to every muscle. She shifted in her chair. *Is there such a thing as a dirty young woman?*

"Angela? Are you still there?"

"I'm here." Her words sounded as if they had come a long way.

"Good. I wouldn't want you to be any place else." He grinned. "Now, can you please pass the green beans?"

"Can" was the right word. She steadied her hands and passed the bowl. His fingers brushed against hers and her tremor was back. For a few seconds the two of them remained suspended, both of them holding the bowl as if it were a large ball of iron. Then she remembered to let go. She was pleased that her hands found their way back to her side of the table in a halfway smooth action. She had to get her mind on neutral things—anything except what was destined to happen later. *How? What subject was safe?*

"At the cabin you said you have . . ." She stared at his face and her voice ran out of steam. Her mind wandered off the track and she had to redirect it. "You said you have brothers and sisters." She smiled, proud that she had finished a rational thought.

"Yeah. I have two sisters and two brothers. They're all younger."

"Big brother, huh. Are you close?"

"Not as close as I'd like to be: DaVita lives in Boston, Robert lives in Houston, and Isaiah lives in Orlando. Jeanine graduated from Tuskegee University as a pilot and moved to Hawaii." He shrugged. "They went where the jobs are."

"You don't see them much?"

"We get together every summer and then for Christmas. In the past we went to DaVita's for Christmas because she's the one with the kids." He looked at Angela and his face softened. "Earline and Benny are six and three. DaVita and Ben would have a battle trying to get Earline to leave home for Christmas." He shifted his knife. "We'll have to come up with a new plan soon, though. Two years ago Robert and Clara had a son. In another year, they won't travel for Christmas, either."

"Are the other two married?"

"Not yet. Isaiah's engaged to a flight attendant; he's a pilot and they met when she was assigned to his flight. Jeanine says she's enjoying the single life." He looked at Angela.

"What about Davita and Robert? What do they do?"

"Davita's a teacher, but she took time off until Ben is old enough for school. Then she'll go back. Robert is a chemical engineer for one of the oil companies."

"And you joined the police force."

"I used to get a lot of questions about that. Not from my family, though. Our parents realized that we each had to follow our hearts."

"You have very wise parents."

"Had. Mom died three years ago last April and Dad died six months later." He stared into space. "I used to think that the phrase 'died of a broken heart' was an old tale. I learned differently." He shrugged. "Anyway, we don't get together much."

"Maybe you can get together during Christmas week?"

"That's probably what we'll do." He finally tasted the chicken. "This is delicious."

"I'm glad you like it."

"'Like' isn't a strong enough word." He looked at her. "Sometimes stronger words are needed, but it's hard to find the right ones." His stare held steady. She couldn't breathe, but she still didn't break the stare. "You know I'm not just talking about food."

"I know." It was a good thing that she didn't have food in her mouth. It was hard enough trying to swallow nothing.

"I know a lot about you, but there is so much more I want to know. I hope you'll give me a chance to find out."

Angela had spent a lot of effort trying to cook a perfect meal. She had measured and mixed with precision that would make a chemist proud. She had taken great pains to make sure that everything was ready at the same time so that nothing got cold. None of that mattered, now.

Food was forgotten as time galloped to meet Angela's destiny with Trent.

They stood at the same time as if given a signal by a director or by fate itself.

"Angela?" That one word—her name—was all that it took. The hunger in his voice caused a hunger to rear up in her. A hunger that had nothing to do with food. Again, as if on cue, they moved—this time toward each other.

Whatever his question, her answer was "yes."

He moved close enough to her for her to feel his body heat before they touched. It mixed with hers. He traced a finger down the side of her face, along her jaw, coming agonizingly close, but not close enough to her mouth. Without thinking, she licked her lips, waiting, wanting.

"Angie." He groaned as he eased her against him.

"Trent." She was finally where she belonged and it was sweeter than she remembered. Sweeter than any memory.

She lifted her face and wrapped her arms around his neck. His lips met hers. *Yes, sweeter,* she thought. And then she didn't think, only felt.

The kiss kindled a desire she never knew she was capable of. She pressed closer, enjoying the crush of her breasts against his hard chest. His body stirred and his maleness nudged against her softness, seeking what she wanted, too. His hands. Oh, his hands were making her lose reality as they stroked her hips, cupped her bottom, drew her closer still. He rubbed against her and she moaned.

One hand found its way to her breast and stroked across the already hard tip. Desire shot through her and a sweet ache built inside her feminine core. Her body prepared itself for what was to come as if this were a usual occurrence.

He pulled his head back, but his hand still slowly stroked across her breast.

"Are you sure?" His eyes were filled with need and desire, but a bit of concern was allowed to show itself.

"I've never been as sure about anything in my life." She cupped the side of his face with her hand. He turned his head and kissed the palm.

She didn't think it was possible, but the ache intensified, grew, demanded relief.

His hand left her breast and she moaned her protest. His mouth swallowed it. Then he lifted her and, mouths still joined, carried her to the bedroom.

He stood her on the floor and looked at her face. "How did I get so lucky?" He held her stare with his as his fingers found the top button on her blouse and eased it free from the buttonhole. His fingers stroked the newly exposed skin. Then he pressed his mouth to the swell that his fingers had just traced.

Angela felt her pulse race in anticipation. He eased the next button free and his mouth moved to the newly uncovered skin, tasting, promising, but stopping at the lace edging.

Angela wished she had worn a lower cut bra. "You've got it wrong," she said, when she finally managed to speak. "I'm the lucky one." Her fingers fumbled with the buttons on his shirt. It took forever to free the first one.

Trent's fingers, moving way too slowly, released the rest of the buttons on her blouse, announcing each new bit of exposed skin with a kiss. Finally, agonizingly, he pushed the blouse aside. It slid down her arms and to the floor, but Trent didn't notice. He was looking at her, only her, busily absorbing the delightful treasure that he had just uncovered. His stare was that of a gold miner who had just discovered the mother lode.

Angela felt her breasts swell under his gaze until she thought the lace bra would give way under the pressure. She wouldn't have objected if it happened. *Why am I not afraid? Why does it feel so right when it's so new?*

Trent's mouth found hers again and it was as if years had passed since the last contact.

His hands stroked down her back, stopping at her waist. Their kiss broke for air, then began all over again. He unbuttoned the waistband of her skirt, then pulled down the zipper, all the while holding her kiss with his.

Her skirt slid to the floor, joining her blouse. Trent's hands found her waist. His mouth left hers and kissed a path to her neck. His hands brushed across the back of her silk panties and cupped her bottom. He eased her closer still. Angela helped.

She placed her lips against his chest. Her mouth kissed across the rough hair, but stopped when it reached the flat buttons hiding there. She licked, then drew one into her mouth. Trent moaned. His maleness pushed harder against the soft mound protecting her inner core.

She managed to unhook his pants and touched the zipper.

"No. Let me." Trent eased her hands away and moved back a few inches. The desire flaming in his gaze mirrored what she felt. "If you touch me there," his husky voice rasped, "this will be over before we get to the next part." He brushed his lips across her forehead. "And I don't want this over, not now, not soon, not ever. I have waited all my life for you; I want us both to savor the experience." He unzipped his pants. Angela reached to help slide them down his hips, but he stopped her. "Not yet. I have to finish calculating the population of Philadelphia multiplied by the number of houses in the city and divided by the average number of people in each household."

"What?" Angela frowned.

"It's a man thing." He smiled as he stepped out of his pants and kicked off his shoes at the same time. "I'll explain it to you later—much later—when we don't have anything else to do." He moved toward her. "As if that time will ever come." He moved closer still. "I think you have on too many clothes." His gaze caressed her chocolate skin peeking through the lace bra and panties. She felt her breasts harden. Much longer and the lace would peel away on its own.

A tiny urge to cover herself from this new experience was overwhelmed by her desire to revel in it and her impatience to have his hands replace his gaze.

She gazed at him—his strong face, his tempting and sensuous mouth, his eyes brimming with desire for her. She allowed her gaze to travel from his face. His strong chest, heavily sprinkled with coarse black hair, made her fingers itch to caress it. Her lips longed to close over the other hard button that she had neglected before. She controlled the need to move close to him, to move against him, to seek release from the pressure building dangerously inside her.

She let her gaze slide lower. Her eyes widened. His manhood straining the limits of his briefs told her that he was ready for her.

"That's definitely a man thing, too, sugar."

She didn't think it possible, but Angela's desire increased. She wanted to know what it felt like to have him inside her, to close around him, to be one with him. She wanted to discover what lovemaking was all about. She wanted Trent.

"No." Protest rose within her as he took another step away from her and picked up his pants from the floor. He couldn't stop now. If he did, she would die from her need for fulfillment.

"I'm not going anywhere." His voice reassured her.

Still, she watched closely, hoping he wouldn't widen the gap between them.

Trent reached into his pocket and pulled out a handful of foil-covered packets.

"I wasn't sure if I'd need these." He smiled at her. "I'm glad I never forgot the Boy Scout motto."

Never allowing his gaze to leave hers, he placed the packets on the nightstand. Then he came back to her.

"I think we were talking about doing something about your overdressed state."

She helped close the space. He kissed her and it felt like ages had passed since she had felt his lips on hers. His hands stroked her back. The kiss deepened as he released the clasp. He inched back just enough to let her bra fall away. His tongue danced with hers as his hands smoothed their way to her waist. His fingers excited a fire as he slowly eased her panties down her hips.

Angela's hands gently brushed the top of Trent's shorts before she pushed down the last barrier between them.

Trent eased her body against his, finally touching his body to hers. Angela gasped at the strength of his desire.

He lifted her and placed her in the center of the bed. Before she could protest, he lay with her.

His hands found her breast again and teased a sensitive, hard tip. Angela moaned as desire centered in her femaleness. His hands, as if he knew her ache, stroked the mound protecting her female center.

Then his finger entered her, and she felt her body close around it in a convulsing tremor. He stroked the nub that she hadn't even been aware of, made it come alive, made her want something, made her need him to assuage her need.

Her hands tightened around his shoulders as she hung on to keep from shattering into a zillion pieces.

"You're ready for me, aren't you?"

She nodded because she was feeling too much to think enough to talk.

Then he eased from her. She groaned her protest.

"It's all right." He smiled reassurance.

She watched as Trent opened a foil pack and rolled protection over the part of him that would release her from her need of him.

Then he was back with her. She smiled at him. He eased his body between her thighs and she eagerly parted for him.

His manhood nudged against the opening of her female center.

Slowly, he eased inside her. She tightened the rest of her body as she felt a sharp pain. Trent went still.

"Okay?"

"Yes," she whispered. And it was. Her hands found his hips and she pulled him closer. It was his turn to groan.

His hands found her hips. Slowly he moved against her, in and out of her.

She learned his rhythm and moved with him. It felt as if she had been waiting her whole life for this.

Trent increased the rhythm and Angela stayed with him. She felt as if she were running up a mountain and dashing downhill at the same time. She felt as if she was finally complete—as if having Trent inside her was her fate. Then she just felt.

She couldn't breathe as fast as she needed to, couldn't get close enough, couldn't keep from breaking into minuscule bits.

She clung to Trent as waves of fulfillment crashed over her, shattering her apart.

Finally, gradually, she came back from wherever Trent had taken her. She still clung to him and he to her. She was exhausted, but she managed a smile. No wonder nobody could explain what it felt like. Words were not meant to describe what they had just experienced.

"How are you?" Trent still held her in his arms as he shifted them to their sides. The tension was gone from his face as he stared tenderly at her.

"Back in one piece." She smiled shyly at him. *How could she be shy after what they had just experienced?* "How about you?"

"Just barely." He traced a finger down the side of her face. "Thank you for the precious gift."

Angela felt her face redden. She led her gaze slide from his. "Thank you for the experience. I . . ." She shook her head. "I never imagined that it would be like that."

"What had you expected?" His hand moved to her back and traced circles across her shoulder blades.

She shrugged. "I didn't know what to expect."

He kissed the side of her face. "Sometimes surprises are good."

She felt her color heighten even more. "That's true." She looked into his eyes and hoped he could see her love.

"Sometimes," he continued, "they are better than good." His hand stroked her round bottom.

"Yes." Breathing was difficult again. She had a problem. *Should I move back for more contact with his hand or away from it and closer to his body?*

Trent helped her with the solution: he kept his hand in place on her bottom as he eased her against his body.

Angela brushed her hands against the coarse hairs on his chest. Then she moved her hands out of the way and to his waist. Her breasts tightened at the contact with his chest. She felt his body harden and nudge against hers. She tried to move closer still.

"Are you sure you're ready for this again so soon?" Trent cupped her breast and brushed his fingertips across the tip.

Angela was surprised at the desire that peaked inside her. She felt as if it had been years since he had made love to her instead of . . . What? Minutes? Hours? She had no idea. She only knew that too much time had passed.

Trent replaced his hands with his mouth. He kissed a circle around, but not touching, the sensitive tip. Angela shifted and tried to get closer still. She wrapped her arms around his neck and pulled his head closer, arching her back, trying to find his mouth with her breast.

Finally, too long a time later, he drew the tip into his mouth and tugged gently. Flames shot through Angela, threatening to consume her. She continued to burn, as he once again quickly rolled protection into place.

His hand found the seat of her desire. She knew she was ready for him.

This time there was no pain as he entered her and made her complete. He held her hips as he rolled her on top of him. Their stares held each other's for a few seconds. Then, as if on signal, they moved together.

Trent held her against him with one hand as the other teased her breast. Angela increased the movement of her hips, matching his rhythm. The pace increased.

Was it Trent or did she change the tempo? It didn't matter. They were together on the love ride once more, climbing together, reaching for the top, ready to soar into nothingness. Ready.

Seventeen

Sometime during the night Trent pulled the top sheet over them. Then he gathered Angela against him. Still asleep, she nestled against his chest. He smiled. Perfect. This felt perfect. He had found the one woman in the world for him. Never, with anyone else, had he felt like this before.

He wrapped his hands protectively around her back. She sighed and brushed a hand across his chest. Trent tightened his hand slightly. He hoped his gut feelings were wrong, and that her accident was just that: an unfortunate accident. Much as he loved their current arrangements, they couldn't stay holed up here forever.

Tomorrow morning he'd make some phone calls to see if there was any news. Tomorrow. He shifted and Angela, still asleep, shifted with him, keeping her body against his. His smile came back. Tonight he would savor finally being with Angela. He closed his eyes and joined her in peaceful sleep.

"What's the matter?" Angela opened her eyes and found Trent staring at her.

"Not a thing." He cupped her face with his hand. "Everything is perfect. At least with me. How about you? How do you feel after your new experience?"

Angela felt her face heat up. Her gaze moved from his face to his chest. "I-I feel all right."

"Just all right?" He frowned. "Are you disappointed?"

"Oh, no." Angela felt her face color even more as he chuckled at her quick answer. "I mean . . ." She frowned. "Are we supposed to talk about this?" I mean, do people talk about something like this? I mean with each other. Not that I could talk about it with anybody else. I mean . . ."

Trent placed a finger against her lips. "I know what you mean, sweetheart. We can talk about anything you want to. Any time you want to. There's nothing wrong with that." He brushed his lips across her forehead. "Or we can not talk about it if that's what you want."

"Oh." Her stare stayed on his chest.

"Does this mean that you don't want to talk about it?" He eased her chin up until he was looking into her eyes.

"I-I don't know." She shrugged and looked away from him. It's—It's uncomfortable."

"Making love?"

"Oh, no." She shook her head quickly and Trent chuckled again.

"You're teasing me." She shifted away and glared up at him.

"Guilty as charged." He eased her against him again so their bodies touched from chest to feet. At his words, a cloud seemed to cover her face. He sucked in a deep breath. "I'm so sorry. Poor choice of words on my part." He smoothed the wrinkle that had formed across her forehead. "We don't have to talk about anything. Or we can talk about everything. Your choice." He cupped her shoulder with his hand. "We can talk about things like love." His smile became even more gentle. "Do you know how much I love you? I have loved you since the first time I saw you. You were huddled over trying to hold yourself together." His hand brushed back and forth across her shoulder. "I always managed to keep my personal life apart from my work until that night. That night it was all I could do not to shelter you in my arms and protect you from all danger. I never felt like that about anybody before—not on the job or in my personal life." He rubbed his hand across her back. "You looked so vulnerable." He pressed his lips to her forehead. "I tried to fight the attraction." He smiled against her shoulder. "It was like trying to put out a forest fire with a garden hose."

"I wasn't aware of very much right after—after . . ." She swallowed hard trying to keep down the panic of that night. "I was still trying to deal with seeing Mr. Hunter killed." She managed to blink away that terrible time, then leaned her head back so she could see into Trent's face. "I did notice you later, though. What other detective would wear a tux on the job?" She smiled. "Of course, if they could come close to looking as fine as you did, they all would."

"Why, thank you, ma'am. Compliments are always appreciated." He smiled. "I had an annual dinner to go to that was being held near that building." He chuckled. "I hadn't wanted to go. The chief had to twist my arm." He kissed her forehead. "Had I known that I was going to make an impression on a beautiful woman, I wouldn't have given the chief such a hard time."

"Maybe it's a good thing you didn't know, then. You wouldn't have wanted the chief to make it part of your regular routine."

"You have a point."

Angela sighed. "At first all I felt was gratitude for your protection."

"Not at first. You mean after you were convinced that I was really a police detective."

"Yeah." She smiled again. "You must admit, you didn't look like the typical police officer."

He nodded. "Okay. I'll give you that."

Her smile softened. "Later, gratitude was just a very small portion of what I felt for you." Her voice got shy, as if it were trying to hide. "I don't know when I fell in love with you. One day, while we were at the cabin, my love for you just poked through and showed itself. I was stunned. I had thought I was in love with Dwight, but I hadn't thought about him since I made that phone call to him."

"The guy who was with somebody else when you called him that night."

She nodded. "That's him. That phone call brought reality home with a vengeance. He wasn't anything but a player. I'm thankful that only my ego was bruised; my heart was untouched. Later, that surprised me more than what I had learned about him."

"I'm sorry you got hurt at all, but I'm glad he did what he did. I don't understand how he could, but I will be forever grateful to him for being so stupid."

"What I felt for him wasn't love; if it were, it would have hurt when he so willingly let me go. It didn't take me long to realize that I was just in love with the idea of being in love. It seemed that everywhere I looked, people didn't come in singles any more—only couples. I felt left out." She shrugged. "Dwight was . . ." She frowned. "He looked interesting. I met him at a wedding reception. He caught the garter after I caught the bouquet." She shrugged again. "We started talking. I have to admit that I pushed us together as much as he did." She smiled. "I had visions of him waiting for me at the altar to make me his bride." She released a sharp laugh. "I couldn't admit to myself that I wanted one thing and he wanted only one thing. He had been pressuring me to sleep with him almost from the time he knew I was interested in him." She shuddered at the memory of her plans for that night in her other life when her world fell apart and on top of everything else, she learned Dwight's true nature. "I'm glad I held out."

"I am, too." Trent hesitated. "I hate to ask, but after the way you thought you felt about Dwight, are you sure that what you feel this time is really love?"

"I've never been as sure about anything before in my life. I've matured a lot since that night. I know what's important and what isn't." She shook her head. "Do you know that now I can barely remember what he looks like."

"Good." He caressed her shoulder. "I don't want you thinking about any other man besides me from now on." He brushed his lips across her shoulder. "Isn't it funny how fate works in a roundabout way? Here we are thrown together by a tragedy and we discover that we were meant to be together." He looked at her. "To get back to the original subject, was last night all you expected it to be?"

She shrugged. "I didn't know what to expect." She looked away again. "And I don't know how I'm supposed to act today."

"You don't act. You just let your feelings come through." He caressed her face. Then he smiled. "Right now what I feel is a need to test the shower." Desire flared in his eyes. "Care to experiment with me?"

"If I do we'll never get to eat, and what I feel is hunger."

"Me, too." His desire strengthened and asserted itself between them.

"For food."

Trent laughed. "Oh. Well, if *somebody* hadn't looked so sexy, so much more delicious than the food, we would have finished our dinner last night." He smiled as her color heightened. "However, since you refuse to participate in my experiment, I will be gentlemanly and allow you to use the shower first." He released her and lay back against the pillow. She didn't leave the bed. "What's the matter? Did you change your mind?" Hope filled his voice.

"I don't have my robe over here."

"Why do you need a robe?"

"I . . ." *Why do I need a robe?* She couldn't answer, but she was still reluctant to leave the bed.

"Okay, sugar. I'll turn my back. Will that make it easier?"

"I know this is foolish after what we just shared, but . . ." She shrugged.

"Not to worry. I don't want you to be uncomfortable." He turned his back to her.

"Thanks."

He felt the mattress shift as she scampered from the bed. When he heard the bathroom door close, he turned back around.

I could get used to this. He folded his arms behind his head and smiled at the ceiling as if it could respond. *Strange how something so wonderful could come from something so terrible.*

He thought about how perfect it would be to wake up with Angela for the rest of his life. He shook his head. She only left the bed a minute ago, and he missed her already. He shook his head again. He had it really bad.

He never expected to feel like this. For years he had envied

Robert and Davita for the love they had found. When Isaiah found Dottie, Trent wondered if it would ever be his turn. He was happy for them, but he had despaired of ever finding a life-long love of his own. When the family got together and he saw their love, he felt more alone that usual. His smile widened.

Now here was Angela, embedded in his heart as if she had been there forever. He loved the feeling, the connection, the completeness. How could he want to make it permanent so soon? He wouldn't question it—just accept it.

The shower started running and his body tightened at the thought of Angela. He imagined her standing with the water flowing over her breasts that he had caressed and teased, flowing over her body that he had explored and stroked with his hands and with his mouth. He remembered how she felt beneath him, on top of him, around him when he was inside her.

He groaned and shifted. He wanted her so much right now that it was as if he had never made love to her and was anticipating the first time. *Give it a rest,* he told his body.

Then he slipped from the lonely bed and went into the powder room, still trying to figure out exactly how to do just what he told his body.

He heard Angela padding down the hall and fought the temptation to go meet her.

"I'm finished. The shower is all yours," she called, as she passed by the powder room on her way back to the bedroom.

He waited until he was sure she had gone into the bedroom before he left the powder room. She deserved better than lovemaking on the hall floor. He shook his head. *Whoever said that teenagers were the only ones with raging hormones were either ignorant or liars.*

He turned on the shower and stepped inside. He started with cold water, changed it to hot, then settled for comfort-able. *May as well,* he thought, as the water ran over him. *The only thing that will get my body back to a normal state is the passage of time.*

He shook his head and turned. When he was around Angela, an erection was his normal state. He adjusted the water temperature again and waited for his body to cool down. The water heater had time to empty and start on a new batch by the time he turned off the water. He went back to the bedroom in a slightly better state than when he left it.

He got dressed, trying not to think about last night, but it was hard since he was still at the scene of the crime, so to speak. He smiled. A lot had happened here last night, but crime was not the word to describe the action.

He faced the mirror as he combed his hair, but he was seeing Angela. Lovely Angela. Luscious Angela. Sexy Angela. He shook his head and put down the comb. *Stop.* He turned toward the door. He was lucky that the body couldn't explode from a perpetual state of arousal. Otherwise, Angela would have a harder time than the king's horses and men had with Humpty Dumpty.

He took several deep breaths before he finally left the room. They helped him gain a little better control. Then he followed the smell of food into the kitchen. He paused at the newly set dining room table and smiled. Every trace of last night's dinner was gone.

"Good morning, beautiful." He tried not to imagine what was beneath Angela's jeans and T-shirt. Then he tried harder. Then he quit trying. "Yeah, beautiful." He wrapped his arms around her and pulled her back against him. Automatically his hands found her breasts and cupped them through her shirt. It didn't feel as good as bare skin would, but he'd have to settle for this for right now. As for later . . . He felt his body tighten at the thought of later.

She leaned back against him and bent her head so his kiss could find her neck. She melted against him as the heat he was generating traveled through her body. Then she eased away from him. "No, you don't. I worked hard to get this breakfast together and we are going to eat it." She gazed up into his face and waited as his mouth came closer to hers. Her eyes closed so she could better savor the feeling. Despite her words, she was disappointed when he let her go and stepped back.

"How are you?"

"Fine." Angela lifted a sausage onto the platter beside the mound of scrambled eggs.

"As fine as you look?" Trent chuckled as a sausage fell onto the table from the fork Angela was holding.

"Behave yourself, Trent." Angela put the sausage where it belonged and reached for the pot of grits.

"Allow me." Trent eased the pot from her hand and began to spoon the cheesy grits into the waiting bowl. "For some reason, you're a little clumsy this morning."

"True." A sparkle showed itself in her eyes. "Aren't we lucky that you're so sure-handed?" She stroked her hand across Trent's behind. Then she placed her mouth against his shoulder blade as she rubbed her body against his. The last spoonful of grits landed beside the bowl.

"We didn't need that anyway, did we?" he asked. Before she could answer, he turned and captured her mouth with his. After a long kiss they separated. "We better get this food onto the table before it joins last night's dinner." He took the platter into the dining room. Angela followed with the bowl of grits and a plate full of wheat toast. "What did you do with last night's dinner, anyway?"

"It's in the refrigerator. It will be tonight's dinner." She pretended to glare at him. "It would have been gone last night, if *somebody* hadn't gotten impatient and skipped right to dessert."

"Somebody wouldn't have persisted if somebody else hadn't encouraged him." Desire filled his gaze. "I enjoyed dessert. I'm sure that the meal you cooked was fantastic, but no way could it be as fantastic as what we had instead."

Angela felt her face redden. Until she met Trent she would have sworn that it was impossible for her to blush. Since they had gotten close, it seemed to be her constant state—that and the ache inside her that needed him to assuage it. "Stop it. Eat your breakfast." She heaped her plate then passed him the platter.

"Yes, ma'am." He smiled at her. "Afterward, can I have some dessert?" Trent put a portion of eggs and sausage onto his plate, but he kept his gaze on her.

Angela held the bowl of grits, but forgot to pass it. She forgot everything except the "dessert" they had shared last night.

"Are you going to share the grits or just hold them?" Trent eased the bowl from her hands and put some on his plate.

"I never heard . . ." Angela's words got stuck. "I never heard of dessert for breakfast."

Still staring at her, Trent put a forkful of eggs into his mouth. "That's because you never experienced it before. Your education has been woefully neglected." His smile was back. "I'm glad." He cut off a piece of sausage and tasted it. "I'll have to introduce you to the concept." He smiled at her. "It's a lot like dessert for dinner, only different. It's always different." He buttered a piece of toast. "I hope you'll find it better."

"Stop it. Don't look at me like that." Her voice softened. "And don't talk like that, at least not now." Her words weakened. "I'm hungry. For food." Angela put a forkful of eggs into her mouth. Her mouth had been watering, but she knew it wasn't for eggs.

"I'm just explaining." Trent chuckled and continued to eat. Angela did the same, trying not to hurry. *It wasn't ladylike to look so forward to dessert, especially right after breakfast. Was it?*

She took a sip of tea to wash down the food so she could take in another forkful. She refused to make eye contact with Trent for the rest of the meal. If she did. . . . She tried not to think about later. That was harder to do that not making eye contact.

"Delicious." Trent laid his napkin beside his empty plate. "That was the best breakfast that I have ever had. Thank you. After we clean up, I want to check to see if Captain Ellers or the chief left me any messages. I'm sure they don't work on Sundays, but if they found out anything they would have left a message at the police stations."

"I'll clean up. You go ahead and make the calls."

"You're sure? You did the cooking. It's only fair that I do the clean up."

"If there's anything left to do when you get through with the calls, you can finish in the kitchen. Okay?"

"Okay." He smiled. "If you work really slow, there will be work left for me."

Angela laughed. "Is that a suggestion?" She stood and took the empty platter and bowl from the table.

"Only an observation, even though cleaning the kitchen is not my favorite thing." He stared at her. "I guess I don't have to go into what *is* my favorite thing?"

"No, it's pretty obvious." Angela smiled before she turned away.

Trent stacked the dirty dishes and followed her into the kitchen, trying not to remember how her T-shirt–covered shoulders felt when his hands reached under and caressed her bare skin. *You got it bad, Trent.* He smiled. *And I like it.* He shook his head as he set the dishes on the counter. "Be right back."

Angela couldn't help the hum that escaped from her as she worked. Neither could she remove the grin on her face. She sighed, but her sigh was full of contentment, not worry.

Last night had been wonderful. Her memories lit a fire inside her as if it were mid August and the oven had been on for hours. She shook her head. To think she had almost given herself to Dwight in her other lifetime. Now she could barely remember his face. Her smile widened. *Yeah,* she thought again, *I'm glad I waited.*

Her hands were busy with the kitchen cleaning, but her mind was definitely somewhere else. It had returned to last night.

Trent had made her feel . . . She frowned as she searched for the right word . . . complete. She never knew that she was capable of such strong emotions—such feelings.

She tingled as she remembered the feel of his hands on her. He had stared at her face. When she was breathless from his kisses, he had moved his hands to her shoulders, then to her breasts. Even now it was a struggle to find enough air for a healthy breath. She had almost gone out of her mind when his mouth replaced his hands on her sensitive tips. Then she did get lost in the desire that overwhelmed her when he moved his hands lower. When his hands stroked across . . .

"Those dishes must really be dirty if they need that much rinsing."

Angela blinked hard. She looked into the sink. The stopper was in place and only an inch separated the water from the spill-over point.

"Oh." She tugged the stopper free. She knew from the sound when the water began to run down the drain, still she watched it as if afraid it would change directions. *Do anything instead of look at Trent.* Surely her face told the direction that her thoughts had taken.

"So." He wrapped his arms around her from the back and pulled her tightly against him. His body tightened uncomfortably at the closeness. He tried to ignore the discomfort. He widened his stance so her body would fit better against his. He kissed along her neck. Then he eased his head back. "Where were you just now?"

"Did you hear from Captain Ellers?"

"You weren't thinking about us, were you? That's not why the kitchen floor almost became the bottom of a swimming pool, is it?"

"How about the chief in Philly. Did he have any information about any activity there?"

"Were you remembering or anticipating?" Trent kissed the other side of her neck.

"Did he?"

"Maybe you were doing both."

"Trent, are you hiding something from me?"

"After last night." He kissed her again. "And during the night." Another kiss found its way to her neck. "You saw everything that I have."

"Trent . . ." She wanted to push away from him for only a few seconds, only until she could think clearly. So why couldn't she? Why didn't she want to do anything except stay wrapped in his arms? She smiled. *When it comes to you, love takes complete control over my life.* Her smile widened. She wasn't complaining. How could she complain about something that made her feel like this? She closed her eyes and enjoyed it.

Trent's hand stroked across the top of her shoulder as he continued. "Actually, you didn't see much last night, did you?" His voice lowered to a sexy rumble. "Neither did I. It was too dark. Next time the day will provide plenty of light." He nipped her neck and desire rippled through her. "Next time will be real soon, I hope."

Angela tried to make her thoughts form a logical order. "Were there any messages?"

"Nothing to worry about." Trent eased away from her. "Really. Captain Ellers left the message at the station that they couldn't find any connection between anyone here and the organization in Philly any more. He said he'll keep digging, but he doesn't expect to turn up anything. When I first talked to him, he had told me that their info says any ties disappeared years ago. There's a world of difference between this generation and the last as far as the organization is concerned. This generation doesn't care about the past: no vendettas. They're in the 'me first' mode. In this case, that's a good thing." Trent smiled. "Captain Ellers also said that Chicago is not known for its careful drivers." He laughed. "I told him that Philly is probably in first place in the terrible drivers category."

Angela stepped away from him. "Speaking of Philly, is there any news from your source there?"

"The chief also left a message. He said that they're still digging, but so far they haven't found anything. He said that things are quiet. A while ago one of the bosses, Big Tic. . . ."

"Big Tick? As in that disgusting bug?"

Trent laughed. "Seemed he used to shake a container of Tic Tacs all the time. Anyway, he died in prison. Had a heart attack."

"I saw that on the news here."

"That was the last news to come from the organization. Everybody else is quietly serving time. Big Tic had a daughter, but females never had any weight in the organization. The sons of the bosses are in control now. They wouldn't stir things up." He smiled at her. "It looks like a case of no news being good news in both instances." His stare heated. "What are we going to do with the rest of the day?" He closed the space between them. "Do you have any suggestions? Because if you don't, I do."

"I am going to do a little work." It was difficult, but she took a step away from him. *"You* can get the newspaper. I saw a box outside the office building last night. When you come back here, you can read it."

"Read the newspaper?" Disappointment crowded his words. "For how long?"

"Only until the basketball game comes on."

"Basketball? You want to watch a basketball game?"

"No, but you do, don't you?" Her eyes were wide with the question, but teasing danced in her stare.

"I don't want to watch a basketball game."

"I thought all guys were into sports."

"The only sport that interests me right now has nothing to do with basketball and will not be televised. In fact, the activity that I'm interested in is not a sport at all. And it's strictly for two people on the same team." He frowned. "How long will you be working?"

"Not long." Angela laughed. "You should see the look on your face. You look like a kid who found nothing but empty space under the tree on Christmas morning."

"Trust me. No kid ever felt like this." He took a half step toward her. "Anything I can help you with?"

"If you come close enough to 'help' I won't get anything done." She laughed. "Really, I only need about fifteen minutes. I just have to update a couple of accounts."

"You never told me what your job is now."

"We have been a little busy what with one thing and then another, haven't we?"

"Especially another."

"Don't start."

"I can only promise not to start right now." He smiled. "Later will have to take care of itself."

Angela laughed. "Fair enough. I'm not working for a company. I decided to try and start my own business. When I approached several businesses in the strip mall where I do my food shopping, they were enthusiastic. A lot of them are new to owning their own businesses and aren't comfortable keeping accounts. Government guidelines for small businesses can be complicated. I relieve them of that responsibility for a modest fee. They can't afford what large accounting firms charge. Actually most of the large firms don't want to be bothered with small businesses. Those accounts don't generate enough income; so the companies consider them nuisance accounts. I make a good living at it and the business owners like the personal care that I give them."

"I don't blame them." Trent crossed his arms across his chest. "I like the personal care that you give, too."

"Trent. . . ."

"But I'm going to wait until you're ready."

"I'm ready right now." She knew that desire filled her face. It had to, the way it was affecting her body. "Wait." She held up both hands when he started toward her. "But I have to wait. That way I won't have to do the work later. I promised to have the updated papers for them tomorrow. "Give me fifteen minutes and I'll be ready to play with you."

"I'm going to hold you to that." Trent stepped close and wrapped her in his arms. He kissed the top of her head. "You do realize that time is relative, don't you? In some cases fifteen minutes can last for hours." He released her and stepped away. "I hope this isn't one of those cases." He brushed a trail of heat along her arm with his finger. "I'll go get the paper and try to read it, but don't expect me to be able to give you a report later."

Angela laughed and went into the dining room. She moved her laptop and briefcase from the floor to the table. She was still smiling as she booted up the computer.

She would have to work hard to keep her mind on names and numbers when what she really wanted to do was concentrate on the fine brown man who would be a few feet away when he came back.

* * *

Trent dropped the coins into the box and lifted out the huge Sunday paper. He hoped he wouldn't have time to read much. He was sure that it was interesting; it was just that Angela was more interesting. Angela. Just thinking about her had him wanting, aching, needing.

He took the paper back to the apartment and hoped fifteen minutes was a huge overestimation.

Eighteen

"Okay." Angela stood in the doorway and stretched. "I'm finished."

When Trent's stare held on her T-shirt, she forgot to put her hands down. Memories of what she and Trent had shared shoved everything else from her mind. She blinked and forced a reasonable portion of her mind back to where it belonged.

"It's about time." Trent folded the section of the paper he was supposed to be reading and set it beside him. "I'm glad I won't have to pass a test on what I just read. It could have been in some obscure dead language for all the sense it made. My mind had other things to contend with." He smiled as his stare held on her.

"Poor neglected Trent."

"You took so long that the sun got tired and let the rain come out and play."

Angela laughed. "I was only fifteen minutes, just like I promised."

"That was the longest fifteen minutes on record." He came toward her, taking his time, knowing she wasn't going anywhere. And he was right.

Angela watched as Trent left the chair. As he came closer, moving much too slowly, she tingled in anticipation of his touch.

Finally he was in front of her—not touching her, just holding her with his stare. It was more than enough. She couldn't have moved if she wanted to and she definitely didn't want to. She wasn't aware that she moistened her lips ready for his kiss. She was only aware of him.

She leaned toward him at the same time that he moved toward her. Their lips touched. Then both mouths opened to get a better taste. Trent's hands found the way to her hips and drew her closer. Not satisfied, she strained closer still. His hands stroked up and down her hips and Angela still couldn't get close enough. He eased his head back and looked into her gaze. "Ready to try morning dessert?"

"Yes." A whisper was all she could manage, but it was enough.

Trent lifted her into his arms. As he carried her to the bedroom, their mouths found each other's again. They separated only when he set her on the floor. His fingers brushed against her breasts as he pulled her T-shirt over her head and her ache grew. Then she returned the favor. She was glad he wasn't wearing an undershirt. She was glad for a lot of things.

Her hands found his chest and she stroked across the rough hairs, hoping he was aching as badly as she was. Touching him increased her ache, but she couldn't stop her hands from moving, exploring. She teased the hard buttons on his chest and smiled at his groan. Then it was his turn to return the favor. His mouth followed the path forged by his hand. He tugged gently on first one, and then the other hard chocolate-drop tip. Finally—but too soon—he lifted his head.

"Again you have on too many clothes." His words rasped as they eased out. "Let's see what we can do about that."

He held her with his arms as his hands found and released the hooks responsible for the barrier between them.

The two lovers eased their bodies far enough away from each other to allow him to slide the bra straps down her arms and off her body. Then he just stood there, staring at her.

The cool room air did nothing to lower the heat of her body. She didn't think it possible, but her breasts tightened even more under his gaze; they grew achingly tight. She stared at him and let his gaze drink his fill of her.

Then he closed the space between them and gently took her hands and wrapped them around his hips. She got the idea and moved her trembling hands to the front of his body. She hesitated a few seconds, took a deep breath, and moved her fingers to the hook restricting his fullness.

She unhooked his pants, grateful that he wasn't wearing a belt; no way could she have managed a belt buckle without looking at it and she couldn't look anywhere except into Trent's piercing, smoldering black eyes.

Her hands brushed lower, across the part of him that had completed her last night and during the night and would soon complete her again. His moan reappeared and he brought her hand from his body to his lips and kissed it.

"Not yet, sugar, not yet."

Angela watched him take the few steps to the nightstand. She didn't protest today as she had yesterday; she knew he was coming back to her. She smiled when he did. Her smile was still in place when he picked her up and gently placed her in the center of the bed. Before she could get lonely, he lay beside her.

Their hands explored each other's bodies as if touching for the first time. When Angela got close to the evidence of Trent's aroused state, he eased her hands away. He moved his body away from her once more, but only for as long as it took to roll the protection into place. Then he was back. Then he was entering her, making her whole once again.

Angela got lost as she and Trent rode once again to their private love place. *I never thought getting lost could bring such pleasure,* she thought. Then she didn't think at all; again she could only feel.

"I think we discovered the ideal way to lose weight." Angela rolled onto her back much later.

"Fantastic sex indulged in often." Trent sat up.

"We've gone beyond the often stage." Angela sat up beside him.

"How about 'nonstop'?"

"That comes closer to explaining our discovery." She pulled the top sheet up under her arms. "Do you see how late it is?"

"Looks like after six o'clock to me. Were you having fun?"

Angela blushed. "You know I was."

"That's it then. You know the saying about why time goes fast." He shifted to look at her. "You don't have any place to go, do you?"

"You know I don't."

"Then we're cool like this." He leaned his head against the headboard and closed his eyes. "What have we got scheduled for tomorrow?"

Angela laughed at the hopeful note in his voice. "I'm getting up." She looked at him. "Right now. I'm going to take a shower. Alone."

"I would say that you're no fun, but I can't lie like that." He shook his head. "I must be getting old. I'm not going to try to talk you into sharing your shower with me."

Angela laughed again as she stood. "Maybe you finally reached your saturation point."

"Not hardly nor likely."

She felt her face warm as Trent's gaze roamed over her body, but she didn't feel self-conscious any more. She felt honored that he felt that way about her. She left the bedroom at a normal pace.

Much more of this and I'm going to die. Trent propped both pillows behind his head. The sound of Angela's shower reached him. *Not in my wildest dreams had I imagined that it could be like this.* He smiled. *When this mess is over, we have to do some serious talking. I can't let her go out of my life again.*

He left the bed and went into the other bathroom. Now he had another reason to make sure that her accidents were really only accidents. It would kill him if something happened to her.

They had eaten a late dinner of leftovers and the kitchen had been cleaned up when Trent brought up the subject of what had kept Angela busy earlier.

"What was the urgency to work on those accounts today?"

"I promised to get the figures to the business owners tomorrow. They have some things to do about expenses and taxes and decisions to make that depend on the work I did."

They were in the living room. Two comfortable chairs flanked the couch, but Angela and Trent sat side by side on the couch, their legs touching from the hip and down as far as possible.

"Can you explain to me what you would tell them?"

"I guess." Angela frowned. Her balloon of contentment had developed a huge leak. "You still don't think it's safe for me to go out, do you?"

"It would probably be all right, but I don't want you to take any risks. We need to give it a little more time to see if any information surfaces." He patted her thigh. "I don't want to lose you now that I've found you again."

"I understand." But understanding didn't lift her spirits. It had been easy to forget why they were here instead of in her home. The reason why she came to Chicago in the first place had started to fade. The turmoil that had changed her life was worth it since it brought Trent to her. She frowned. She wished it could have happened without anybody getting killed.

"Good. We can go over what I need to know later." He smiled at her, not aware of what was running through her mind. "I promise to take good notes; I won't mess up with your clients, okay?"

"Okay." She tried to push enthusiasm into her answer.

"If it wasn't for the fact that you're more beautiful than I am, they would never know that it wasn't you explaining things to them. That's how thorough I promise to be." He used the remote and turned on the television. "But there will be plenty of time to go over everything later. This is supposed to be a good movie coming on. The fact that you're watching it with me will make it even better, although maybe more difficult for me to concentrate. I am ashamed to say that I missed this Denzel movie in the theaters and also on video." He smiled at her. "Promise that you won't tell Denzel. If you do, he'll put me out of his fan club."

"I promise." Angela knew that Trent was trying to get her mind away from the reason they were here instead of in her home. She managed to smile at him, hoping he would think that he had succeeded.

"I don't think there is any danger of you discussing me if you ever did meet Denzel. I'm sure you would have other things on your mind. All the women think he is one fine brother."

"He is, but if all the women knew you, they'd know that, on the Fineness Chart, Denzel ranks well below Trent Stewart."

"You do know how to flatter a brother, don't you?" He brushed his lips across hers again. "And you know that flattery will get you everywhere."

"It's not flattery. It's the truth."

"Miss Baring, you do say the nicest things."

"I try."

"You succeed." He leaned over and gave her another quick kiss.

The title came on the television and Angela struggled to concentrate on the movie instead of what—or who—might still be waiting for her somewhere out there.

The movie ended and, after the evening news was over, it was perfectly natural for Trent to hold out his hand and for Angela to take it and walk arm in arm with him into the bedroom. Making love and then falling asleep in each other's arms was perfectly natural, too.

"Okay, go over it one last time." They had finished eating breakfast and Angela was preparing Trent to meet with her clients.

"Woman, you missed your calling. You would make a perfect inquisitor. I feel like a suspect repeating an alibi to a detective who doesn't believe him."

"I just want to make sure that you have everything right."

"You do know that everybody has telephones these days

and that it will be easy to check with you if I do forget something." He shuffled a stack of papers. "Although there is no way I could forget anything since you wrote everything down." He held up a thick pile of papers clipped together in sets. "Probably more than once."

"I had to make sure that I covered everything." She shrugged. "Maybe I did kind of repeat the information in different ways; I wouldn't want you to fumble for answers if somebody had questions."

"I won't, sweetheart." He stood and kissed her. "You covered every possibility." He smiled. "When I return, I expect a reward for doing such a great job."

"You'll expect a reward regardless." Angela wrapped her arms around his waist.

"That's right." He kissed her again. "I have become addicted to your dessert."

Angela brushed her hand across his chest, then settled it over his heart. She smiled as the beat sped up at her touch. "I know the feeling." She pressed her lips to his chest. "I think it's contagious."

"I can think of worse ailments to catch." He captured her mouth with his own. The kiss deepened, threatening to get them both lost again. He pulled back and sighed.

"I'd better go while I can." He smiled. "The sooner I go, the sooner I can come back."

"True." Angela took a step back at the same time that he did. Their hands were still clasped in each other's as they walked to the door.

"See you soon." He brushed his lips across hers quickly. "Wish me luck."

"Luck doesn't enter this. You have the information and you scored perfectly on my test."

"I intend to score perfectly when I get back, too."

"You are terrible."

"I hope you mean terribly good." He opened the door.

Angela laughed as she shook her head. "You are something else."

"Yeah, I am." His smile widened.

"Trent." Angela's smile disappeared. "Be careful. I couldn't stand it if anything happened to you."

"I am always careful." He tried to ignore the look that flashed across her face. He knew that she was remembering the time that being careful didn't keep him safe. He was sorry he had had to tell her about it, but he didn't like keeping secrets. He went on, trying to put ease back on her face. "Besides, we know that nobody is after me. And nobody knows we're here or that you're with me." He winked at her. "Stay sweet. That's a waste of breath. I know you can't be any other way." Then he opened the door. He tried to be nonchalant as he looked carefully around before he slipped out, but Angela saw him.

She still stared at the door after he had been gone long enough to be in the car. *Please keep him safe. I couldn't take it if anything happened to him.*

She took several deep breaths and let them out. *I will not think about what might happen. Trent is right. Nobody knows that I'm here, and that's the only thing that would put him in danger.*

She waited for peace to return. When it did, she left the hallway and went into the apartment to try to find enough to do to make the time until Trent came back to her go faster. When she made her mind find another subject, it returned to what had developed between Trent and her. Her fears disappeared completely and she smiled.

Finally she understood why people had such a hard time explaining or describing love. How could you explain something that made you smile while you ached for someone?

She went into the bedroom, but instead of making the bed, she stared at it with a silly grin on her face. *Love.* Her grin widened. *And lovemaking was indescribably delicious.* She laughed and hugged a pillow to her. It was also addictive. She felt her body tighten at the most recent memory of Trent making love with her. She shook her head. *How in the world did people in love get anything done?* She laughed and corrected her thoughts. Anything *else* done. Love didn't make the world go around; it threatened to make it stop. She sighed. Maybe Trent would finish quicker than they expected.

She finished in the bedroom and went to the kitchen. Fifteen minutes tops was all it would take to get the room sparkling. She was glad that the Sunday paper was so big. If she read every word, including all of the classifieds and every word in the ads, maybe Trent would be back by the time she finished.

Trent drove to the first shop, forcing his mind to stay on the directions instead of on Angela. He managed, but just barely.

He pulled into a parking space in front of the neighborhood grocery store in the tiny strip of shops. "Jack's Groceries" was written in large, but plain, black letters on the worn sign that hung over the storefront. Trent took the top set of papers from the folder beside him, grabbed a deep breath, and went inside.

The bell over the door announced his entrance before he could. Shelves, crammed with goods, stood on each side of the door and continued around the sides, broken only by freezer cases on one side. *How can they find anything?* Trent wondered, as he made his way into the store, stepping around cardboard displays holding everything from canned soup to dish detergent taking up floor space all along the small opening leading to the counter that looked as if it belonged in an old-fashioned kitchen. Miss Delsey's store popped into his mind.

"I'm Trent Stewart, Mr. Hoffman. Jane Johnson sent me," Trent told the gray-haired store owner after he had finally reached him. He held out his hand, but the man only pushed his glasses back up on his nose and stared up at Trent from behind the battered counter that looked as if it had been in place for decades. He kept his hands to himself.

Floor-to-ceiling shelves filled with floor-to-ceiling canned goods and boxes and packages of products flanked the wall behind him and only stopped when they reached the side walls. The man was small, but the massive jammed display made him look smaller than he was. His frown stayed for so long that Trent felt that Angela should have given him a password. Even that might not have worked.

Trent waited because there wasn't anything else he could do. Finally the man released some words, but they were laced with suspicion.

"Where is Jane? Why didn't she come herself? She never told me anything about working with anybody else. She didn't say nothing about having a partner." His frown deepened. "I don't like folks I don't know getting in my business."

"I'm not her partner—just a good friend." *Trent wasn't about to tell Mr. Hoffman exactly how good a friend he was.* "Jane twisted her ankle. Nothing serious, just a sprain," Trent added, when the man's eyes widened. "She just needs to stay off it for a little while but she wanted to make sure you got the work that she did. It is her work. I'm just delivering it for her."

Trent felt as if he was in front of a grade-school principal trying to explain himself out of trouble. He sighed. And he hadn't done anything wrong.

The man stared a while longer. "We store owners been having a bit of trouble around here lately."

He stayed in his spot as if something was holding him. Trent had to consider that maybe something was. A lot of the owners of small shops had guns for their protection. Trent had to admit, even though he had been a policeman, that he couldn't blame them. There weren't enough police officers to give protection to every store owner and the smaller businesses couldn't afford security personnel.

"I can understand that." He'd let the man take his time.

"How do I know that what you say is true?"

"You can call Jane, if you want, but she did give me these." Trent slowly put the papers on the counter in front of the man. "She gave me these papers and told me how to go over them with you. I'm meeting with a lot of her clients today. You can call her if you want to. I'm sure she gave you her cell phone number."

"She did." The man nodded slowly, but he didn't move toward the phone nor did he come from behind the counter. His intense stare stayed fixed on Trent.

Trent felt as if he were trying to sell Mr. Hoffman something that he didn't need or want—like bungee-jumping lessons from the top of the Andes Mountains. He waited some more and watched as trust and distrust wrestled on Mr. Hoffman's face. How could he go back and explain to Jane that he had failed with the first client?

Finally Mr. Hoffman spoke. "I reckon you're telling the truth. It would be easy enough to check on you." At last he held out his hand. "Hal Hoffman." He smiled. "Before you ask, no, not Jack. Jack was my father. He built up a reputation with this store, so, when he passed on, I didn't see a reason to change the name." His smile widened. "You know: don't mess with success." He moved from behind the counter. "Come on over here and let's see what you got for me." He led Trent to a table set to the side and covered with papers and boxes. He shifted some things from it onto a plastic crate on the floor beside it.

Finally, Trent began to go over the papers and to explain what Angela told him. Mr. Hoffman had a few questions, but nothing that Angela hadn't covered.

Trent hid his relief until he left the store. Then he smiled and made his way to Della's Barber Shop and Beauty Salon at the end of the same strip. He shook his head. He hoped this was a case of the first one being the hardest. If the others gave him as hard a time as Mr. Hoffman had, it was going to be a long day and his work would probably spill over into tomorrow. On the other hand, maybe he'd get lucky and the next one would balance out.

Trent finished at Della's without too much trouble. She was as suspicious as Mr. Hoffman. At Trent's suggestion, she called him before she welcomed Trent. When he had finished, he drove to the next client and then the next.

He took a quick lunch break at Mamie's Soul Food Restaurant, another client. From there he called Angela to reassure her that he hadn't lost any of her clients. Next he drove to another client, Kim's Dry Cleaners and Laundromat, three blocks away.

By then Trent had resigned himself to this not being the easy job he had expected it to be. He'd be finished when he was through. It didn't matter when. Angela would be waiting for him like the mythical pot of gold at the end of the rainbow but Angela wouldn't be at all elusive.

Between stops he allowed one quick daydream about Angela, but he kept himself from dwelling on what would happen when he got back to the apartment. He had to for several reasons: he might cause an accident and, for certain, his body would tell anybody who looked at him what he was thinking about.

Finally, after having to reassure every shop owner that Angela had really sent him, he finished with the visits. Only two out of the ten owners had taken his suggestion and called Angela to check up on him. It took a lot longer than he had expected, but each owner was satisfied with the report.

He started back to the apartment, proud of the way he had handled things. The fact that this was new for him never showed in his presentations; the only calls made were to verify that he was who he said he was.

He relaxed against the back of the seat. He was tired from this new routine. *Give me a good old stakeout or a chase any day. This mental tiredness is worse than physical.*

He pulled into rush hour traffic and didn't frown. It would take longer than it would have an hour ago, but he was going home to Angela. An SUV dashed in front of him to squeeze into a space too small for a compact. Trent slammed on the brakes and let it in. Instead of frowning at the driver, Trent just smiled. *Home to Angela. I like the sound of that.* He imagined being able to know that, at the end of every day for the rest of his life, she would be home with him.

His look of contentment stayed as he made his way through some of the worst rush hour traffic he had ever experienced.

He wouldn't have been so quick to congratulate himself on a job well done if he had known that he had relaxed too soon—he had left a trail.

By the time Angela heard Trent's key in the lock, she had cleaned the apartment more thoroughly than the maid would have. She was trying to find something else to do when he walked in.

Between every task she had to convince herself that he was all right. The two calls from her clients probably made him wonder if he was doing something wrong, but she welcomed them as she had the call he made to reassure her. The calls let her know that he was safe.

She rushed to him while he was still in the hall and greeted him with a kiss that threatened to eliminate any possibility of conversation for a long time, but she did manage to break it off.

"I am so glad to see you."

"I would never have known if you hadn't told me." Trent set a bag on the table and cradled her within his arms as he smiled at her.

"I was worried. You were gone for so long."

"I told you that you had nothing to worry about. I can take care of myself in danger, and there was no danger today, just nontrusting store owners." He ran a finger down her nose and tapped the end. "You have some suspicious clients. All of them. They probably stopped believing in Santa Claus when they were three years old. Maybe even two." He chuckled. "I know the police never have to worry about any of them being victims of scams."

Angela smiled. "They are a savvy group, aren't they?" She sounded like a proud parent. "Other than that, how did it go?"

"Perfectly, of course. I was always an excellent student."

"Nobody had any questions?"

"Nope. At least none that I couldn't answer. You prepared me perfectly." He cradled her in his arms. "I told you that when I called you."

"I know, but you weren't finished then. Mr. Hoffman didn't have a problem?"

"Not after I convinced him that you sent me and showed him the papers you gave me. I don't want to accuse him unjustly, but I think I know the reason why he stayed behind that counter until he was convinced of who I was." His forehead creased. "I hope he got training so that if he has to shoot, he'll hit what he aims at." Trent frowned. "Personally, I'm always uneasy about civilians having guns, but I'm realistic enough to admit that sometimes it's necessary for protection."

"Mr. Hoffman is very methodical. I'm sure he did what was necessary to prepare himself." She frowned. "Several of the businesses in that area have been robbed. For a while, it was one every week. The police increased their patrols and the robberies stopped." She shrugged. "Maybe that was the reason or maybe the robbers just decided to move on." She frowned again. "How about Mr. Matthews? He didn't have any questions?"

"Nope." Trent kissed the side of her face. "In fact, I think Mr. Matthews was the one who asked if I wanted to do his accounts from now on."

"Yeah. Right." Angela pulled back and poked his chest. Trent chuckled.

"Really, sweetheart, everything went perfectly. Your notes covered everything." He drew her back against him. "When anybody asked where you were, I told them that you sprained your ankle and would see them the next time."

"My ankle? Why my ankle?"

"If I said you had a cold or the summer flu, they might have questioned the accuracy of your figures." He ran his hand smoothly down her back, then brushed over her behind and left his hand there. "They don't know how perfect your figure is at all times." He eased her against him.

Angela felt his need for her. A matching need grew and spread inside her. "First . . ." She was having trouble breathing. "First we eat . . ." He kissed her neck. "Lunch."

"Uh-huh." He nipped her neck. "Then we finish with dessert." He stared into her eyes. "I guess you'll insist upon having lunch first?"

"Absolu . . ." He swallowed her word with his kiss. She broke the connection. "Lunch first." Angela managed to find her thought in spite of the way his kiss was jumbling her mind. She eased back a bit. "Otherwise I'll never get to eat lunch."

"Okay, if you insist." Trent allowed a space between them. "But I expect to enjoy dessert more than the rest of the lunch.

Oh, I almost forgot." He handed her the bag from the hall table. "Mamie insisted on sending this. She said it's your favorite."

"Just about everything on her menu is a favorite. Since I already fixed lunch, we'll have this later."

"Later as in later today or as in tomorrow?"

"Trent. What am I going to do with you?"

"I have a couple of suggestions."

"Later. In a little while," She added when his face filled with disappointment. "Let's see if your theory holds true, since you don't even know what I fixed."

"It can't compare with your dessert."

"No matter what I fixed?"

"No matter what you fixed. Baby, there isn't anything you can serve that can surpass your dessert."

Angela laughed and led him to the dining area. "The same goes for me, too."

They finished a lunch that neither tasted and proceeded to dessert, shutting the common world out as they entered their own.

Nineteen

Karen worked hard Saturday afternoon after she traded her rental car for another one. She knocked on every door to every house on the street where she had almost been successful in her payback, starting with the house where it had almost happened. When there was no answer, she tried the other houses. Whenever she found someone at home, she used the same story she had used at the hospital: her organization wanted to reward good deeds. Then she mentioned the story of the woman who saved the little girl.

Everybody she spoke to had seen or heard the news about the incident, but none of them had any information she could use. She made herself smile and thank them anyway. Then she moved on to the next house.

She kept at it all day as if she were working a job that paid high overtime rates. When it became too late to knock on doors without arousing suspicion, she stopped for the night.

Early Sunday she started again. Maybe this morning somebody would be home now at the house where she had failed. Her smile was for real when she saw a woman come out of the house. Finally. She wasn't sure that this woman had any information, but when she had looked in the rearview mirror before she had zipped around the corner Friday morning, it looked as if the so-called helping voice had come from this house or one of the ones on either side. In any case, this woman must know something.

In the suburbs, neighbors talk to each other, especially close neighbors. If it wasn't this woman it was most likely a neighbor on one side of her—a neighbor who would have told her what happened. This time Karen's smile was genuine as she made herself walk slowly from the car.

The woman was picking up her morning paper from the lawn when Karen introduced herself and told the same story that had worked so well. She hoped that this woman was anxious to see Jane "get what was coming to her" as Karen had worded it since the first time she told it at the hospital.

"I'm Louise Dalton," the woman had said, when Karen finished the story and had given her a business card. "Come sit on the porch. We'll be more comfortable talking up there."

The last thing Karen wanted was to waste time sitting on somebody's porch, but she went. Besides, maybe it would be time well spent.

Karen tried not to let her hopes grow as she followed the woman. She scrounged up some more patience when what she wanted to do was rush the woman through her story and get to the part where she gave her the information that she needed. *I've got time,* Karen told herself. *Little Miss Witness Protection isn't going anywhere. She thinks she's still safe.*

Karen had to hold in her laughter. The witness protection program had a flaw: it couldn't protect the witness when decent citizens weren't aware that a person needed protection.

"I remember the story." Louise nodded. "In fact I saw the young woman just the other day. Now isn't that a coincidence?" She frowned at Karen. "Where are my manners? Can I get you something? A glass of iced tea, maybe?"

"No, thank you. I'm kind of in a hurry." She forced the smile to stay in place. *Why was it taking her so long to get to what I need?*

"Do you know she was almost hit by another car the other day? I saw it with my own two eyes. If I hadn't been out here getting my newspaper at that time and yelled to her . . ." She shuddered. "I don't want to think about what might have happened." She shook her head. "I don't know what this old world is coming to. Decent folks can't even walk the streets safely in broad daylight. Like I told her, everybody is in too much of a hurry, if you ask me." She stared at Karen. "Actually, they're in too much of a hurry even if you don't ask me. You know what I mean?"

"Yes, I do." Karen took a deep breath hoping it would help her words sound casual. "Did she say where she lives?"

"She was such a nice young thing," Mrs. Dalton said. "Didn't want any fuss made over her. Wouldn't let me call an ambulance even though she took a hard fall. I just know she woke up stiff and bruised in the morning." Mrs. Dalton shook her head. "Like I said, I recognized her from that time a little while ago when the little girl almost got hit at the playground down the street. We talked a bit about careless drivers, then she insisted on going home. I offered to drive her, but she was determined to walk." She stared at Karen. "I thought that was foolish. After all, I offered her a ride, and I know she was shaken up a lot."

"Did she say where she lives?"

"No, just that she lives nearby. It's got to be a short walk, though. The way she was limping, she couldn't go far."

Did she say where she works?"

"I don't rightly remember, but I don't think so." She frowned. "You know, she was coming from work when she saved that little girl, so she must work near here."

Karen thanked her, gave her a real smile, then left to circle the neighborhood. Angela had to live in one of these houses.

By the end of the day she tried not to be disappointed. She shouldn't have expected it to be so easy, but it seemed as if it was going to be as hard as finding the right numbers for the lottery. Karen frowned.

Angela had been studying to be an accountant when she worked for that dog, Mr. Hunter. Karen clenched and unclenched her fist. *I have to keep my mind clear.* She exhaled slowly. *Maybe she has a job doing that now. A lot of time people stayed with their old work when they relocated.* A hard look settled on her face. *Had Lester found another job as a hit man? He was next. Then Big Tic could rest peacefully. He deserved it.*

She located the business area, grabbed some take-out from

the soul food restaurant, and then went to her hotel room to work on a plan.

How could she use Angela's job to find her? Every business used accountants. She shook her head, gave up on that idea, but latched onto another. Everybody, even Miss Perfect, had to go to stores. She must use the stores in the neighborhood some of the time. Maybe somebody at one of the shops had some information. She bit off a piece of barbecue rib and chewed slowly. *As good as this is, I know Angela has eaten there.*

She took a deep breath and let it out slowly. *Patience,* she told herself when she felt her control trying to slip. *No hurry. She's not going anywhere until I send her. Tomorrow. If I don't find her then, I'll try the next day. And the next.*

On Monday just after daybreak, Karen settled into a parking spot across from a strip mall and waited for the stores to open. If Angela lived nearby, she probably shopped nearby, at least some of the time. Everybody needed a loaf of bread or a quart of milk every now and then and didn't want to bother with supermarket lines. If not this mall, then maybe the one two blocks down the street.

Unfortunately she didn't have a picture of Angela, but she could give a good description of her. She'd never forget what Angela Baring looked like, even though whenever her mind formed a picture of her, Angela was dead just like Karen's father.

She looked across at the mall. If not today, then tomorrow. However long it took that's how long she'd look.

She watched as the shops came alive; metal screens were rolled up and closed signs were flipped to open as doors were unlocked. Karen made herself wait until they were all open. She wanted to hit them all before they had a chance to talk to one another; she didn't want anybody to have enough time to think about why she was interviewing them. Della's Barber Shop and Beauty Salon was the last to open.

Just as Karen started to get out of the car, a car parked in a space halfway down the strip. She watched as the tall driver got out and went into the restaurant. *What is he doing here?*

She leaned back against the seat. The widest smile in a long time flashed across her face. The news broadcasts and the papers might not have shown a picture of Angela, but the night that Mr. Hunter had been killed, they had been kind enough to name the first detective on the scene. He'd be involved later since it was his case. A nice, clear picture of him was in the paper the next day, dressed in a tux as if to disguise the fact that he was the police. She frowned. *What was Trent Stewart doing in Chicago? It had to be more than a coincidence.*

She didn't know how or why, but Angela had to have something to do with it.

Karen nodded and smiled. Patience had finally paid off. *Daddy would be so proud of me.* Of course, a little help from fate didn't hurt. She nodded again. This was meant to be. Why else would she have stumbled across Stewart like this? She shrugged. *I have to give myself some of the credit. I did figure out to come here.*

"I should get my detective's license myself." She smiled. "Logic does help." Karen mumbled and scribbled notes. She made a quick note. Her smug look would have made the cat who caught the canary envious. *Soon, Big Tic. Soon. Payback day is coming, Daddy.*

She took a few minutes to savor her victory. Then she frowned. What if that's not him? What if it's just somebody who looks like him? She sighed. She'd waited this long, a few minutes more wouldn't make a difference. If it was Trent Stewart, all she had to do was follow him. He'd lead her to Angela. To keep from biting her nails, she picked up a tissue and began to tear it into tiny pieces. When that was gone, she reached for another. Her stare never left the restaurant door.

The front seat and floor looked as if a snowstorm had hit by the time the one she had been waiting for came out. *Almost there,* she thought as she started the car.

Her smile disappeared when she tried to drive away. She knew what the wobble was before she got out of the car to look. She had had enough flats to recognize one when she had it.

Her patience hid from her and her temper took over and almost drove her the rest of the way over the edge. Of all the times to have a flat.

Karen watched as Trent drove down the street. He never turned onto a side street so she had no idea which street Angela lived on. Or if he was on his way to her house. To even say that he was in Chicago with Angela was an assumption, but she had to make it or she would really lose it.

She threw the yellow notepad into the backseat. The pen followed after it bounced off the windshield. She picked up a handful of the confetti that she had made and flung it against the windshield, too, sorry that it wasn't a handful of marbles instead; something to make a noise. *How dare they give me a defective car.* She released a string of curse words that would have made even Big Tic cringe.

She was still fuming as she used her cell phone to call the company. The poor receptionist felt the full force of Karen's temper. So did the young mechanic unfortunate enough to responded to her call two hours later.

"I have been waiting for you for two hours. Two hours." Karen rushed up to the truck before the driver could get out. Her hands were bunched at her side when what she wanted was to wrap them around his neck. He was lucky that she needed him. "What kind of business are you people running?"

"I was at the scene of an accident down on the highway. It was a big pile-up. A lot of us were there with our tow trucks. That's why you had to wait so long. Some of the trucks are still there. A big rig lost its load of steel girders. The rescue teams had to use the jaws of life a couple of times to . . ."

"I don't want to hear your sorry excuses; just fix the tire."

"Yes, ma'am." He got out and walked around to the front passenger side tire. "I see the problem. You ran over a nail; it's still in your tire."

"It is not *my* tire and I don't care what the problem is. Fix it. Now."

"Yes, ma'am."

She hovered over the mechanic even though she knew that

time didn't matter any more. He could take hours and it wouldn't hurt the situation one bit. Trent Stewart was gone and he took her chance of finding Angela Baring with him.

She paced back and forth on the sidewalk as if she were in a too-small cage. Is this how Big Tic felt in that cell? Is that why he died? Did he just quit fighting and decide to let his damaged heart stop, rather than go back to prison from the hospital? *It wouldn't have happened if he had been home. He'd still be alive. Angela will pay; I'll see to that.*

She stepped up her pacing as she searched for self-control. She needed it so she could think. She was still looking for it when the car was ready.

She got behind the wheel, but didn't start the motor. She was so close right here.

Much as she was tempted to continue with her quest, she didn't dare right now. If she was going to expect the shop owners to believe her story, she'd have to present a pleasant face to them. There was no way she could manage that without cooling off first. The way she felt and the way she knew she looked, nobody would believe that she wanted to find Jane to honor her. They wouldn't believe that she had anything good in mind for anybody.

She took a deep breath. Besides, she could wait until tomorrow. There wasn't any hurry, now. Trent Stewart was gone.

She went back to her hotel, still struggling for control. By the time she reached her room, she had reached a level of calm.

At least I have more information now than I had before this morning. Important information. She knew the key detective on the Mr. Hunter murder case was here in Chicago. Now that she thought about it, he *had* to be here because of his connection to Angela; it couldn't be a coincidence that he was not only in the same area, but in the same small suburb.

She had to make a few phone calls. She had to find out why the Philly police department sent Trent Stewart to Chicago. *Was it in conjunction with the other charges against Big Tic's organization? Were the feds finally planning to file additional charges?* She laughed. The organization was involved with the drug trade from the fields until the products reached the hands of the users, and the feds were planning cases for income tax evasion. Her smile disappeared and she shook her head. *The feds usually used their own people. Why pull Stewart into this?* She frowned. *What am I missing? Is he working for them now? Are they planning to relocate Angela again?*

After Big Tic died, she had lost touch with everybody associated with him, even her relatives; she hadn't wanted any reminders. She sighed. Maybe she should have kept in contact with somebody.

Anger welled up in her but she shoved it down where it couldn't interfere with her thoughts. Anger was counterproductive. She had to make plans. *They can't move Angela. Not now. Not when I'm so close to getting her.*

She nodded slowly and a little anger slid from her face with each nod. Maybe fate had given her a bonus. She hadn't found Angela today, but she had stumbled across Detective Trent Stewart. If she was lucky, she could get both of them. She *did* owe him, too. After all, he was the one responsible for Angela being here in the first place. *If he hadn't been so persistent the night Mr. Hunter had been erased, Angela would have been taken care of back home and Lester wouldn't have talked and Big Tic would be okay and I would have my life back.*

They would have gotten him released because of his health. They had been working on it the day he died. Why couldn't he have held on a little while longer? Her face tightened. She couldn't change that, but she could see that Big Tic could rest easy.

Trent Stewart was too smart. The guys waiting at Angela's house that night were the best the organization had, but somehow Trent had known they were there. They never did find that leak, but there must have been one. The guys had gotten there fast. Why else would Angela not go to her house, at least to get some things before she left for good?

Karen nodded again. *Oh, yes. Trent Stewart needed to be gone as much as Angela did.*

Karen smiled. Yeah. She could make this little setback work for her. *I just have to plan a different strategy and hope that the feds haven't picked this time to make a move on the case based on the information Angela uncovered when she poked her nose where it never belonged. She's taking up way too much of my time. I need for this to end.*

She lay down and let her mind go to work.

Twenty

"Hi." Angela walked over to the sofa and kissed Trent's cheek, then slowly eased away. "I finished with the last ten accounts. After we deliver these tomorrow, the owners will be set until they need the next quarterly report."

"Very good." He ran his hand down her arm. "I have finished my job, too." He pointed toward the kitchen. "As you will see, the kitchen is ready for your white glove inspection. There is no sign of the late breakfast that we enjoyed." He ran his fingers up toward her elbow, found the sensitive inner spot, and drew lazy circles. "Of course, we didn't have dessert with our breakfast, but that wouldn't involve the kitchen anyway." He smiled. "At least I don't think so." He smiled. "Maybe one day we can explore the possibility." He moved his hand slowly back down her arm and touched her thigh. His fingers brushed a slow trail up to a midway point, back down and up again. "You never know where you will have dessert until the time comes." He moved his hand to her waist. "However, I can wait patiently because I know that dessert will come later." He eased her down onto his lap and kissed her. "Not much later, though, I hope. It seems that lately I am always hungry for dessert." He brushed his lips across hers. Their kiss intensified, then Angela separated from him.

"We have to go over these last reports so you'll be prepared when you take them to the store owners tomorrow." She eased herself to a place beside him, but still relished the touch of his body against hers. They could have been in an easy chair and had space left over. She smiled. If this was all a dream, she hoped she stayed asleep.

"I guess you're right." He captured her fingers with his. "If you don't watch out, I'll get so good that the next time I can do them by myself and we can eliminate the middle man." He squeezed her hand. "Or in this case, the middle woman."

She didn't laugh in response and, instead of getting the reports, she just stayed there. Still not saying anything, she eased her hands from his and twisted them in her lap.

"Sweetheart? What's the matter? You know I'm kidding. I promise to do a good job this time, too. You didn't get any complaints about my presentation from your clients the last time, did you?"

"No." She shook her head, but she didn't look at him. "It's not that."

"Maybe this time nobody will even call you to make sure that you sent me. You don't have another Mr. Hoffman as a client in the next group, too, do you?" He laughed, but again Angela's laughter didn't join in.

"It's not that, either. I know that you'll do a good job." She glanced at him. She looked as if she had tried to find a smile, but couldn't. Instead, she sighed.

"What is it? What's wrong?" He turned to face her.

"Trent," she frowned. "How long do you think it will be before I can go home? I love being here with you. You know that. I never dreamed it could be like this, but it's like living a fantasy. I'm ready to go home. We could be together like this at my house." This time her sigh was heavier. "This is a nice place and I appreciate it, I really do"—she squeezed his hand—"but I feel as if I'm stuck in place while the rest of the world is moving forward. I want things back to normal, back the way they were, but I want this time with you to stay, of course." This time she did smile at him. "We could still be together at my house, couldn't we? It doesn't matter to you if we're here or at my home, does it?"

"How could you ask that? You know that where we are doesn't make a difference to me. You should know that what I want more than anything is for us to be together, too." He kissed her forehead. "But we still have to make sure that you're safe. One of the chiefs would have called me if you were still in danger, but you know me. I have to make sure." He brought her hand to his mouth and placed a kiss in the palm. "I plan to call Captain Ellers today to see if anything new turned up, anyway. After that I'll call the chief one more time." He smiled. "Then we can make decisions based on what we find out. Even if we can leave here, we still have to go over the reports, don't we? Your clients have to have those reports no matter what we find out." He laced his fingers with hers and squeezed. "Right?"

"Right." She stood. "I'll go check them one last time. Then we can go over them together as soon as you finish with your calls."

Trent watched her go. Did she remember the last time she had talked about getting her life back to normal? He hoped not because then she would also remember the normal that she had hoped for never came. If it had, she would be in Philadelphia instead of here in Chicago. There was a possibility that she could go back to Philly, but he didn't want to mention it and take a chance on getting her hopes up. He shook his head. He wasn't even sure if she still wanted that. He wasn't sure what she wanted. He didn't even know if she wanted him in her life after this was all over. He was ready for forever, but was she? Had she even thought about it? He sighed. One thing at a time.

Maybe when he finished with his phone calls, he'd have some really good news for her. Then they could take it from there. He didn't want to consider the possibility that she might have to move to yet another city. He'd think about that when and if he had to.

He called Captain Ellers. That was the easy call to make. Trent didn't expect anything new from him and that's what he got: nothing new.

"Any underworld ties that might have existed between Philadelphia and Chicago at one time have been gone a long time and there's no trace left here," Captain Ellers said. "We've got a completely new organization in charge of the drug trade, now." His laugh was sharp. "The department has the same type of trouble, but the suspects have changed. Same story, different characters."

"I'm sorry that the problems still exist, but glad that Angela isn't in danger because of some connection."

"You don't have anything to worry about. Our most reliable informants didn't even know who we were talking about when we asked around; the names meant nothing to them. It looks like your lady friend is safely out of the loop."

Trent thanked him and hung up. It didn't matter to the police who was breaking the laws, they still had to go after them. But as far as Angela was concerned, it meant that nobody from Chicago was responsible for her accident. So far, it looked as if it might have been just somebody behind the wheel who didn't know how to drive.

Trent hoped that the chief back home didn't have anything to report either. He sighed. Still, he and Angela had to be prepared just in case.

If the chief did uncover something in Philly, we'll get through it. It might not be what Angela hoped for, but if necessary, she can relocate again. We can relocate. This time it would be different. We'd be together. He sighed again. *If that's what she wants.* He hoped it wouldn't come to having to move, though. She'd been through enough, and none of it was her fault. He refused to allow himself to consider that maybe she wouldn't want to be with him on a permanent basis. He had a hard time keeping uncertainty away. He made himself move to the next phone call.

Only one way to find out the last piece of information. He punched in the 215 area code and said a prayer before he entered the other numbers. *Let it be over for her,* ran through his mind as he waited for somebody to answer.

"Okay, sweetheart." Trent turned off the phone after his short conversation and smiled as Angela came back in the room. "This is our final report." His smile widened. "Final report. Doesn't that sound great? It looks like things are okay both here and back in Philly. The chief took one last look for us. The old bosses' kids who are in power seem to have moved on. They don't care about the past. Their only concern now is keeping the opposition from taking over their territory and businesses." Trent shook his head. "Loyalty isn't what it used to be. In this case, that's a good thing."

"What about the federal case based on the information that I uncovered while I was working on my term paper? They acted excited about that."

"The chief said the feds are going at it from a different angle. The case they had planned based on that information is unnecessary. Most of the guys they were after are serving sentences that won't end until they die, or else they are already dead. They're going after the others on cases stronger than income tax evasion. The federal government is after the new organization now, and your information doesn't have anything to do with them." His voice softened. "You're out of it, sweetheart."

"I can go home?" Angela felt as if somebody had moved a ton of steel from on top of her. "The accident was just an accident?"

"Looks like just another incompetent driver on the loose."

"I can go home?" Her eyes seemed to light up. "I can even go back to Philadelphia if I want to?"

"You can go wherever you want."

"I can have my own name back. I can be Angela Baring again."

"If that's what you want."

"That much I am sure about. Do you know that after two years, I still have trouble answering to Jane Johnson sometimes?" She laughed. "I don't have to anymore. I have choices. I can put Jane Johnson to rest." She laughed again. "Now that I do have choices, I don't know whether I want to stay here or go back to Philly." She twirled around. "It is so great to have choices again, to have control of my life again." She glanced at the papers clutched in her hand. "Oh, I forgot the account book. Be right back." She hurried toward the bedroom, but turned and smiled at him. "I don't have to brief you on the reports, now, do I? I can give the clients these reports myself, can't I?"

"You sure can. If you want to abandon me like that, you can."

"Hey." She ran to him and kissed his forehead. "I want you to come with me." She smiled again. "Isn't this great?" She turned away, but turned back to face him. "Be right back, okay? I have to get those books." She laughed as she left the room.

"I'll be here waiting for you."

Trent's smile faded after she left the room. *I've never seen her so happy.* His time with her had been anything but. He shook his head. He wished he dared to feel at least a little of the happiness that she was showing. He exhaled slowly.

This time his concern didn't have anything to do with Angela's safety; it was purely selfish. Both chiefs had assured him that she was in no danger. She was so filled with happiness. Had she thought about how this would affect their relationship? He shook his head. He was being selfish.

Would she choose Chicago or him? Of course, he could operate his business anywhere, but would she want to be in his life on a permanent basis? Their time here had been a fantasy, just as she had said. What would happen between them when reality settled in? He wanted her for always. He had from the start, but things weren't right for a commitment with everything up in the air as it was before. *Now it's up to her.* He didn't want to think about what he would do if she didn't want what he wanted.

He would propose to her as he had planned to do all along. He had just been waiting for the uncertainty to end. Now it was over. Tonight he'd take her out for a nice dinner to celebrate. When they came home, he'd ask her to marry him. He frowned. *Maybe I should wait until after we move back to her house. We could go out to dinner again and I can propose when we get back.* His frown deepened. She might be too tired after moving and getting settled back in at her house. Maybe she'd rather have take-out for dinner. They could stop by Mamie's and get some platters. He could still propose to Angela afterward.

Maybe I won't wait until we move back. We're paid through the end of the week. Tomorrow we'll take the reports to her clients together. Then, when we come back here, maybe I'll ask her.

He shook his head. It didn't matter where they were or under what circumstances. What did matter was that she said "yes." She wouldn't say no, would she? He thought about her reaction when he had told her what he was doing now. *She got upset, but she hadn't mentioned it since then, so she must have accepted it. Right?*

"Here they are." There was a lightness in Angela's voice that he had never heard before. "Let's work at the table." She sat and opened the top file folder. "I know you don't have to know this now, but you can pretend to be the clients and ask questions."

Trent sat beside her. He tried to pay attention to what she was saying, instead of listening to the doubts whirling through his mind. He was glad that he didn't have to give the reports by himself this time.

"Oh, man." Angela stopped in the middle of the third report and frowned. She slapped the table. "There's one thing that I didn't think about." She forgot the open folder in front of her. "I have to make sure that my clients have somebody to take my place. I can't leave them hanging."

"What did they do before they hired you?"

"They kept their records themselves."

"Do you think they can do them again?"

"I don't think they want to go back to that. They were all so grateful to have me do the books for them. Many of them were making costly mistakes because they weren't aware of changes in the regulations and guidelines." She frowned and slowly tapped her pen on the table. "The university has a business majors track. I'll call and see if the department head can recommend a graduate who is still in this area. After that I'll have to interview them. I can't just give my clients a name and say 'so long.'"

"Sounds like a plan."

"This is more complicated than I thought." She shrugged. "I'm not really on a timetable. I can take as long as it takes. I'd better make that call before I deliver the reports. I want to give the owners some prospects before I tell them that I'm leaving." She smiled. "I won't leaving for at least a couple of weeks, not until I'm satisfied that the new accountant can handle the accounts to my clients' satisfaction." Her smile widened. "But I *am* leaving Chicago after everything is settled. I'm going back to Philly. I am going home."

"Great." Trent tried not to let happiness fill him, too. She hadn't promised him anything or discussed her decision with him before she made it. They had never talked about a future together. Despite all this, in spite of his trying not to, he felt light enough to float.

Angela took out the phone book and Trent let his hope grow. She knew that he'd be in Philadelphia. Maybe she took it as a given that they would be together when they got back.

He watched her as she responded to the person she was talking to. She kept her patience as she was transferred to several people and put on just as many holds. He could tell when she finally got some needed information because her smile widened.

He watched her hand as she wrote down some information. He couldn't help but imagining that hand on him later in response to his hand on her. Things would work out for them. They had to.

Twenty-one

She made herself wait until evening, then Karen dialed a 215 number in Philadelphia. It had been a long time, but she still remembered the phone number. She frowned. She hoped they hadn't done something stupid like move or change the number. She shook her head and sighed.

Big Tic had always said that family was important. "That's who you can count on when things are rough," he used to say. "That's all you got. Family. You don't got them, you got nothing." She should have remembered that. She should have kept in touch with the family, especially after Big Tic died. They were at the funeral, paid their respects, but she hadn't wanted anything to do with them. *They should have protected Daddy.* She had cut all ties with them. Somebody answered at the other end and she shoved her resentment away.

"Yeah," she said, when a woman answered. "Is James there?" *Who did he think he was fooling by keeping his serious name?* "Yeah, Aunt Lucille, this is me." She sighed. *I should have known that she would recognize my voice.* "I'm fine. How about you?"

Karen didn't interrupt as her father's sister detailed the list of her latest ailments. It wouldn't have shortened the list if she had; in fact, it would have taken more time. Aunt Lucille had been at death's door ever since Karen could remember—except on bingo nights. Then she almost 'skipped out the door,' as Big Tic used to put it. *A short distance from the grave her whole life, yet she had outlived her brothers and sisters. Including Big Tic. How was that fair?*

During her aunt's breath break, Karen broke in. "I was hoping to find James there. I know this used to be family dinner night. I figured it still is. I need to talk to him." She nodded. "Yes, Aunt Lucille, I promise to keep in touch." She nodded again. "You take care, too." She took another deep breath, proud of her patience as the next person picked up the phone.

"Hey, Pretzels," she said, when another familiar voice came on. "I know it was a long time ago, but I'll bet you're still addicted to them. You probably have one in your hand right now." She laughed. "Yeah, I guess Aunt Lucille would be insulted if you ate them instead of her pot roast." She got rid of her laughter and got to the reason for the call. "I need a big favor." She shook her head. "Not that kind of favor." She frowned. "You guys still in that business?" She shook her head again. "You're right. I don't want to know. I'm calling because I need some information and I hope you can help me."

"Anything for you, Cousin Kay Kay."

"I knew I could count on you." She nodded. "I already promised Aunt Lucille that I'll keep in touch." She reminded him of the case involving her father, as if he needed reminding. His own father had gone down, too. "I need some information. Can you see what you can dig up about Trent Stewart? He was the cop responsible for Dad's death and the other troubles of the family."

"I remember the name. What do you have in mind?"

"Don't worry about that end of it. I just need for you to find out if he's still with the force."

"I don't need to check around. We were sitting around talking the other day. You know the reporters rehashed the whole case when that key witness, that Angela Whatever, showed up on the news from Chicago." He laughed. "I never knew anybody to blow protection like that before. Good thing we're not still interested." He laughed again. "Sitting duck." Again his laughs skipped over the phone. "They did a whole program around that case, dredged up anything and everything they could find from back then. Trent Stewart's name came up. The reporter mentioned that he left the force after he got shot during a crime bust. He's private, now."

"Too bad the shooter didn't finish the job."

"Trent Stewart is old business. That television program had no business pulling it up again. Every opportunity they get, they shine a light on us."

"Trent Stewart is why my father is gone."

"Look, I loved Big Tic. You know that. He was like a second father to me. But he knew the risks going into the business."

"Stewart got your father, too."

"Pop took it like a man. He'll be out in three months. They couldn't make enough stick to keep him for long."

"Don't you care?"

"Pop said that's the chance they took. He said it goes with the territory. They all knew that. They figured it was worth taking a chance. He said he's using this like a vacation. He said he's through. When he gets out, he said he's going back to the island." He laughed. "Of course, Ma said she ain't going nowhere." He laughed again. "We'll see who wins."

"Trent Stewart and Angela Baring killed my father."

"Too many years of too good eating was what killed Uncle Tic. It would have happened no matter where he was. Fact is, being in there might have bought him a little more time— no lobster with melted butter in prison."

"How dare you say something like that? If it wasn't for those two, he'd still be alive." Her voice climbed. "And how could you say that he was better off in prison? How could you think that he was happier in prison than he would have been at home with me?"

"That ain't what I meant. Of course he would rather have been at home. They all would. But it wasn't meant to be."

"Because of Trent Stewart and Angela Baring. That's why."

"Karen, you got to let it go. Big Tic would."

"No, he wouldn't. Neither should your father. What happened with him? That's not the Uncle Ken I used to know. I waited all this time for him to do something, but there wasn't anything from him. Did prison make him soft?"

"He's just tired, is all. He's just putting in his time and waiting to get free."

"Once they all believed in payback."

"That's why so many of them are gone."

"What happened to love of family? They preached that all the time: 'Take care of family. Family is all we got.' When did that change? You guys took over what they built. How can you forget something as important as family?"

"We didn't forget. We still honor their memory. We just move on. Anything else is a waste of time. You got to do the same."

Karen swallowed her response. She needed more information and arguing with Pretzels wasn't going to get it. Besides, if he didn't understand what she was saying, she couldn't make him. *She needed to get this over with. Was it possible to disown a cousin?* "Have you heard anything about the federal case that was tied to the Hunter case?"

"That we *were more* than a little interested in, even though we erased our tracks." Arrogance rode his words. "I guess the feds realized that they can't tie us into nothing from back then. The best they could have done was push an income tax charge and that was a weak case. Besides, all of the family members involved with the old business are inside or gone."

"Including Daddy."

"Yeah. Anyway, that case is history. They don't need Angela Baring, excuse me, Jane Johnson." He laughed. "Can you believe that she picked a name as common as Jane Johnson? But then, that's probably why she picked it. Must be a million in the country with that name. Kinda like Smith. Anyway, she's on her own, now. Hey"—he interrupted his own thoughts—"Why are you interested in all that old stuff now? Is it because the news of her heroics brought back memories? Why you asking questions? What you got in mind?"

"Nothing that concerns you."

"Where are you? Are you at home?"

"Thanks for the info."

"Kay Kay, don't do nothing stupid."

"Be talking to you, Pretzels." He was still talking when Karen hung up.

Too bad Stewart got shot two years too late. If he had been

*on his own that night when her world started to unravel.
. . .Karen* took a deep breath. *If he hadn't been playing bodyguard to nosy Angela Baring. . . .*

She shook her head. *I can't change what already happened, but I can see that he pays—that both of them pay. I
have to look at the plus side.*

*He's just a private citizen. Hitting him won't bring as much
heat as if he were still a police officer; they are so protective
of their own.* She nodded. *Oh, they'll try to solve his murder,
but they won't feel the kinship; it won't have top priority.* She
shrugged. That's one thing she and the police had in common:
loyalty to family. Determination was another.

She leaned back in the cheap chair, ignoring the creaks.
What were the chances that he just happened to come to the city
where the person whom he protected two years ago had relocated? About the same as winning the Powerball Lottery.

Even if he were still with the Philadelphia police, he was
way out of his jurisdiction here in Chicago, but he wasn't and
his private detective license was only a used sheet of paper.

She thought about the chill that seemed to be a constant in
the air. This certainly wasn't the best time to play tourist. She
shifted positions.

*I never did believe in coincidences and, at the age of forty,
I'm not about to start now. I just have to find him and use him
to find Angela. I know that's why he's here.* Her jaw tightened.
*In spite of losing him this morning, I'm a lot closer today than
I was last week at this time.*

She pulled the writing pad on the desk closer to her, picked
up the pen, but she only chewed on it. She had to make sure
she didn't blow this chance; she might not get another one.
*Two for the price of one was always a bargain when it was
something that you wanted.*

Her mind worked as her hand began to move. No words appeared. Instead doodles of points and sharp edges and bold
lines took their places on the page in front of her.

The shops? How could she best use the shops to help her?

Twenty-two

Angela hung up and walked over to Trent. She was so busy concentrating on the conversation that she had just had that she didn't notice how subdued Trent was. He smiled at her but it wasn't strong. She never noticed. He tried not to mind.

"I made arrangements to meet with whoever can make it. Dr. Case, the department head, was kind enough to offer to arrange things for me and to offer the use of his conference room. If he can set it up, we'll meet with them this evening or hopefully at least tomorrow so nobody has to take off from work on such short notice. I doubt if everybody's schedule will mesh. If necessary, I can meet with them at another time. My schedule is the most flexible."

"Don't worry; it will all work out."

She frowned at him. "You don't mind all of this, do you? I mean, it might delay your going home."

"I'm here with you for however long it takes."

She smiled. "Good. I told him that I don't expect anybody to dump their schedule for the interview. After he makes the contact, I can meet with them anywhere. It doesn't have to be at his office. If necessary, another meeting can be scheduled with the clients." Her smile widened. "It may take time, but I feel good about this. Dr. Case mentioned four names and gave me a short bio and résumé on each one. He's going to fax copies to me." She laughed. "He said that so many of his former students were using him as a reference that he made them give him résumés." She chuckled. "He said he told them that it cuts out part of the time if somebody comes to him looking for an accountant." She nodded. "He sounds like a really nice man. Anyway, from what he said, all four of them seem more than capable. Two are already handling accounts on their own and are looking to expand the number so they can work strictly for themselves. If all things are equal, I'll probably recommend one of them." She shook her head. "But I won't rule out anybody without an interview first. If my clients hadn't given me a chance, I would have had to take a nine-to-five job working for somebody else instead of building my own business."

Trent eased her into his arms. "Ah, but then you wouldn't have had the opportunity to be a superhero; you wouldn't have been walking home from work when that little girl was almost hit, because you wouldn't have been working walking distance from your house." Trent kissed her. "And you wouldn't have made the news and the Philly stations wouldn't have picked up the story."

She wrapped her hands around his shoulders. "And we wouldn't be here like this because you wouldn't have found me."

"Uh, uh." He shook his head. "Not true. I would have found you; it just would have taken me longer."

She kissed him and rested her head against his chest. Then she eased from his arms. "Now for the hard part. I may as well get started. I have to call my clients and tell them what's going on. I'm going to suggest that they meet the prospects with me and decide for themselves. This decision is too important for them to allow anybody else to make it for them." She laughed. "A big consideration is how well the personality of the accountant fits with that of the owner. You run into snags and clashes even when you're usually in agreement."

"What kind of snags? I figured you follow the guidelines and that's it. Isn't it just a matter of how long it takes to process the numbers?"

"It's not that simple. Often decisions have to be made about timing and about the pros and cons of each choice. I've had some hard times convincing somebody that one way was best when a different choice looked more favorable on the surface."

"I want to meet the accountant whose personality meshes with Mr. Hoffman's."

Angela laughed. "Mr. Hoffman is okay. He just has a strong personality."

"Yeah, and a giant redwood is just a tree."

"Okay. I'll admit that he can be strong willed. Anyway, one of the prospects is sure to fit." She frowned. "Hopefully, I'll be able to coordinate the times that the clients are available with the times the accountants can make it without lot of trouble. I think it would be easier all around if we can meet as a group at first." She shrugged. "After that they can meet separately if they want. I'll be out of it by then." She shrugged again. "They might even decide on different accountants. There's no rule that says that they're a package deal." She sighed. "I'm going to miss all of them. They're like family, now."

"You can come back and visit." He lifted her chin. "It's not like it's halfway around the world, you know."

"I know."

"And there is a thing called a telephone that lets you reach out and touch someone even when your arms aren't long enough."

"Yeah." She smiled. "You're right. You are so good for me." She kissed him.

"And don't you forget it." He kissed her.

"As if I could." She rested her head against his chest.

They were together with their bodies touching each other's, but each one's thoughts were on different paths. Finally Angela eased away.

"We still have to go over these reports and take them to my clients. I'll have to tell them today that I'm leaving because I need to check with them about setting up the interviews. I can't do that until I hear from Dr. Case." She chewed on her lower lip. "We should be able to have at least the initial meeting with some of the accounts in a day or so."

"Probably so."

She sat at the table and went back to the beginning of the report she had been reviewing, but again she stopped before she finished. "The clients who have shops in the area and I can probably meet with the prospects at Mamie's after the first meeting. It will be more convenient than going all the way to the campus. I know we'll need more than one meeting." She laughed. "We can even have a dinner meeting like the big executives do."

"Why not."

"Okay. Back to work." She went back to going over the report out loud and didn't stop. Then she put it aside and opened the next one.

Trent listened even though he knew he wouldn't have anything to do with them. He wasn't needed. She didn't need a guard anymore. Would she decide that she didn't need him period? He tried to drag his mind away from that thought.

"Okay," Angela said an hour later. "I think that's enough." She closed the last file after going over the contents one final time just as she had the others. Then she set it on top of the pile on the table beside her. She glanced at her watch. "That didn't take too long. We're ready for tomorrow." She stood.

"Wait a minute. Ready for tomorrow? After going over the reports only one time?" Trent stared at her as he scrambled from his seat. "When we went over the last reports, you acted as if I were studying for a test that an examiner wanted me to fail. Today it's as if my mama is the one who's going to decide if I pass or fail, and she has already written my name in the pass column and turned it in."

"Oh, poor, poor Trent." Angela gave him a quick kiss. "I hate to tell you, but today you're just a handsome face." She kissed him again. "Tomorrow, too." She smiled. "A very handsome face, I might add, but just a handsome face. Arm candy, I think is the way they put it."

"Really?" He cradled her within his arms. "I'm your arm candy?"

"Nobody else's." She rested her hands on his arms.

"Well, if that's the case"—he brushed his lips gently across hers—"I guess it's okay."

She laughed as she tucked the papers into her briefcase. "We can't do anything else until I find out how Dr. Case made out."

"You mean we have time on our hands and nothing to do with it?"

"You sound as if you have something in mind."

"Since I met you, I always have one thing in mind."

"Do I get a prize if I guess what it is?"

"I hope you consider it a prize and you get it without having to guess."

They met halfway across the room. As they walked into the bedroom, their thoughts were the same: *I hope Dr. Case takes a long time setting things up before he calls.* Then thoughts of Dr. Case were replaced by thoughts of love.

Angela turned from Trent's arms and reached for the ringing phone. Trent stirred and wrapped his arm back around her. It was difficult, but he kept his hands still and his lips to himself as she spoke.

"Okay." She turned toward him after a short conversation. "Miraculously, Dr. Case was able to set up a meeting with all four of the prospects for tomorrow evening at eight o'clock. I'll call the owners. Most of them close at seven. Those who don't, have somebody else working in the shops with them, so I hope most if not all of them can make it." She got up to get her appointment book. "I'd better call them now." She took a few steps and turned back. "You know, we have to stop meeting like this." A twinkle danced in her eyes. "You are throwing a twenty-four-hour schedule way out of kilter."

"I couldn't do it without a little help from you."

Their laughs mixed as if they belonged together.

Angela sat on the edge of the bed and began making calls. Trent forced himself from the bed to keep from distracting her. He went to the kitchen and started dinner. He smiled. *Is this a late lunch or an early dinner?*

He put the potatoes into the oven to bake. Then he started cutting the vegetables for the salad. The steaks had been marinating since he and Angela got up this morning. His smile widened. *Late* this morning. Lunch or dinner—what did it matter as long as they were together?

"Yes." Angela danced into the kitchen. "As George Peppard used to say on the *A-Team*, 'I love it when a plan comes together.'"

"I take it you met with a modicum of success."

"More than a modicum." She laughed. "Every last one can make it. A few had to adjust their schedules, but they said they'll be there." She stared at nothing. "All of them were sorry that I'm leaving. Mamie and Della took it hard." She shrugged. "I guess I should feel flattered." She shook her head. "What I do feel is guilt. I feel as if I'm abandoning them."

"Come here." Trent put down the salad tongs and opened his arms. Angela walked into them. "No guilt trips allowed. You will see that they are in good hands before you leave, right?"

She nodded. "Yeah."

"Okay then, Mother, it will be safe to leave your children with somebody else."

"You're right." She sniffed. "Something smells good."

"It's just a typical man's dinner: baked potato, salad, and steak."

"I want you to know that there is nothing typical about this male." She kissed him.

"Thank you, kind lady." He let her go. "Now come eat before it gets cold." He held a chair out for her.

"Yes, sir." Her smiled stayed on him as she sat down.

During the meal, excitement filled Angela's voice as she filled Trent in on the details of the conversations. He was content just to listen.

Wednesday morning, as soon as the stores were open, Angela and Trent left so she could make the last trip to her clients. She refused to allow her mind to hang on to the fact that this was her last visit in this capacity.

They talked about nothing and laughed about nothing as they rode to the first client in a strip mall a few miles away.

Angela tried to remember when she had felt this happy, this light, and she decided that the answer was never. The only cloud was seeing her clients after telling them that she was leaving.

She met with all of them and cried with a few, but she got through it. Sarah, who owned a small grocery store, was the worst.

"Child, what do you mean you're leaving?" The small woman put her hands on her hips. The top of her head would have reached just under Angela's chin. "First you come in here and convince me that I need your services. I ain't complaining about that. You were right. You showed me where I was throwing money away because of what I didn't know." She pinned her with a stare. "Whoever said what you don't know won't hurt you never found out the details of what he didn't know. Anyhow, you let me need you. On top of all that, then you go and crawl deep into my heart and sit there as tight as my grandchildren do. Now you're talking about abandoning me to some stranger."

"Miss Sarah, I promise, I won't leave until you're satisfied with my replacement."

"Humph. Can't nobody replace you."

"That's sweet of you." Angela kissed her cheek. "Of course, when I first introduced myself to you, you insisted that you didn't need me, that you were doing perfectly well on your own."

"Young folks ain't got no corner of the dumb market." Her stare softened. "You sure you got to go?"

"I'm sure."

"He got anything to do with your decision to leave?" She stared at Trent.

"No. I just want to go home. Dorothy was right: 'There's no place like home.'"

"Well, if you're sure you gotta go . . ."

"I'm sure."

"Child, I am gonna miss you something fierce." She wrapped her strong arms around Angela.

"I'll miss you, too. You're one of my favorites."

"Bet you tell that to all your clients."

"I do not." She held the woman close.

"Well, I guess I best not let on at the meeting tonight. Don't want to cause no hurt feelings." She laughed. "I am gonna miss you." She gave Angela a quick squeeze and let go. "You best move on to the next heart you're fixing to break."

"Miss Sarah. . . ." Angela shook her head.

"Go on with you, now. I'll see you tonight. Don't you be late."

"Yes, ma'am. I won't be late."

Angela wiped her tears, even though more were still falling. Trent patted her shoulder and opened the car door for her. He let her cry it out as he took her to the next client, hoping it wouldn't be as bad on her.

Twenty-three

Hours later the sun was slanting its light through the trees along King Street as if it were weary from a trying day. Angela knew how it felt. She had explained her leaving to each store owner over the phone, but she had to do it all over again in person for every one of them. They accepted it, but everybody let her know that they didn't like it. She should have felt flattered; instead, no matter how encouraging Trent was, she felt as if she were letting them down.

When she finally finished with the last client, she felt as if she had shed the tears stored up for the rest of her life.

"You made it through." Trent pulled her close after they left Tony's Shoe Repair shop. He held her close as if trying to ease her loss. She nestled close and just stood within the circle of his arms.

"I don't know what I would have done without you with me."

"You would have done all right." He kissed the top of her head.

"I don't know about that. I'm glad I didn't have to find out."

"I'm glad I was here." He stepped away. "How about stopping some place for dinner? We'll be pushing it if we go all the way back to the apartment and try to cook something before the meeting with Dr. Case."

Angela glanced at her watch. "Wow. I didn't realize that it was so late."

"When you have to take a difficult oral exam, not once but ten times in a row, plus the time it took to get from one place to another, it's understandable that time got away from you." He smiled. "From us."

Angela smiled back. "That's right." Her face brightened. "How about someplace different?"

"Fine with me."

"I haven't taken you to Needa's. Let's go there. It's not far from campus. My house isn't very far either, so we can stop before or after the meeting. I need to pick up my mail. Who knows what's waiting for me."

"Maybe you won a million dollars and they decided to send it to you instead of delivering it in person."

"Yeah. Or maybe a spaceship from Venus is parked in the yard and the space travelers are waiting for me to welcome them."

They both laughed. By the time they reached the restaurant, Angela's eyes had been dry for a while.

They made their way to the small restaurant that was squatting in the middle of a small lot. The sign read Needa's, as if everybody knew what they'd find there. From the looks of the parking lot, that was true.

"It's crowded. Will we have enough time before the meeting?"

"They're always crowded. They're also very fast. Needa's is proof that you can get good food fast."

They were lucky enough to be seated right away.

"Hi, Miss Bessie," Angela greeted the older waitress as she set two glasses of water on the table. "What's good and yet fast today?"

"You been here before, so you know it's all good and fast. Raheem, in the kitchen, holds the record for getting a meal on the table in record time." She laughed. "We tell him that he should be in the record books." She laughed again. "If it's got to be super fast, though, you might want tonight's special: fried catfish with the trimmings."

"You are speaking my language," Angela said.

"I know what you mean." Bessie leaned close. "I sneaked a taste of the first batch. It will make you wish you had a bigger stomach. Raheem had to chase me out of his kitchen. And of course you can't have catfish without cornbread. His cornbread will melt in your mouth as fast as the butter on it. That and a side of greens and sweet potatoes make a perfect meal. We'll talk about the peach cobbler later." She leaned close again. "I made that."

"Needa should pay you for advertising."

"I told her that. She said it's the least her sister can do for her."

Angela laughed. "You know I have to have that whole package."

"What about you, handsome?" Bessie looked at Trent.

"I'll have the same."

"Sure thing." She looked at Angela. "Is this handsome prince special to you?"

"Yes, ma'am." Angela's smile softened. "Trent is very special to me."

"Well, that don't matter none. If I was twenty years younger, I'd battle you for him." She glanced at Trent again. "Better make that thirty."

They all laughed as she walked away.

"Needa's not one of your clients."

Angela shook her head. "No. She has a son who is a CPA." She shrugged. "I can't handle all of the accounts in Chicago anyway." She looked at Trent and smiled. "That doesn't make her food any less tasty. Everything I have ordered is delicious. I don't know what the secret seasoning ingredient is, but wait until you taste it for yourself."

"How did you find out about Needa's?"

"Would you believe, Mamie told me?" Angela laughed. "She said she eats here when she wants to get away from her own cooking."

"You're kidding."

"I said something about competition and she told me that there are more than enough hungry folks to go around."

The restaurant lived up to its reputation about being fast; Bessie brought their meals fifteen minutes later.

After they both agreed that the food was the best they had ever tasted, neither Angela nor Trent let words get in the way of their enjoyment of it.

"Ready for dessert?" Bessie smiled at them.

"You have got to be kidding." Angela patted her stomach. "Another crumb and I'll burst."

"Same here." Trent leaned back.

"There's always tomorrow. You don't want to get up tomorrow morning with a taste for something sweet and remember that you didn't get some of my cobbler. Then you'd have to come all the way over here because your stomach, not to mention your mouth, won't give you no peace until you do." She laughed. "It don't need nothing else, but you warm it in the oven, drop a scoop of vanilla ice cream on it and you'll hope the angels serve it when you get to Heaven."

"Okay, okay." Angela laughed. "Two cobblers to go."

Bessie returned so fast it was as if she had anticipated their order and had it ready.

They got to the campus and parked without too much trouble. It was 7:45 when, after asking a couple of students, they found Bailey Hall.

"Wait a minute," Angela said, when Trent reached for the door. She took a deep breath and let it out slowly. "Okay. I guess I'm ready for this."

Trent touched her shoulder and put his hand on her back. She relaxed as they made their way down the hall.

When they reached Dr. Case's office, Angela paused in the hall. She was about to lose what had been a big part of her life for the past two years. *Is this how empty nesters feel?*

Trent squeezed her shoulder. "You can do this," he whispered in her ear and she believed him. She straightened her back and walked into the room.

After introducing herself and Trent, the two of them followed Dr. Case across the hall and into the conference room. She stopped just inside and greeted the large group.

All of the owners were there already. Those who had spouses brought them along. A young woman and a young man sat apart from the others.

"I told them that you'd be early." Mr. Hoffman sat at the far corner. "Never known you to be late."

"Nobody said anything different," Mamie said.

"So. These are the folks you been spending your time with, huh?" Mr. Hoffman said, as he looked around the room.

"It's nice to meet the rest of the family." Sarah nodded at Angela. Angela swallowed a lump and hoped the tears that were threatening went with it. She couldn't manage any words, so she smiled and hoped that was answer enough.

"Don't seem like nobody else is as ornery as Hal." Mamie smiled at Mr. Hoffman.

"I'm not ornery. I'm just thorough." He smiled at her. "You keep talking like that and I might forget to let you know when I get a shipment of that tea that you like so much."

"And I just might forget to send you a piece of my coconut cake when I make it."

As they all laughed, two more people came in and greeted Dr. Case and then spoke to everyone else.

Dr. Case introduced the four, then excused himself. "My part in this is over." He turned to Angela. "I'll be in my office when you're finished."

Then it was Angela's turn. She told them what she had been doing and how she approached the records. Then it was time for the candidates to speak.

All of the owners listened without asking questions; even Mr. Hoffman, but when the candidates finished, everyone had questions. Angela mostly sat and listened, but several times she had to fill in information to clarify the questions.

Two and a half hours later, Angela was confident that every owner would be satisfied with one of the candidates. From the way the questioning went, she would be surprised if they all picked the same one. In fact, after having sat in on the meeting, having heard their questions and the way they interacted, she was amazed that *she* had managed to work with all of them successfully. When the questions stopped, she stood.

"If there are no more questions, I guess that's it." She blinked and tried to do a good imitation of a brisk business person. Maybe that would help her get through this. "You owners have the information you need so you can contact your new accountant directly." She paused and swallowed hard. "You don't need me anymore." Again she had to stop. Trent reached for her hand and squeezed gently. "Still, you know how to reach me." She managed a smile even though tears were closer. "Again, thank you for coming on such short notice. I really appreciate it." She waited for them to leave, for somebody to stand, for anybody to say something. Finally Della got up from her seat at the far side of the table.

"We want you to know how much we appreciate what you did for us. Even though, from what I heard"—she looked at Hal—"you had to drag some of us from the Dark Ages. We want you to know that we are grateful for what you did. We have this small token of appreciation for you."

The tears that Angela had been holding back escaped as if somebody had suddenly removed a barrier. She could only watch as Della reached beside her chair and pulled out a set of luggage with a huge red ribbon tied around it. Angela's tears increased.

"Just so you don't think we don't wish you well in your move," Sarah added.

"You guys." Angela shook her head. "You shouldn't . . ."

"Don't say we shouldn't have," Mr. Hoffman said. "Because of your fine work, we can afford to do something like this." He frowned and stared at the table. "I'm gonna miss you," he mumbled. Then he cleared his throat as if he could cover the words before anyone else could hear them.

After being hugged by everyone, Angela felt, more than ever, that she was losing her family.

"I know you don't have no business with us no more, but you better not go away from here without coming by to say good-bye." Sarah hugged her again before she left the room wiping her own eyes.

They worded it differently, but one by one each client said the same thing. Angela had to promise to stop by each shop before she left. Finally the last one was gone. She stared at the empty seats until the last footsteps had drifted away. Then she turned to Trent.

"I guess I'm ready to go."

Trent brushed a tear from her cheek before he picked up the luggage. After a final thank you to Dr. Case, they left the building.

During the ride to her house, Angela struggled to gain control of her emotions. She sniffled a couple of times. Trent reached for her hand and held it the whole time.

"It's going to be okay. The worst is over and you got through it as well as anybody could." He squeezed her hand.

It was well after eleven by the time Angela opened the door to her house. She stared at the sweet grass basket on the small mahogany table in the hall. This wouldn't be her home much longer. Should she take the basket with her?

"Something the matter?" Trent touched her shoulder.

"I was just thinking about how I'll miss this house."

"The end of one thing always leads to the beginning of another." He kissed the side of her face. "I'll be there to help you make the change." He stepped away.

"I'm counting on it." Angela gathered the mail covering the floor. "I hope most of this is junk and won't take much time."

Trent helped pick up a batch. "Since it's so late, do you want to spend the night here?"

"I think that's a good idea. There's no reason why we have to go back tonight." She went into the dining room and Trent followed her.

"True. We're both here. Where we are doesn't matter as long as that doesn't change." He kissed her, then went to get the wastebasket from the kitchen. When he came back he set it down beside her and went to the back of the house.

From force of habit he checked each room. When he got to her bedroom, memories of what had happened between them since they left here flooded back to him. He relished reliving them.

After he was satisfied that everything in the house was just as they had left it, he went back to the dining room and sat opposite Angela.

Love and desire for her filled him. What had he done to earn this? Why did he deserve to have her in his life? He couldn't think of a single thing.

"Trent?"

"Huh."

"You were so far away from here it's a wonder you got back so quickly. Where were you?"

"With you."

"I mean just now?"

"So do I." He looked sheepish. "I didn't believe that old Willy Nelson song until I met you."

What song?" Her eyes opened wide and her mouth hung open. "Willy Nelson? The country and western singer? You listen to country and western?"

"Shh. Don't tell anyone. They might put me out of the brotherhood."

"You listen to country and western." She shook her head.

"I listen to everything. Classical, jazz, contemporary, oldies, and, yes, occasionally, country and western. A lot of them tell great stories. The particular song that I was thinking about is 'Always on My Mind.'"

"Oh." She smiled. "I've heard that one."

"Ha. Gotcha."

"I'm sure somebody else recorded it, too." She tried to act indignant but it didn't work. She shrugged. "I have to admit, there's something about his delivery of a song." She smiled again. "Is it true? What you said about the song being true, I mean?"

"Absolutely."

"Well, I can think of several songs that remind me of you, but they are a little closer to the hood. Luther, James Ingram, early R. B. Kelly." She sighed. "Anything and everything by Luther." She sighed again.

"Hey, you're going to make me jealous."

"I'm thinking of you when I listen to him."

"I guess that's okay, then."

She laughed. "Anyway, I asked if you want me to wait until tomorrow to go over the rest of this mail? There's so much of it."

"There won't be any less if you wait until tomorrow. Go ahead and finish. I know how it is when you have a ton of mail and you want to check it right away. I've been in that fix several times when I had to go out of town on a job and I was gone longer than I expected." He was so busy smiling at her that he didn't see the frown that flitted across her face. "I'll still be here when you finish."

Her smile came back and she continued.

Trent left once to get a pitcher of water and two glasses. Then he settled across from her. He picked up a magazine and was glancing through it when she caught his attention.

"Here's something you can do."

"Something I can do? What do you mean?"

"You can teach classes."

"Teach classes?"

"Yeah, you know, self-defense, how to make your home safe. That kind of thing." She held up a brochure that came in the mail. "They always have classes like that for the community. I know they have them at home. The universities offer them to the students. Unfortunately, there's always a need for training like that."

"I have a job. Remember?"

"I mean instead of being a private detective."

"I like what I do."

"But it's not safe."

"I thought we went over this already."

"We didn't discuss you doing anything else specifically."

He stared at her. No softness showed on his face. "What I do was good enough when I was protecting you."

"I-I'm not saying it isn't good enough. I'd worry about your safety every time you were on a job."

"Case."

"Huh?"

"Case. I have cases." He leaned back in his chair. "Some people are policemen. Some build skyscrapers. Some fight fires. Some fight wars. My work is nothing compared to what they do. I could get killed crossing a street. You could have been, too."

"Those were accidents. You said so yourself."

"That's true and that's my point. At any given moment somebody could be in danger at any given place. I learned that along with the rest of the country." His jaw tightened. "I'm a private detective."

"I'd worry every time you went out of the house. I couldn't stand going through that every day."

He stood and stared at her. "Are you saying that I have to choose you or my work?"

"I don't know why you can't consider it."

"And I don't know why you have to change me."

"I-I'm not trying to change you. I just want you to be considerate of me."

"I haven't been considerate?"

"You know what I mean."

He stared at her. "Yeah, I think I do." He left the room.

"Where are you going?"

"I'm going to take a little walk."

"Think about what I said?"

"I'll think about anything I damn well please."

He closed the door quietly behind him, leaving Angela with the silence that filled the air.

A few minutes later she put aside the rest of the mail. She had no idea what the last two pieces were about. Then she leaned her arms on the table and waited for Trent to come back to her.

Twenty-four

Somewhere a church bell had sounded its maximum allotment and had started over with one. Still Angela sat at the table as if tied to the chair. *How did we go from "Always on My Mind" to this?* She blinked hard. *More importantly, how are we going to get back?*

She was still trying to figure that out when she heard Trent at the door. She wanted to run to him and fling herself into his arms. She wanted to tell him that nothing else mattered as long as they were together. She wanted to, but she didn't because it was a lie. She knew that she'd die a little each day he went on a job. She shook her head. A case. She shook her head again. It didn't matter what you called it, the danger was still there.

"You're still up?"

"I-I was waiting for you."

"You shouldn't have. You've had a long, hard day."

"You've been up just as long."

"Angela, I think it's best if I sleep in your guest bedroom tonight."

"What?"

"We have a lot to work out." He sighed. "We both need to take a step backward. We can't if we're acting as if we're joined at the hip."

"Do you want to talk about it?"

He laughed, but bitterness was where happiness belonged. "I think we talked enough for tonight, don't you?"

"I . . ."

"I'll see you in the morning."

He left the room and Angela stayed in the chair, waiting for reality to sink in and free her. Finally she trudged into her bedroom.

When she crawled between the sheets, she tried not to remember how it felt to have Trent's arms wrapped around her. The tears that fell to her pillow didn't help get rid of the memories. She ached for him. How could he decide to sleep apart so easily? He must not love her as much as she did him.

She turned over onto her back. *What about me? I gave him an ultimatum.* She shook her head. She wished she had found a better approach. Could she fix things tomorrow? Would he let her try? And how could she if he did?

The brightness flooding the room was a lot different from the way Angela felt. Sleeping on the situation hadn't helped her at all.

She got up because she felt she should and got dressed because that was what people did in the morning. She heard Trent stirring and, for the first time since they had been together, she didn't look forward to seeing him. *You can't stay in here all day,* she told herself. She took a deep breath and followed his sounds.

"Good morning." She tried to search his eyes for the warmth that usually greeted her. Not a trace was showing.

"Good morning." He stared at her for a few seconds and then poured his coffee.

"I-I thought I'd make pancakes. I know how you like them."

"Whatever is easy." He shrugged. "It doesn't matter." He shrugged again. "I'm not very hungry."

"Pancakes it is." She knew he wasn't talking about just food. Would he ever want her again? Why was he being so stubborn?

She got out the box of mix and the frying pan. Trent took his coffee to the dining room table.

He can't even stand to stay in the same room with me any more.

Angela mixed the batter, wishing she were making the pancakes from scratch. She'd have to concentrate more on that and maybe the rift between her and Trent wouldn't hold her attention. She sighed. She doubted it even as she thought it. The rift was too new, too wide, too deep.

She went to the cupboard. Syrup. She had never bought more after she used the last of it three weeks ago.

"I have to go to the store for syrup."

"Do you want me to go?"

Was he anxious to get away from her again today? "That's okay. I'll go."

His answer was a shrug.

She left not expecting a good-bye kiss and didn't get one, either. *How can we fix this? Things are worse than they were last night.*

"I never saw this coming," Trent said to the empty house. He put down the days old paper that he had taken from the coffee table. It didn't matter that the paper was old; he had no idea what he had read anyway. *What are we going to do?*

He went to get another cup of coffee as if that would help.

When the phone rang about half an hour later, he still hadn't formed an answer. He doubted that such a thing existed. "Hello."

"I'm sorry. I must have the wrong number."

"Wait. Is this Miss Sarah?"

"Yes. Why, you're Jane's young man."

Not right now, Trent thought. *Maybe not ever again.* "This is Trent."

"I'm probably ruining a surprise, but I never could keep my big mouth shut on good news." She laughed. "I got no trouble stifling bad news, but good news, well, that's another story. I just got to let it go when I get hold of it."

"Jane had to run to the store. I'll bet you decided on a new accountant. I'm glad you could decide so quickly. I know An . . ." He stopped. It was too complicated to explain Angela's name change. Besides, it didn't matter. She was leaving the people who knew her as Jane. "Jane will be happy. She feels so guilty about leaving."

"I didn't mean for her to feel guilty. I understand that young folks got to move on." She laughed again. "Old folks, too, sometimes."

"I'll have her call you when she gets back."

"Hold on, now. It's true that I settled my mind on Mindy Calhoun for my new accountant. Notice I didn't say as Jane's replacement. Nobody can replace her. She's real special."

"Yes, she is." *And I'm letting her slip away from me as if she doesn't mean a thing in my life.*

"Anyway, that's not why I'm calling. I got good news for Jane that's about her."

"What kind of good news?"

"You won't believe this. I had a visit a few minutes ago from a nice lady looking for Jane."

"What lady?"

"This lady, Sara Willis, was by here. Ain't it something that we got the same name? Spells her different, though. Anyway, she came by here looking for information about Jane."

"What kind of information?" Trent straightened. "What did she want?"

"She said her organization wants to reward Jane for saving that little girl's life. She said not enough is done to recognize good deeds. I agreed with her. You know, every day the paper is full of dreadful news. We need to read about good things every now and again."

Trent stood and started for the door glad for the invention of the cordless phone. "Tell me about it. What organization was she from?"

"She . . . Just a minute. I got to find that business card. Now, where did I put it?" Trent heard papers crackling. "I swear, I got to clean up this mess. I can't find nothing." The rustling of papers replaced Miss Sarah's voice.

It seemed to Trent that it took Miss Sarah ten hours to come back. It was good that she put the phone down. If she hadn't, he would have yelled at her and flustered her and it might have taken her twenty hours. *Should I go look for An-*

gela? What store did she go to? Which way did she go? Will she come straight back?

"Here it is. Let's see. Her name is Sara Willis and she's from the Citizens' Appreciation Association. I never heard of them but anybody doing good for somebody is all right. Like I said, she asked me not to tell, but I can't keep my mouth shut on good news. I lasted about twenty minutes."

"She left your store twenty minutes ago?"

"Give or take a few." She laughed. "That's a record for me." She laughed again. "My old age must be slowing me down. There was a time when I would have burned up the phone lines before the person left."

"What did you tell her?"

"At first I gave her Jane's phone number, but she wanted her address. Miss Willis said she liked to see the faces when she gave them the news."

"You gave her this address?"

"Yes. It's all right, isn't it?"

"Is there a phone number on the card?"

"Right here. You got to go get a pen or do you have one?"

"I'm ready." Trent forced his hand to form clear numbers on the memo pad beside the phone. Then he forced himself to be polite as he ended the conversation after promising to let Miss Sarah know what happened. *I hope I won't have anything except good news to tell her.*

Maybe it's legitimate, he thought, as he dialed the number, but deep down he knew it wasn't.

"The number you have called," the fake voice repeated the number, "is not in service. Please . . ."

He didn't wait for the rest of the instructions.

Damn. How did I mess up? Who did I overlook?

He dashed out of the house, ignoring the protest coming from his leg. After all the trouble he went through to bring his gun with him and register it, he had left it back at the apartment. *Sloppy. Careless. Incompetent. Please don't let it cost Angela.*

He got outside and took the steps down two at a time. His left leg continued to fuss and hung on to its stiffness, but it held him. He saw Angela at the corner and everything happened at once.

The air filled with enough cacophony to form a perverse orchestra with just a little lag time between the unusual instruments.

"Angela, get down." Trent cursed the stiffness in his leg slowing him down as he ran toward her.

She turned from the side of her car and toward him. A bang split the air before she finished following his direction. A fire like the tip of a lightning bolt slammed into her and she went the rest of the way down.

Immediately Karen turned toward Trent and released another bang before he could take his own advice. He stumbled and fell as if imitating Angela's movement.

Next, with her gun hand outstretched, Karen moved into the street and toward Angela, who was sprawled on the sidewalk closer to her than Trent was.

"Hey, lady!"

Air brakes squealed, tires squeaked, a horn blared, one heavy shout, and a host of weaker voices joined in. Then all of the loud noises shut up, leaving just voices and running footsteps to take their places in the air.

A black shoe lay on its side all alone in the street as if marking the spot for somebody.

Twenty-five

As if somebody were giving directions, the crowd divided into three, each picking a person to form circle around. Even though the three people had been some distance apart when the action started, by the time everything stopped, the three circles were not far apart at all.

"What do you think that was all about?" A short woman stopped at Trent, but spoke to the man who was able to answer—the one standing nearby.

"Unless the dealers have gotten older and females are involved, I doubt if we have to worry that this is about some drug mess moving in on our street." He frowned and shook his head. "Who knows what this is about."

"I called 9-1-1." A younger woman came from the house on the corner.

"Anybody know any of them?"

"This one lives over there next door to me." The older woman standing near Angela pointed to a house a few doors down. "Her name is Jane Johnson. I welcomed her to the block when she moved in, but I haven't seen much of her."

"I've seen her on the street, too. Kind of keeps to herself, but she spoke friendly like when she saw me," another said.

"Any of you folks know this lady?" The truck driver stood over Karen. "She stepped right in front of me." He shook his head. "I never saw anything like it." He struggled to breathe. "I got a clean driving record. I wasn't speeding." His stare wouldn't leave her. "I never even got a ticket." He swallowed hard. "How could she not see my rig, big as it is?"

"She was too busy with this here gun." An elderly man touched the gun beside Karen's hand with the toe of his shoe.

"I never seen *her* around here. Anybody ever see her before?" A small woman looked around. Her question, loud enough to be heard by all three groups, was met with head shakes and mumbled "nos."

"Shouldn't we do something?" A tall gray-haired man stepped closer to Trent and leaned over. "Don't seem right that we should just wait. They might be dying or something."

A young woman stepped in the middle of the groups. "I'm a nurse. We shouldn't move anybody. I'll see if anyone needs emergency aid until the ambulances get here." She started toward Angela and noticed the fluttering of her chest.

"This one just moved," a man standing over Trent announced.

"Here comes the ambulance," a teenaged young man announced, as if the others couldn't hear the sirens crying closer.

"This lady hasn't moved a finger." A thin woman standing near Karen said. She bent over as if to make sure she had spoken the truth. The nurse rushed to her.

"You wouldn't move either, if you were hit by a big truck." A young woman wrinkled her nose and stepped back.

The nurse knelt and felt for a pulse. Carefully she rolled Karen over. She hesitated, then began CPR. She was still trying to bring her back when the EMT arrived and one took over for her.

All three crowds retreated, but they stopped when they got on the sidewalk. A police car arrived as did another ambulance. The crowd stood as if watching a movie up close.

Two little boys and a girl chased around in a game of tag weaving in and out of the adults as if they wanted to do something, too, but this was all they could think of.

The man working on Karen stopped first. He shook his head and covered the body. "Call it," he said to his partner.

"You got her name?"

The other man pulled a wallet from the purse beside the body. "Her driver's license says Karen Weston, but she has a bunch of business cards that say Sara Willis." He shrugged and kept looking. "Everything else says Karen Weston so I guess that's it." He frowned. "From Philadelphia." He shook his head as he handed the wallet to the man recording the information. "She came a long way to get killed."

The policeman finished gathering information from the driver. Then he moved to the crowd. The look on his face said that he hoped all of their stories were alike.

"Did you say Karen Weston?" Trent struggled to sit. The top of his shoulder felt as if the devil had touched him with a finger and left it there.

"That's what her ID says."

How had he missed this possibility? He was so busy thinking with a different part of his anatomy instead of his head. His sloppiness almost cost Angela her life. He stared at her and tried to stand.

"Don't try to get up." The woman technician touched his other arm.

Angela moaned when they slit her sleeve and put a temporary bandage on her arm. She moaned again when they lifted her onto a stretcher, but she didn't open her eyes with either moan.

"I have to get to Angela." He stood in spite of the hand on his shoulder trying to hold him down. The finger of fire poked around in his left shoulder and dizziness moved through his head; still he stayed on his feet.

"Which one is Angela?" He glanced at the technician speaking to him and then at the stretcher being placed in the ambulance.

"Over there." He started toward it.

"Hey, come back. What's your name?" She followed him. "You need to stay here."

"Trent Stewart and I need to be with her." Between his shoulder and his left leg, which he had twisted when he went down, he understood firsthand the term "walking wounded." He ignored the pain. "I'm riding with her." The stare he gave the technician closest to him kept any disagreement away.

"Are you a relative?"

"Just about."

The man hesitated, then helped him into the truck. The red on the bandage around Trent's arm spread.

"You shouldn't move that arm. In fact, you shouldn't do anything except wait until a doctor sees you."

"How is she?" Trent dropped down on the bench opposite the stretcher. He eased Angela's hand into his.

"The bullet is still in her shoulder. A few inches lower and to the right and I'd be a whole lot more concerned." He sat beside Trent. "Or maybe no longer concerned at all. Also, she banged her head pretty hard, so she might have a slight concussion. Nothing life-threatening, though." He stared at Trent. "Are you her husband?"

"Not yet." He brushed the hair from Angela's forehead and kissed her.

"You say her name is Angela?" The technician started to fill in the first space of the form on his clipboard. "Angela what?"

"She's known as Jane Johnson. I call her Angela." He shrugged instead of giving an explanation. No sense complicating the situation right now.

The technician glared at him, ripped the top sheet from the pad, and started all over.

When he got to the part about insurance, Trent took Angela's wallet from her purse and found the information.

He had to concentrate to answer the questions when he had to give information about himself.

The ambulance roared down the streets with the siren warning everybody to get out of the way. Trent rubbed Angela's hand, trying to move her pain to him. *I almost lost her.* He closed his eyes and gave thanks for a second chance.

They got to the hospital in fifteen minutes, where, despite Trent's protests, they separated him from Angela.

"Mr. Stewart, the sooner you let us examine Miss Johnson, the sooner we can let you be with her," the nurse told him. "Besides, you have to be examined, too. Don't try to tell me," the nurse added when Trent started to speak, "that it's just a scratch. I've seen enough scratches and enough gunshot wounds to know the difference between the two. Bullets do not cause scratches."

Trent sighed and let Angela's hand go. The nurse was right. If nothing else, he had to let them make sure that there wasn't something the matter with Angela that the EMT missed.

He watched as they took her into an examination room. Then he followed the nurse into the next one so they could examine him. *I almost lost her.* He shook his head, trying to dislodge that thought as they checked him.

After they finished with him, Trent called the chief back home. His reaction when Trent filled him in matched Trent's when he had learned Karen's identity.

"I never considered this. Big Tic died of a heart attack. Everybody knew he had a bad heart for years. Before we got him, some of the guys were taking bets on who would get him first: us or death." His sigh drifted over the phone lines. "I must have lost a step." Another sigh eased out. "I'm glad my mistake didn't cost Angela her life. I am truly sorry."

"You can't take all of the blame. I should have considered this possibility. Instead I let love affect my common sense."

He hung up, but what might have happened kept him company as he waited.

What seemed like hours later, the nurse came to get him from the waiting room. The pain in his arm had dulled to an ache. The one in his leg had calmed to a hard throb, but he stood.

"You can see her now, if you want to."

"Is she okay?" *If he wanted to? It was clear that the nurse didn't understand what was between them.*

"She's going to be fine. We removed the bullet. We're admitting her and keeping her overnight just for observation, but we expect to send her home tomorrow morning." She told Trent Angela's room number and directed him to the elevators.

Trent lied his way into her room by claiming to be her fiancé. If she allowed it, that would no longer be a lie. He sighed. *How could she not allow it?*

He slanted the chair beside her bed and sat. His leg spiked one protest when he bent it and then settled back to a throb.

Trent eased Angela's hand from the top of the blanket to his. *It's cold.* He slowly rubbed soft circles, willing warmth back. Then he sat, just holding her hand.

As if sensing his presence, Angela turned her face toward him. "Are you all right?" Her voice was thinner than usual.

"Am *I* all right? I'm not the one in the hospital bed."

"Are you?" She moved to sit up but grabbed her shoulder and lay back down.

"I'm fine, now that you're back with us."

"You're hurt." She nodded toward his shoulder.

"There's a lot of that going around." He pointed to hers. For the first time in what seemed like weeks, he smiled.

"What happened?"

After Trent filled her in, she continued to stare at him. She squeezed his hand. "You saved my life. Again." She blinked. "You're good at what you do. I . . ."

"Angela, I've been thinking . . ."

"Let me finish. It was unfair of me to ask you to give up your career. I love you. If you still want me, I'll take you as you are. I can learn to live with the dangers." She smiled. "After all, you never know what fate has in store for us. I'm an accountant and I've almost been killed four times." She brushed a finger along his hand. "I'll bet that's more than you have, in spite of your work."

Trent brought her hand to his mouth and kissed it. "I've had time to think." He shook his head. "If I hadn't stumbled, I might have been able to keep you from being shot."

"You probably would have gotten killed." She swallowed hard. "If you hadn't gone down, the bullet would have hit your chest."

"It took something like this to realize that my time working cases is past." He rubbed his leg. "The shoulder will heal. I don't think the leg will ever be back to the way it was before I took that bullet in it." He smiled at her. "And I'm okay with that." He squeezed her hand. "The only thing I wouldn't be all right with would be if you don't agree to marry me."

"Marry you?" Tears started trickling down Angela's face. "You want me to marry you?"

"Why so surprised? Did you think that I'm one of those love them and leave them guys?"

"No. I just . . ." She shrugged.

"So, what do you say? Will you marry me?"

"Of course I will. How could you think I'd say anything else except yes?"

"I don't take anything for granted after what happened." He shook his head. "I should have seen the possibility. When I think of how close I came to losing you . . ."

"The chief didn't, either. Don't get stuck on what might have happened." She squeezed his hand. "Look at it this way: it brought us back together."

"We would have gotten over the rift anyway. While you were gone, I had decided to tell you that I was changing careers."

She laughed. "And I had decided to tell you that I'd live with whatever you do as long as we're together."

"Do you know what this means?" Trent stood and leaned over her.

"What?"

"An endless supply of dessert." He brushed her lips with his. She wrapped her good arm around his neck and deepened the kiss.

The same thought settled in both minds: A lifetime of desserts.

Twenty-six

Mamie's looked as if a fairy godmama had waved her magic wand and transformed the restaurant into a wedding chapel, but in reality, Angela's clients had spent hours performing their handiwork to make the transformation.

White crepe paper curled with colored to form swags crisscrossing the ceiling in a loose weave. A large white paper wedding bell was fastened to each end when it reached the wall.

More bells, in strong shades of blue, pink, yellow, and purple hung from what were normally plain brass sconces scattered along the walls. A white lattice-work arch, decorated with lilies and flowers of every variety to be found, was in place at one end of the room as if it belonged there all the time.

The chairs, divided in two to make an aisle, faced the arch as if waiting for the show. People, most of whom knew each other, introduced themselves to those who didn't. They all had one thing in common: they all knew Angela and Trent.

The chief was sitting with Captain Ellers and Trent's other friends from Philadelphia. Miss Delsey had surprised Trent by flying for the first time.

"I couldn't let my June Bug take a wife without me there to see it," she had explained. "I owe it to Sadie and Joe."

Trent's brother, Robert, sat with his wife Clara, and their son to witness Trent's day of happiness. Isaiah sat with his fiancée, Dottie, who had announced after the dinner the night before, "I'm getting married next whether I catch the bouquet or not."

DaVita and Ben sat with their two kids who looked longingly at their little cousins sitting two rows in front. Their faces said, "Hurry up so we can play." Jeanine, still suffering from jet lag from her flight the day before, was in the back room with Angela and the others, even though the older women didn't let her near her soon-to-be sister-in-law. She stood back and smiled as the women fussed around Angela.

"I reckon that's as good as we can get it." Sarah patted the crownlike headpiece on Angela's head.

"Wait a minute." Mamie smoothed out a sleeve. "There."

"Not quite." Della brushed the other sleeve.

"We have to stop this. Everyone's waiting." Angela took a step away from the women hovering around her. One step was all that was possible since every one of her female clients had insisted on helping her get ready. Mamie had shifted things in her office to turn it into a bride's dressing room, but it was never meant to hold so many people.

"Let us check things one more time." Sarah stood as straight as her barely five feet would allow her and stared at Angela.

Angela smiled at them; her adopted mothers and grandmothers were each dressed in a different deep rainbow color. She was glad that Trent had agreed to have the wedding here instead of Philadelphia. These people had become her family.

Her smile widened as she caught the glance of her soon-to-be sister-in-law. Soon she'd have a new family.

"Lovely, just lovely." Della sighed, as she looked at Angela in her lace-covered calf-length wedding dress, bringing her attention back to the moment.

Angela touched the locket, a gift from Trent, settled against her skin. The scalloped neckline of the cream-colored dress provided a frame. The hem of the dress was edged with scalloped lace that matched that at the neckline.

"These lace sleeves really set the gown off," Mamie said.

"Perfect," Della added, and they all nodded in agreement.

"What's holding you up in there?" Mr. Hoffman's voice accompanied a knock on the door. "Everybody's waiting. I told the fellas that we never should have let all you women into that room at one time. You all are probably smothering that poor child. Are you all right in there, Jane? I mean Angela?" His voice stretched another decibel as if he were across the street instead of outside the door.

Angela chuckled. She didn't blame him for stumbling over both of her names. She hadn't gotten used to Jane when she changed her name back to Angela. Her smile softened. The last name didn't matter. In a few minutes that would change. She sighed as she thought of Trent waiting for her at the altar.

"Are you all still in there?" Mr. Hoffman banged on the door again. "You got a room full of folks waiting out here."

"Yes, sir. I'm coming right out." She looked around at the circle of women. "We have to go."

"I guess you're right." Sarah wiped her eyes to keep tears from dripping onto her rose-colored dress.

"Don't start or I'll start," Mamie sniffed.

"Then I will," Angela added.

"We can't have that." Della dabbed at Angela's eyes. "I guess we're ready to let you go."

Each woman picked up her bouquet with a ribbon that matched her gown. One by one they hugged Angela gently before leaving the room. After they left to stand in the hall, Jeanine stood in front of her, dressed in a golden shade that highlighted her skin tone.

"I just met you yesterday, but already you seem like family. I have never seen Trent so happy." She hugged her. "Thank you for loving my brother." She stood back and winked. "See you in a little bit, Sis."

Angela took a deep breath as the music sounded to announce the women. She stared in the mirror one last time as Angela Baring straightened a curl and shook her head at the young woman staring back at her.

She had been through so much, including name changes. The change about to take place was the most pleasant one. She smiled again. And it would be the last.

Trent is waiting for me. She shook her head. *For me. It was worth everything I went through to end up with him.* She thought of Nick and Mr. Hunter. *I'm sorry people had to die for me to meet him.* She swallowed the tears that threatened to surface. *Not today.*

The music changed to announce her entrance and she took the bouquet of lilies and roses from the desk and left the room. She stood at the entrance of the transformed restaurant.

The appearance of the room had been changed drastically for her wedding, but that wasn't what she was noticing. For all the attention she gave the room, there could have been tables and chairs filling the space as usual.

Her focus was on the man waiting for her at the end of the aisle; he was staring at her with all the love possible shining in his eyes—love for her.

He does look great in a tux. Her mind skipped to that other time that he was dressed like this—a time with no happiness. Quickly that long ago instance was replaced by this moment.

She smiled at him and walked toward her future with Trent. A future with a lifetime of love, happiness, and desserts.

To the Reader:

I hope you enjoyed *Escape to Love*. I turned up the tension and action just a tiny bit. I hope it kept you up past your bedtime, made you neglect your work, caused you to ride past your stop on the public transit system, and all that good stuff. I have not been a stay-at-home anything. I spent six weeks in Hawaii this past September and half of October. I will be setting a novel there, but my next novel will be set in the Orlando area. It involves corporate espionage and includes an interesting hot air balloon ride. (It is a romance, you know.)

Meanwhile, keep reading and I'll keep writing.

Alice
www.alicewootson.net

ABOUT THE AUTHOR

Alice Wootson was born in Rankin, Pennsylvania, a small town outside of Pittsburgh. She came to the Philadelphia area to attend Cheyney University and stayed to teach in the Philadelphia School District. Writing is her second career. She didn't do much writing while her three sons were young, except for an occasional short story. After they were grown and computers became readily available, she began writing in earnest.

Alice is an avid reader of just about every genre, but she also admits to being a television junkie. She travels a lot with her husband, Ike, and is always looking for new settings.

She often visits schools to conduct writing workshops.

She is a member of Romance Writers of America, Mad Poets' Society, and the Philadelphia Writing Conference.

COMING IN AUGUST 2003 FROM
ARABESQUE ROMANCES

__SAVING GRACE
by Angela Winters   1-58314-335-1 $6.99US/$9.99CAN
Grace Bowers is determined to bring down the company that discriminated against her father thirty-five years ago. Hiring Keith Hart to handle the expansion of his growing restaurant is her first step. Suddenly she and Keith are working together—and fighting a potent attraction that makes becoming real-life partners incredibly tempting . . .

__MEANT TO BE
by Mildred Riley   1-58314-422-6 $6.99US/$9.99CAN
When a young boxer turns up dead, nurse Maribeth Trumbull is determined to find out what happened. But police officer Ben Daniels is dead-set against her digging up evidence on her own. While she may be drawn to the irresistibly sexy cop, Maribeth has no intention of surrendering her hard-earned independence . . .

__CAN'T DENY LOVE
by Doreen Rainey   1-58314-432-3 $5.99US/$7.99CAN
Tanya Kennedy longs for something her dependable boyfriend Martin can't seem to provide. Disillusioned, Tanya refuses his marriage proposal . . . and runs straight into her ex, Brandon Ware. Once, Brandon filled her life with passion, but he also left her feeling bitterly betrayed.

__MY ONE AND ONLY LOVE
by Melanie Schuster   1-58314-423-4 $5.99US/$7.99CAN
Determined to recover from her brother's disastrous mismanagement of her career, star Ceylon Simmons has worked herself to near collapse. She's come to find refuge on sea-swept St. Simon's Island. But when she discovers that the man she's always loved from afar is also visiting, she realizes there's no safe haven from their desire . . .

Call toll free **1-888-345-BOOK** to order by phone or use this coupon to order by mail. ALL BOOKS AVAILABLE AUGUST 01, 2003.

Name _____

Address _____

City _____ State _____ Zip _____

Please send me the books that I have checked above.

I am enclosing $_____

Plus postage and handling* $_____

Sales Tax (in NY, TN, and DC) $_____

Total amount enclosed $_____

*Add $2.50 for the first book and $.50 for each additional book. Send check or money order (no cash or CODs) to: **Arabesque Romances, Dept. C.O., 850 Third Avenue, 16th Floor, New York, NY 10022**

Prices and numbers subject to change without notice. Valid only in the U.S. All orders subject to availability. **NO ADVANCE ORDERS.**

Visit our website at **www.arabesquebooks.com**.